THE CONSIDERATE TERROR

THE CONSIDERATE TERROR

THE UNCONVENTIONAL AGENT BEAUFONT™ BOOK 4

SARAH NOFFKE

MICHAEL ANDERLE

This book is a work of fiction. All of the characters, organizations, and events portrayed in this novel are either products of the author's imagination or are used fictitiously. Sometimes both.

Copyright © 2022 LMBPN Publishing
Cover by Fantasy Book Design
Cover copyright © LMBPN Publishing
A Michael Anderle Production

LMBPN Publishing supports the right to free expression and the value of copyright. The purpose of copyright is to encourage writers and artists to produce the creative works that enrich our culture.

The distribution of this book without permission is a theft of the author's intellectual property. If you would like permission to use material from the book (other than for review purposes), please contact support@lmbpn.com. Thank you for your support of the author's rights.

LMBPN Publishing
PMB 196, 2540 South Maryland Pkwy
Las Vegas, NV 89109

Version 1.00, May 2022
eBook ISBN: 979-8-88541-447-0
Print ISBN: 979-8-88541-448-7

THE CONSIDERATE TERROR TEAM

Thanks to the JIT Readers

Dorothy Lloyd
Jackey Hankard-Brodie
Veronica Stephan-Miller
Diane L. Smith
Deb Mader
Angel LaVey
Dave Hicks
Christopher Gilliard

If we've missed anyone, please let us know!

Editor
The Skyfyre Editing Team

For all the great librarians out there—for shelving all those books, over and over and over again. And being awesome resources.

— Sarah

*To Family, Friends and
Those Who Love
to Read.
May We All Enjoy Grace
to Live the Life We Are
Called.*

— Michael

CHAPTER ONE

The Great Library, Timbuktu, Mali

Chaos tore through the Great Library. Books flew off shelves, and torrential winds sought to tear the magical structure in half. It was as if a cyclone had burst through the glass walls that enclosed the largest library in the world but left the exterior of the Great Library unscathed. What was terrorizing the place had simply appeared, and it wasn't going to stop until it got what it came for.

The Great Library wasn't a place just anyone could enter. Every book from history could be found in the Great Library. As soon as a book was completed, no matter if it was published or not, it appeared on one of the thousands of shelves inside the building. If a volume was edited or updated, that was also in the Great Library.

Many books could be lethal if they got into the wrong hands. Plans for making the most advanced bombs in the world could be found in the glass building perched casually on a street in Timbuktu. Deadly spells filled many of the pages of hundreds of books, and along with fictional books, there were also dangerous nonfiction writings that could do a lot of damage.

This was why, from the outside, the Great Library blended in with the city. Most people who looked at it saw nothing of particular interest and ignored it. Only people with special access due to their status could even find it, much less enter.

Dragonriders and fairy godmothers were allowed entry into the place, which was run by one man—the Great Librarian, Paul. Mortals weren't allowed in, nor were most of the magical races. On the list of those forbidden from entering were demons, yet one had found a way of entering the Great Library, and it appeared that he might destroy it.

"What is happening!" Paul yelled as he sprinted down the main aisle. It ran the length of the Great Library, which was miles long.

Pages from books as old as time, written by Papa Creola, spiraled around the Great Librarian as he struggled to grab them. Paul's long beard tangled around his face from the wind as his blue silk robes tangled around his feet, nearly sending him down.

He jumped, reaching for the pages assaulted by the winds, but for each one he grabbed, there were hundreds more to catch. Confused and scared by the strange activity that had befallen the usually quiet Library, Paul abandoned his attempts to grab the books.

Instead, he ran in the opposite direction from the chaos to the front. Whatever was happening to the place he'd vowed to protect was bigger than him, and Paul knew it. He needed help. Something had invaded the holy space, and he had to find someone who could protect him and the Library. Paul had no idea that the monster who had unleashed this chaos was only going to make things more horrible.

It would take more than a dragonrider or a Warrior from the House of Fourteen to stop the evil loose in the Great Library. It would take more than a demon hunter to stop this beast.

In the end, it would require someone most didn't think of as a fighter to fix what was about to be unleashed. Only someone whose mission was to protect love could fight that which was coming.

The world would need to rely upon the fairy godmothers.

3

CHAPTER TWO

The violent wind vanished as quickly as it had started. As books clattered to the floor and pages settled, a large figure stepped through a dark and shimmering portal next to a set of tall shelves. The storm hadn't just been for effect or to lure the Great Librarian away. It had been how the ancient demon, Tomár, could enter the place that should have been forbidden to him.

One important aspect of the Great Library was the versions of the books it held. They were, of course, all first editions. They also held magic since, in essence, they were organic beings. As the originals were changed, so did the versions in the Great Library.

Incredible power existed in the words in each of these books. Spells whispered from these texts were more powerful than from copies of the same books out in the world. The fictional stories were more alive when read from an edition inside the Library. Dark magic never attempted before could be done with books in the Great Library—but it would only work from these volumes. Tomár had mastered that magic and was about to do something most would never dream possible.

The demon gazed around, studying the many rows in front of

him. No one would mistake Tomár for a human, although he wore normal clothes consisting of black jeans, a plain ripped T-shirt, and boots. This demon hadn't been human for many, many centuries, which was why he was about to unleash a brand-new evil.

Tomár was tired of his perpetual state of being—unable to die unless slain by a demon hunter. That wouldn't be his fate. Instead, the demon that had spawned so much hatred during his reign would take the planet down with him. It was time for Tomár to die, and so would the world and its people. They had only ever caused him anguish.

Tomár stood over seven feet tall. His tattooed skin was red, and he had large, curved horns protruding from either side of his bald head. Many who had found themselves in a dark alley with the demon had mistaken him for a bull. His black eyes would pierce their souls as the large silver ring in his nose caught the light. None could ever report what they saw since once all the energy in them had been leached, they'd been left to die alone.

Although demons were the antithesis of love, they ironically survived on it. It was soulless demons who sucked the positive emotions from mortals, stealing their life force, sending them into great despair. Most had no idea they'd been a victim to a demon, losing their purpose and all hope in the world.

Love fueled the world. It kept people happy, and conversely, it kept demons alive. Suck all the love from the world, and the planet would die. It was that simple and was all Tomár wanted, the earth dead, along with its people, and his chance to finally pass in peace.

Extending his large hand, Tomár pointed a long black fingernail at the nearest shelf. A thick book slid out before turning on its side and hovering a few feet from the demon. With a small jerk of his wrist, the book flicked open, an errant wind riffling the pages before it stopped on a particular one.

The words Tomár spoke weren't ones that most would understand. It was a forbidden language of the demons and held diabolic power. It didn't take long to know that the spell had worked.

An instant after the hissed words fell from Tomár's lips, a hand shot out of the pages. Like blindly slipping into the world from a dark closet, the pale hand felt around in the air. Then, as though it was being sucked into this world, the creature was yanked from the book, flapping his wings and staring around the Great Library in total bewilderment.

Before the mostly naked winged creature who was holding a bow and arrow could ask any questions, Tomár pulled two more figures from the book. Like being birthed from the pages, the two women who appeared, one after the other, stared around in confusion. The sight of the huge red demon kept all three ancient creatures from attacking or protesting.

Tomár narrowed his eyes, appraising the gods he'd brought through the pages of history. He glanced at Cupid flapping his wings and hovering, his bow and arrow in his hands but not pointed at the demon. The god of love and desire wore a scrutinizing expression on his young face. Appearances were deceiving because Cupid was neither young nor innocent. This magical creature from Rome had been banished for a good reason—he was heartbroken and therefore dangerous.

Tomár's gaze settled on Freyja, the Norse goddess of love. She wore animal pelts over her broad shoulders, and her black hair hung in several braids. The many rings she wore were all talismans from battles, but she was missing her famed necklace. This was part of the reason for the vengeance in her eyes as she lifted her jaw and tightened her hand on her sword.

Not saying a word, Tomár glanced at the Egyptian goddess, Hathor. She appeared as royalty in a gown of gold silk and wore a tall headdress over her straight black hair. One would be unwise to underestimate the beautiful woman. Hathor was known as a goddess of love, but she was also the goddess of war and had earned the latter title by trying to destroy mankind.

"I have summoned you three from the dead for a very specific mission," Tomár began in a deep raspy voice. "You will take your wrath out on this world, punishing those who punished you long ago."

Looking up at Cupid, Tomár waved his large hand, and the god's bow and arrows disappeared, replaced with a modern black crossbow. "They took Psyche from you. Love is not the answer. It is the reason for your suffering. Go out into the world and take it back."

The winged creature nodded, his eyes slits full of hostility.

Tomár's chin lowered, and his gaze fell on Freyja. "Your husband is dead. Lovers are to blame. Go out in the world and punish them."

The warrior who had scoured the planet for her long-lost love during her time released a single tear from her eye and then shook, vengeance in her every movement.

"You," Tomár said as he focused on Hathor. "You aren't strong enough yet, but you will be. The destruction these two bring, the love they erase, will be your fuel." The demon waved his hand at Cupid and Freyja, saying they would be the ones to bring Hathor back to full strength.

"When you are strong enough, you will finish what you once set out to do," Tomár continued. "You will destroy mankind, ending this planet once and for all."

The Egyptian goddess didn't nod or say a word, but by the expression in her eyes, Tomár knew he had her compliance. These three had been charged with creating and protecting love, but in the end, all of them had been punished for it. They'd waited in the underworld of the gods for a long time to come back and seek their revenge. Now they could have it.

"Go!" Tomár yelled, his voice shaking the walls of the Great Library. Without a word or a backward glance, all three gods turned and strode down the long aisle of the Library, out into the world that had banished them.

The book that had been the vessel to bring back the god and goddesses of love clattered to the floor, shutting at once. Tomár strode away, leaving the powerful copy of *Magical Creatures* to be found by the Great Librarian.

Only the author of the book would be able to explain what had happened there. Only Bermuda Laurens could unravel the dangerous mystery, and only one person could stop what was coming before it was too late.

CHAPTER THREE

Little Pleasures Farmhouse, Outskirts of Boulder, Colorado

"I'm not up for this job," Paris Beaufont said, shaking her head at her Uncle John.

He gave her a sympathetic look. "There's no job. You simply have to show up."

"Wearing that." She pointed to the frilly bridesmaid dress that had arrived in her size and which she was expected to wear to his wedding that weekend.

He chuckled. "It's a dress, Pare. Not a torture device."

She rolled her eyes. "Oh, do tell. How many corsets have you worn? They are torture devices. If I can't see my feet, I'll trip and fall. Then everyone will be looking at me and not your gorgeous bride. So please, let me do this favor for you and wear my good leather jacket and not taffeta."

"I appreciate that you're trying to make this sound like you're helping me out, but you're in the wedding, and everyone, including your mother, is wearing a bridesmaid's dress."

Paris lowered her chin. "My mother?"

"The allergy to wearing dresses is hereditary. I guess she's taking a Benadryl that day," he joked.

"Bu-but…it's purple," Paris complained as she looked at the pile of fluffy material sitting on the dining room table in the restaurant like it was nuclear waste.

"According to my lovely bride, it's lilac," Uncle John corrected. "You'll look beautiful."

"I'll look like a plum," she argued. "Why couldn't Aunt Alicia choose black as her wedding color?"

"Because we're not the Addams Family," he said.

"Oh, wow, that was a timely reference. Thanks, Gomez."

"Hey, I have to wear a cummerbund and a bow tie," he offered.

"Do you get to see your feet?"

He smiled at her. "You'll look beautiful, and it will make me happy. I mean, I get to marry the woman I love with you beside me, along with your mother and all the people we treasure most in this world. I get to do it at Little Pleasures, the most magical place. I really can't think of how my life could get better."

Paris sighed, resigning her stubbornness. "I'm really happy for you, and it *will* be magical. You and Alicia deserve this wedding after everything you've been through, being separated from each other. Little Pleasures will be really beautiful."

On the heels of her words, the lights all over the dining room went out, followed by a loud crashing sound.

Paris straightened and closed her eyes for a half-beat, then opened them again. "Faraday, what have you done?"

"Nothing!" the squirrel chirped from a back room.

Hemingway strode in from the back, shaking his head. There was black grease all over his hands and streaks of it down his face. "If by nothing, he means he blew the breakers trying to set up an elaborate light display for the wedding."

"Thanks for ratting me out! You're dead to me, farm-boy!" Faraday yelled from the back.

"That's Mr. Farm Man to you," Hemingway called over his shoulder with a laugh.

Paris turned to her boyfriend, shaking her head. "What is going on?"

He leaned forward, careful to keep his dirty hands off her, and kissed her affectionately on the cheek. "Nothing for you to worry about. Once you take that squirrel to work with you, there will be less for me to worry about."

"What about the lights?" Paris asked, looking around, grateful for the many windows that allowed natural light into the large space.

"Oh, Clark and I can get them back on," Hemingway answered. "We're used to Faraday tripping the power, spilling chemicals, and blowing things up. We have contingency plans for all situations."

"Wow, out of context, he sounds like a real pain in the—"

"I can hear you," Faraday yelled from the back room.

"Butt," Paris finished saying. "However, he's a pain in the butt who also helps us to save people and stop lethal virtual realities and shut down bad guys like Jackson Zelle."

"So, we're not putting him in the soup yet, then?" Hemingway asked.

"It's usually Paris who threatens to cook me," Faraday said, scurrying into the dining room, also covered in black grease. His tail looked like he'd fried himself with electricity.

Hemingway shrugged. "I get why she wants to cook you." He grinned at Paris. "Speaking of food, you want me to pack you two a lunch?"

Paris shook her head. "No, we have tea with Sherlock Holmes."

Uncle John chuckled. "Most would think you were making that up."

"I know, my life is a farce," Paris remarked, pulling out her sunglasses to get ready to go. "When is teatime anyway? Sherlock said to meet him on Roya Lane at teatime."

"Between three and four," Uncle John answered.

"Oh, well, then I'll grab something for lunch at FGA," Paris said, smiling at Hemingway. "It's good for me to socialize with the others in restaurant settings. I've got two new departments and need to seem approachable and relatable."

Faraday snickered. "So, is that why you refuse to wear the uniform of the agents or the fairy godmothers and dress like a motorcycle cop?"

"I don't look like a motorcycle cop, Squirrel," Paris said, seething.

"You're like everyone else, blending in with that demon blood that gives you superpowers and an extra spark," Hemingway said proudly.

"Not to mention being the only half-magician, half-fairy in the world," Uncle John added.

Paris rolled her eyes as she headed for the door. "Fine, I'm a little different than most."

"All, Paris," Hemingway called. "You're different from all. There's no one like you in the world."

At the exit, Paris turned and smiled at the two men, Faraday beside her. "Well, you two are pretty unique too. Good luck with the wedding plans."

Uncle John beamed at her. "Thanks! Good luck with Sherlock Holmes and the new departments."

"Try not to get into too much trouble." Hemingway waved, grinning at her.

"I'll try," Paris replied, pulling back the door.

"I was talking to the squirrel, actually," he retorted. "I think we all know wherever you go, trouble will find you."

Paris pulled out her wand and brandished it in the air. "Yes, but since I know that, I'm always ready."

CHAPTER FOUR

Lobby, First Floor, FGA Tower, New York City, New York

"Why is everyone staring at us?" Paris asked when she and Faraday entered the skyscraper, making their way across the marble floor of the FGA lobby.

"Besides the usual obvious reasons that we just reviewed?" the squirrel supplied. "You know, motorcycle cop, halfling, demon."

"Yeah, besides those reasons," Paris muttered, looking around. "That's all been the case since I started here. Why are people gawking more impolitely than usual?"

"Well, before rumors were that you were given an agent position as the first female as a political move by Saint Valentine," Faraday began, "many thought you didn't really deserve the role, and it was based on your name."

"Right, because being named after a city where people eat snails makes me so cool."

The squirrel gave her an annoyed look. "The Beaufont name. Now that you've been assigned two more departments, well, some agents might have to admit that you're successful."

Paris stuck her tongue out at an agent who was gawking particularly hard when they walked by.

Faraday sighed, rolling his eyes. "They will also admit that your maturity didn't get you promoted."

Paris ignored the squirrel and wagged her finger at the ogling agent. "Hey, you might want to blink every so often there, Peeping Tom."

"My name is Agent Onyx," the guy said, sounding offended. He shook his head and looked away.

"Rules on blinking still apply regardless of your name," Paris sang, striding past Fairy Grounds, certain the pixies who ran the establishment would give her dirty looks and volley insults at her. To her surprise, the manager Ivy flew out of the coffee shop at the sight of Paris. She was holding a cup of something steaming in front of her as her little pink wings flapped double time.

"Agent Beaufont!" Ivy called. "I have coffee I want you to try."

Paris tilted her head to the side, giving the tiny fairy a look of surprise. "How much poison is in there?"

The squirrel, either in an effort to help or because he wanted Paris to throw him across the lobby, kicked her in the shin. Paris glanced down at her sidekick and narrowed her eyes at him. "That tickled a little."

He shook his head at her. "Maybe if you didn't insult the pixies at Fairy Grounds, they wouldn't file complaints about you."

Remembering the tidbit of information Agent Barney Jasper had told her, Paris glanced up at the pixie. "Yeah, about that. I explained why I said you couldn't make coffee when I made the scene in this lobby. Why did you complain about me?"

The pixie blushed. "Well, because you didn't drink your coffee that day you were in the shop with your friends."

"Your coffee isn't really something you drink as much as chew," Paris remarked.

Ivy narrowed her eyes, the blush falling away. "It's because of comments like that. I've heard rumors that you're often saying our coffee isn't good, not just that once to create a diversion."

"Man, you fairies and your rumors," Paris said loudly, looking around. "What are y'all gossiping about now?"

Many who weren't already staring looked at Paris. The squirrel tried to assault her shin again.

"Hey, you might want to make less of a scene if you don't want to be the subject of gossip," Faraday offered.

Paris squinted at the rodent. "Why don't you fatten up? Right now, you'd make a really small purse, and I want something my Kindle can fit in."

"You don't carry a purse," he replied, "and you don't have a Kindle."

"Because you took it apart," Paris fired back.

"Regardless of all the negative things you've said about Fairy Grounds," Ivy said, trying to recapture Paris' attention, "we, the pixies, were hoping to make a truce with you. We understand that not only did you protect us from Agent Josh Emerald, but you also fought Agent Jackson Zelle, which is why you've earned yourself a promotion. So, I wanted to offer you a cup of coffee on the house. I made it myself. I followed the directions for brewing, which was very complicated."

Paris offered a smile. "Why, thank you. That's really appreciated. Making a fine cup of coffee is an artform that many work to master." She took the mug and took a sip. She nearly spewed out the liquid, which could hardly be classified as steaming hot.

"Okay, mastering it is one thing but really making it is as easy as boiling water!"

The ever-persistent squirrel thumped Paris in the shin again.

She looked down at him with a hooded expression. "Another attempt on your part to make me behave?"

"They say that with science, all things are possible, but Paris Beaufont proves theory wrong, once again."

The pixie, apparently thinking this was all about her, screamed and flew off after snatching her cup back from Paris.

She nodded casually and pursed her lips. "Yeah, that went about how I expected."

"You can't be polite, can you?" Faraday questioned.

Paris shook her head. "No, I can't enable it. Do you really want me to tell that little runt of a fairy she makes good coffee when it isn't true? That will do no one any good."

Faraday groaned. "Fairies don't care. They put so much syrup and sugar in their coffee they never notice it's burned. They mostly go to Fairy Grounds for the scones. You're the only one who cares since you drink your coffee black."

She grinned. "Yes, like my soul."

He huffed. "You're not fooling me. You might have demon blood, but you're all goodness and pixie dust."

"I'm not either," Paris argued, pretending to stomp and throw a tantrum, earning her more attention. "I've got demon blood and will eat kittens to prove it."

A few fairy godmothers passing by heard this and veered the other way. Paris' heightened hearing caught the phrase, "Let's hope she gets eliminated in the corporate restructuring. I just bought a Siamese."

Paris rolled her eyes and cupped her hand around her mouth, shouting at the fairy godmothers. "The cats are seriously inbred. I'd do you a favor by eating that thing."

Once more, Faraday kicked Paris in the shin. "Seriously, if you don't want them to fear you, stop pretending you eat kittens. Besides, you're a vegetarian."

Paris laughed as she regarded the rodent trying his best to assault her. It felt like little pats. "They don't know that, and beet juice looks like blood."

"You're such a weird and wonderful person."

"Hey, what do you think they meant by the corporate restructuring thing?" Paris asked, her eyes trailing after the fairy godmothers.

"Well, Saint Valentine hinted at it in your last meeting, right?"

"Yeah, but nothing specific."

"You know who is always in the know because no one knows he's always listening and would know," Faraday sang.

"You know you said 'know' like a ton right there."

"You know I do," Faraday chirped, hurrying for the second floor.

CHAPTER FIVE

Dwyer's Polishes, Second Floor, FGA Tower, New York City, New York

The second floor was full of more people regarding Paris like she was a zoo animal. She would have reasoned it was because she was with a squirrel, but since those kinds of animals weren't in zoos, she thought it might be for another reason. She was the source of most rumors. After the incident downstairs with Ivy, she was giving the rumor mill a fresh and ample supply.

"Hey, Dwyer," Paris said, having waited until the shoeshine station was free of people so she could have a private conversation. "What's the special today?"

Dwyer, the owner of Dwyer's Polishes, turned and smiled to greet Paris and Faraday after cleaning up after his last client. "Well, hey there. If it isn't the subject of all whispered conversations and my part-time assistant."

"Yeah, I think I'm talked about more now than ever before. Faraday can help you with side tasks as time permits."

"Well, I don't have any jobs for you, little buddy," Dwyer said, looking down at Faraday with bright eyes. "Check back."

"I was hoping you could fill me in on what you've been hearing," Paris began in a low voice. "First, what's today's shoeshine special? That Sneaky Feet one you did was really helpful the last time."

"Oh, yes, that's a good one," Dwyer remarked, wiping off the seat and offering it to Paris. "Today's is also helpful. It's Listening Ears."

"Wait, you polish her shoes, and it makes her ears listen better?" Faraday asked, climbing onto the chair next to Paris.

"Well, it makes her a better listener," Dwyer said. "You know, most people don't listen. Not really. They are thinking about what they are going to say while the other person is talking. Imagine how communications would change if people were actually present, listening to one another?"

"I like the idea in theory," Paris said, stretching out her legs. "I might have to stop by Sundry Charms and get some of that Quiet-Down-Gum, or Holly might talk me off during today's morning meeting. She really only responds to 'Shush it.'"

"Don't worry," Dwyer began, pouring bright green polish onto her boots, "the polish simply makes you good at listening, using that skill as a superpower of sorts. You'll still have the ability to talk, but you'll do it when it makes sense, rather than just to get your chance to."

"Amen, brother," Faraday said, nodding like Dwyer was preaching his sermon.

Paris shot the squirrel a disgruntled expression before glancing back at the guy shining her shoes. "Well, speaking of listening, what have you been hearing around the rumor mill regarding corporate restructuring?"

Dwyer paused and looked up at her, then leaned forward. "Agent Jackson Zelle is gone."

"Yeah, I know, I was there."

"Yeah, but he has been replaced," Dwyer continued.

"Already?" Faraday asked. "By who?"

"By what, you mean," Dwyer corrected. "Saint Valentine outsourced the finance department."

"Yeah, he mentioned he might do that because it would erase any bias caused by finances."

"I like the altruistic reasons," Dwyer continued. "Saint Valentine isn't making any friends with this decision. People here like money, and guess what we're running out of without a finance department?"

"Money?" Faraday guessed.

"Bingo," Dwyer said, rubbing a rag over the goop on Paris' boot. "Budgets are getting slashed, and many aren't happy. The board is angrier than ever. They are demanding Saint Valentine generate revenue streams fast to recover the funding."

Paris sighed. "That's ridiculous. That's why Saint Valentine outsourced. We need money to operate, but it shouldn't be our goal. We're about creating love."

"Yes, but people have gotten accustomed to things being a certain way and don't like the budget cuts," Dwyer said. "It's affecting everything from salaries to benefits to department spaces, and many think you're the reason why."

Paris groaned and threw her head back. "Of course I am. I get rid of a deadly traitor bent on monetizing love rather than promoting it, and I'm the problem. I don't benefit either way. We have and always have had zero funding. I don't even have a used coffee maker."

"Why would you want a used coffee maker?" Dwyer asked, looking up at her intently.

"This makes sense," Faraday reasoned in a low voice. "People are talking about you not because you're seen as a hero, but a mixed bag. Yes, you saved people when Josh imprisoned everyone in the virtual reality simulation, but now you've gotten rid of Jackson Zelle. Most didn't know he was bad and didn't witness his treason. They only see that you got rid of him, and now they don't have any funding. They think you're using demon witchcraft to take over the place."

Paris was about to laugh at how ridiculous this was, but

Dwyer nodded adamantly. "That's exactly what a lot of people think."

Paris groaned again. "The fact any of you are thinking at all is the biggest shock," she said loud enough for everyone close by to hear, as she planned.

Faraday leaned over and cupped his mouth. "Again, this is when I'd kick you if I could. Quiet down before you make a scene."

"Go away before I throw you," Paris threatened.

"Well, that would definitely create a scene," Faraday said, sinking back.

"I know you're trying to make this place better," Dwyer said, smiling brightly. "Jackson was a bad guy. He was a lousy tipper, rude, and always about profit. You're doing the right thing, Agent Beaufont, but sometimes people with the most important jobs aren't liked by those who aren't ready for change. Keep doing what you're doing and when things are better, everyone will be happier for it."

Paris offered the shoe shiner a look of gratitude. "Thanks. I wish I knew how to help this place. I have created a lot of problems and have not given a lot of solutions. We don't have a Director of IT and Operations for Finance."

"Well, you can't renovate a house until you clear it out," Dwyer said, running his rag over her boot one final time. They weren't too shiny, but they were clean, and she somehow felt ready to hear from others rather than give orders. Since it was her first day with her new departments, that might come in very handy. She hoped so since she was overdue to have luck on her side.

CHAPTER SIX

Casual Romance Department, Third Floor, FGA Tower, New York City, New York

On the way up, Paris and Faraday had been smooshed on an overcrowded elevator with a bunch of fairy godmothers and agents with judge-y eyes and silent stares. She would have told them all she wasn't the problem and that it was their propensity toward complacency and low standards that were the issue, but Faraday was pinching her the entire ride up to the third floor to the Casual Romance department in an attempt to make her behave. Needless to say, she was ready to rip into the squirrel when they exited the elevator, but more pressing matters stole her attention at once.

"What are you doing to my assistant?" Paris asked after disembarking from the elevator to find Holly with a razor and shaving cream, standing in front of Doris Frederickson—the oldest employee at FGA. Behind her, with her hands hovering over the old woman's shoulders, was Isha.

"I'm using reiki massage to heal the lady," Isha said, running her hands over Doris' shoulder but not touching her. The old woman was sleeping soundly in her chair and wasn't waking any time soon, it appeared. "It's an ancient Japanese form of healing where the energy radiates from one's palms and into the patient's skin, offering a multitude of benefits."

Holly wiped the shaving cream in one of her hands onto Doris' face, covering her chin and not even startling the old sleeping woman. "Please tell me that you didn't pay someone to hover their hands over your body and call that a massage?"

Isha gawked with an offended look on her face. "Not only did I pay for a massage, but I enrolled in a twelve-week course. I'm now a certified reiki massage therapist."

"You're a certified idiot," Holly said, wiping the excess shaving cream on a towel and brandishing the razor close to Doris' sleeping face.

Paris sighed loudly. "I'm going to start with my original question once again. What are you doing to my assistant?"

"Her chakras are blocked, so I'm giving her a reiki massage," Isha said, still hovering her hands close to Doris. The old woman was snoring and seemed very happy, her blue head of hair was tilted back, and her mouth was wide open. She looked like Santa Claus with the shaving cream dripping off her chin.

"No, I believe she said something else of hers was blocked, which is why I gave her that kale smoothie," Holly argued. "I put a sleeping pill in it so I could shave her mustache. She's going to wake up a brand-new woman."

"If she wakes up at all," Paris nearly yelled. "You drugged an old woman?"

"Yeah, she pretty much naps every hour," Faraday argued. "You really don't have to encourage her to sleep."

"She's never asleep for long enough for me to get a clean shave," Holly said, tossing her fake blonde hair off her shoulder. "She is always so restless, talking in her sleep. I figured a good barbiturate would knock her out."

"How is it that you two don't have enough to do that you're

shaving my assistant and pretending to give her massages?" Paris asked with her hands on her hips.

"Reiki is a real massage," Isha argued, offended. She blew a piece of short black hair off her forehead. "Do you want one?"

"Maybe later," Paris said, waving off her employee.

"She's really productive, surprisingly," Holly said. "Doris has decoded many cases, and they are stacking up without you to assign them to us since you've been slacking off, sleeping, and playing with your rodent."

"Sleeping and eating and taking care of my vital needs," Paris corrected. "I went home for nine hours to sleep and try on an atrocity of a dress. Then I returned here where you all are an atrocity that I must deal with."

Holly pursed her oversized, collagen-filled lips and nodded to Isha. "See, she's over there playing dress-up while we keep this place afloat."

"Did you really work all the cases I gave to you?" Paris asked.

"Of course," Isha said as Holly replied, "Nope."

"Which is it, Mary Kate and Ashley?" Paris asked, narrowing her eyes at her employees. One was a new-age hippie, and the other didn't know how to act or look her age.

"Well, we worked all the cases," Isha answered.

"We made matches with half of them," Holly added.

"What about the other half?" Paris asked.

"They require funding, resources, and a little thing I like to call cash," Holly said.

"So, you couldn't fulfill them."

"Well," Holly drew out the word. "We did, but you know what happens when you show up to a ritzy club wearing last year's fashions?"

"I have a feeling you'll tell me," Paris muttered.

"You get called out and thrown out," Holly informed her. "So that's what happened, boss. We failed. So, we are putting our efforts where they need to be." She leaned forward and ran the razor over Doris' face.

"Your efforts could be better served doing just about anything else," Faraday said, jumping up on a table and inspecting the barber's work.

Holly halted and pointed at the sleeping old woman. "Have you looked at this woman's mustache? It's a hazard. I bet it obstructs her vision. The other day, she had a piece of onion lodged in it for an hour. Do you know how bad her breath is already without her talking breathing into an onion?"

"Okay, carry on," Paris said, waving at the pair and her sleeping assistant as she made her way back to her office. "I can't believe I'm saying this, but you're doing good work."

"Where are you going?" Isha called after her.

"To assign you cases you can work," Paris said. "Then I've got to meet with my other departments."

"Oh, yeah, that's right. We're no longer your favorite children," Holly said.

Paris paused and swung around to face her. "When were you ever my favorite…I'm not calling you children, although the term is accurate."

"Well, you get the point," Holly explained. "You've got two new shiny departments, and they'll be your favorite because they listen and do what you say and don't use your email address to send requests to your boss or sleep in your office or have your assistant do your taxes."

Paris blinked at Holly for a long moment. "You get that Doris isn't an accountant. You use my email. Wait, I don't even know where to start with this!"

"It's better to let it go then," Holly encouraged. "I've got a lot on my plate anyway." She turned around and apprised the old woman. The shaving cream was dripping onto her chest at this point.

Paris realized she was defeated. "How is the matchmaking

coming with the guys from Sad Lion Gaming Company? Any progress?"

"Great," Isha said at the same time Holly muttered, "They'll all die alone."

Paris shot the two a disgruntled look. "Finish whatever you're doing to Doris and then get back to helping them. They aren't a lost cause, and we're going to find them happiness. Then I'll have new cases for you with creative ways to get around funding problems."

"Okay, and if you want a reiki massage later, I'll give you one, boss," Isha offered. "I could give you one right after lunch, say around three or four when I usually nap."

"Although that's a very thoughtful offer and a deliberate admission of guilt, I've got tea with Sherlock Holmes," Paris said, heading for her office.

"I get that it's totally bogus science that Isha is doing but don't lie to her face. At least give her a real excuse," Holly said.

Paris turned around once more and rolled her eyes. "Fine, I can't because I'm getting the Mickey Mouse tattoo on my back laser-removed."

Holly glanced up at Isha. "I told you she's made tons of horrible mistakes in her time."

Isha nodded in agreement. "At least she works to fix them."

Both women smiled at Paris. "Good luck with your laser treatment."

CHAPTER SEVEN

Paris' Joke of an Office, Casual Romance Department, Third Floor, FGA Tower, New York City, New York

It took longer than Paris would have expected to review and assign all of the cases Doris had decoded. The old fairy wasn't awake a lot and moved like molasses, but when she worked, she got stuff done somehow.

Still, the results weren't good because Holly was right. Without funding, many of the cases couldn't be worked. Even with magic, it took funds to get things done in the world. There was no way around it. Paris consoled herself with the fact she was meeting with Sherlock Holmes that afternoon. He was going to help her track down Subfar, the Protector of Wealth.

According to Papa Creola and Mama Jamba, that was who Paris needed to create a viable revenue stream for FGA. This would allow them to promote love and not be biased as Jackson Zelle and Josh Emerald had been with their greedy ways. Paris hadn't deluded herself into believing tracking down the Protector of Wealth would be easy or fast. These kinds of things never were. Subfar had gone into hiding because his brother, Subner, the Protector of Weapons, wanted to kill him. There was a lot to unpack, but Paris would, and then she'd be that much closer to doing her job.

Currently, Paris didn't feel like she was doing her job so much as shuffling reports into piles labeled Holly, Isha, Needs Funding, and Needs-a-Miracle. There were a lot more cases in the last two piles than in the first.

"Okay, well, that gives the dimwits out there a bit more to do after they finish with Doris," Paris said to Faraday, apprising the piles she'd made on her sad excuse of a desk. "Ready to go and meet my new departments?"

Faraday looked up from the notes he'd been working on, which looked like blueprints. He was doing a good job of hiding them from her, so it was hard to tell. "I would go, but I think taking a squirrel with you lessens your credibility when you're being scrutinized so much already."

Paris regarded him carefully. "What are you hiding, Squirrel?"

"Nothing," he chirped, putting the blueprints behind him and covering them with his tail.

Paris sighed. "I don't have enough energy to fight you on whatever trouble you're crafting."

"I'm not crafting trouble," he argued. "I'm an investigator. A seeker of truth. A discoverer of knowledge. A—"

"Blower-upper-of-my-property," she interrupted.

"That's not a thing," he said, disagreeing.

"Well, I have to go and do introductions with the Practical Love and Refinement Departments, so if you're not coming, so be it. Try not to get into trouble because the last thing I need is to have to go and rescue you from some sub-atomic-gamma-ray-nuclear device."

He shook his head at her. "You get that's also not a thing, right?"

"I get very little at this point," Paris said. "I've got meetings with departments which may or may not think that I'm the problem because of the talks of budget cuts and layoffs floating about. Then I have a meeting with my boss and the hiring committee for the IT director where we'll be planning our next meeting."

"Always the model of efficiency," Faraday hummed.

"You got it," Paris said. "Then we have tea with Sherlock Holmes. You'll make that, won't you?"

"I wouldn't miss it," he told her.

"Unless you're stuck in a high-voltage-negative-ion-deliberator machine."

"Again, that's not a thing," Faraday said, folding up the plans he'd been reviewing and grinning at her with mischief in his eyes.

"Okay, well, I'll meet you for tea," Paris said, making for the door. "I'm off to…well, actually, I have no idea what I'm doing or supposed to do." She paused and looked at him with utter terror in her gaze. "Do you think anyone knows that I'm clueless?"

He shook his head. "That's the thing about you, Paris. You appear to know exactly what you're doing at the worst of times. If there is one thing you're best at, it's pretending to know what you're doing."

Paris grinned with relief. "Okay, good. Well, good luck with your tectonic-current-emulator machine."

"Less talking might help convince others that you know what you're doing," Faraday offered.

Paris pretended to zip her mouth shut and throw away the key before trudging for the elevators and to the upper floors where her new departments were located.

CHAPTER EIGHT

Casual Romance Department, Third Floor, FGA Tower, New York City, New York

If Paris was honest with herself, she was nervous about taking over as an agent for these two departments. What did she really know about practical love? She knew what her knowledge consisted of when it came to refinement, and it was almost zero.

However, her boss, Agent Barney Jasper, said she'd been promoted because she'd been resourceful in utilizing the talents of others when working the big cases. Paris did seem to take a holistic approach to management. This was most likely a result of being both a practical magician and an emotional fairy, mixed with a little demon blood.

Paris reasoned she didn't know much about casual romance, and still, she'd been somewhat successful in running that department despite all the odds against her. She'd been set up to fail in the beginning because Barney thought she was a lost cause who would spread trouble. She thought he was a pompous jerk who did nothing at all. They'd come a long way even if they still butted heads.

Also, in the beginning, Paris started her agent career with two worthless employees she'd had to whip into shape pretty fast. Holly and Isha weren't really bad employees. Under the previous management, they'd gotten lazy, but now they were proving to be successful when given support and guidance.

From the start, Paris didn't have resources or money, which made it nearly impossible to work any cases. Nearly, not entirely.

Paris had figured out how to persevere and hoped she could take many of the same practices she'd employed before and use them to lead her new departments. She didn't think she needed to know everything about practical love to help the fairy godmothers, nor did she need to know the latest fashion trends to be a good manager in the Refinement Department.

People quit bosses, not jobs. If she was doing her job as an agent, then she was fostering the skills of those assigned to her. That meant she didn't need to know a whole lot about casual love or refinement. Not knowing a lot was to Paris' benefit. Then she could be open to new ideas and the imaginations of others.

Paris really wanted to believe her lack of experience was going to be her saving grace. She wasn't bogged down by knowing too much about how things worked, just as she didn't know the history of FGA. Paris had her instinct and her raw desire to create love. She didn't care about bottom lines or performance reviews. She only cared about love, and hopefully, it was enough to get the job done.

She realized the problem she had to face was more rudimentary as she stood in front of the elevator, frozen in confusion. Paris didn't know where her new departments were located in FGA Tower.

CHAPTER NINE

Casual Romance Department, Third Floor, FGA Tower, New York City, New York

"Wilfred, will you help me, please?" Paris asked.

She prepared herself to wait for the hologram AI magitech support to show up. After Agent Josh Emerald terrorized FGA, many were afraid to go anywhere on their own and had asked that Wilfred go with them, which took up the majority of his time.

Paris was pleasantly surprised when the distinguished butler-looking man with white hair and wearing a gray three-piece suit arrived. The AI was called Wilfred, and he bowed with a pleasant expression on his face.

"How may I assist you, Agent Beaufont?"

"Thanks," Paris said with relief. "Don't tell anyone, but I don't know where my new departments are located."

"Your secret is safe with me because you asked."

"Right, you have to be told to keep things private, or you're an open book. Thanks for the reminder. I need to know where the Practical Romance and Refinement Departments are located."

"Of course," he said with a short nod, his hands pressed

behind his back. "They are on the fourth and fifth floor respectively. Would you like me to accompany you?"

Paris smiled and pressed the button for the elevator. "I would, and not just for moral support. Faraday abandoned me, and on my own, I'm certain the possessed elevator would take me to the basement without my permission or somewhere else entirely. That thing really has a mind of its own."

"I don't think it has a mind at all," he corrected and held the doors to the elevator open for her when it arrived. "I'm happy to accompany you. I sense by you saying moral support that you're experiencing nervousness about your new responsibilities."

Paris sighed and boarded the elevator. "Well, I'm lost before even beginning. I didn't even know where to look to find my departments."

"I understand. Loss is hard. I lost my job as a stage designer," Wilfred related.

"You what?" Paris asked, confused as she pressed the button for the fourth floor. "Stage designer, but you work here."

"Yes, that was before, but I left without making a scene."

Paris' eyes widened. "Oh. My. Angels. Did you just tell a joke?"

"Yes. Did it make you feel better? You said jokes improve moods, and yours is low."

Paris shook her head. "It wasn't bad. Delivery was a little stiff, but you get credit for the effort. I was so confused about you being a stage designer."

"Before that, I had a job at an aquarium, but I lost that one too."

Paris gave him a quizzical look. "Oh, yeah?"

"Yes," he answered. "Incidentally, did you know that a piranha can devour a human in thirty seconds?"

"Wow, Wilfred, those aren't bad," Paris said proudly. "You even have a theme connecting them. You've got potential."

"So, you feel better then?" he asked as the doors to the elevator opened.

"Yes, thank you. I'm not lost."

A sad expression covered his wrinkled face. "As I get older, I remember all the people I've lost along the way."

"Oh, I'm sorry," Paris said, not accustomed to the AI having feelings. She didn't think he was truly capable of them, but at her insistence, he was doing a good job of acting.

He shrugged. "Alas, maybe a career as a tour guide wasn't for me."

CHAPTER TEN

Practical Romance Department, Fourth Floor, FGA Tower, New York City, New York

Much like the Casual Romance department, one floor down, the workspace seemed much larger than was necessary. The small department had an entire floor that appeared much better furnished than the Casual Romance department.

When Paris started as an agent, her boss Barney moved the Practical Romance Department to the empty fourth floor, saying later he didn't want Paris spreading her wrong ways of doing things to others. She felt smug, knowing how much the tables had turned.

The agents in charge of Casual Romance and Refinement had tucked tail after the virtual reality simulation incident and quit, pursuing jobs in Fairyland or Las Vegas or one of the other areas where fairies did well career-wise.

Unlike the Casual Romance department, Practical Romance wasn't a mix of unmatching furniture. There was no Wellness Area, a Cozy Corner for napping, or a Team-Building Conference Space, but it did have a kitchen nook.

"A coffee maker," Paris said, gravitating toward the neat area with clean mugs and a percolating coffee machine. She some-times had conversations in her head she finished out loud, and this was one of those times. A few fairy godmothers wearing the blue gown and sporting the blue old-lady hair glanced up at her as she studied the space where they sipped coffee.

"Can we help you?" one asked, giving her a scrutinizing expression, looking her up and down.

"I think you're lost," the other one said. "The Casual Romance department is on the third floor."

Paris sighed. Of course Agent Punk Face, her nickname for her boss she thought he'd outgrown but realized he hadn't, didn't tell her new department about her or that she was their new boss. This was going to be more fun than Paris had bargained for, and she'd budgeted for zero fun.

"Hi, I'm not lost," Paris said, standing tall. "I'm here because—"

"We don't have any kittens," one of the fairy godmothers interrupted.

Paris bit her lip and considered shrinking the woman. She was probably named Etsy or something else equally as hippyish.

"Yeah, I don't eat kittens," Paris said. "I'm here because—"

"Who let her in here?" a high-pitched voice Paris recognized and hadn't missed at all sounded behind her.

Exasperated, Paris turned around to find who she had expected. It was none other than her arch-nemesis from Happily Ever After College, "Becky the Bully" as she liked to call her, although she was actually named Rebecca Montgomery. Her mother, Virginia Montgomery, thought she ran the school but really just had a strong influence over the FGA board and was able to put pressure on them financially. That influence was even more pervasive now that FGA was hurting for money.

"What are you doing here?" Paris asked. She looked over the snooty fairy godmother. Becky's expression was pinched, and her usually brown hair was now gray and pulled back in a high pony-tail. She was wearing the fairy godmother gown.

Then Paris noticed it. Becky had a pink sash around the hood of her gown, showing she'd graduated from Happily Ever After College.

"I've been assigned to the Practical Romance Department," Becky explained. "Clear off, Paris. I don't want you trying to embarrass me like you always did at school. It's my first day, and I'm waiting for our boss, Agent—"

"Agent Beaufont," Penny Pullman supplied, striding over and taking a spot next to Paris. She gave her a proud expression as the other fairy godmothers gasped in horror. Penny held out her hand to Paris in a presenting manner. "This is your boss and the new presiding agent over our department."

CHAPTER ELEVEN

Practical Romance Department, Fourth Floor, FGA Tower, New York City, New York

"How do we know this is true?" one of the fairy godmothers asked, crossing her arms and giving a challenging look.

"Yeah, Penny Poorman is always in cahoots with Paris," Becky said, sidling up next to the other fairy godmothers.

"Her name is Penny Pullman," Paris corrected and narrowed her eyes at Becky. She hadn't changed and was still bullying people she thought she was better than.

"You'd know this was true if you read your email," Penny said confidently. She wasn't the same pushover she'd been when Paris had arrived at Happily Ever After College and had saved her from Becky's tricks and taunts.

The protesting fairy godmother pulled out her phone and started reading something. A moment later and she looked at her friend and then Becky. "It's true, this...halfling is our new boss."

"I go by Agent Beaufont, and I will eat your kitten if you refer to me as 'this' anything ever again."

"What happened to our boss?" the other fairy godmother asked, checking her phone.

"He left," Penny said. "He was scared and burned out and ineffective at his job. We have Agent Beaufont now, and she's innovative, brave, and full of great ideas."

"Thanks, Pen," Paris said to her friend with a smile.

"That's not the Paris I know," Becky said, staring up at the ceiling.

"I go by Agent Beaufont," Paris corrected sternly. "Do tell me. You just started at FGA? I thought you'd failed all your requirements at Happily Ever After College and had to retake them? Or did Virginia pay the board to pass you?"

"That's not what happened," Becky fumed, her fists by her side.

"Someone was paid," Penny said to Paris and shook her head.

"That's not what happened," Becky repeated. She had never been the master of words or math or really anything that didn't involve bullying.

"Regardless, you're here, and I am too," Paris began. "I am your new presiding agent over Practical Romance. So, I'd love to meet everyone, get a tour, and learn about what you all do here."

"Don't you want to assign us cases?" one of the fairy godmothers asked.

"Yes," Paris said, drawing out the word. "First, I need to understand what exactly you've been doing, then I can make an informed decision."

"Our department assistant didn't come in today," the other fairy godmother said. "I think she quit if our agent did."

"Yeah, she was on her way out and would have followed him," Penny said.

Paris shrugged. "Well, I have an assistant in Casual Romance who can decode the reports from the tele-eventor, so that's not a problem."

"You mean Doris Frederickson?" one of the fairy godmothers asked. "Is that old rock still alive?"

Becky laughed rudely. "Mother says they can't fire her at FGA, and each year she costs them more in benefits than ten departments combined."

The other two women laughed.

"Doris," Paris began, her voice stern and commanding, "is a hard-working fairy who earns her keep with her superior work ethic and commitment to details. Old means experienced, and I happen to have the most experienced assistant at FGA. You will be kind to her, or you will be reassigned to Advanced Love Branch in the basement."

The three women gasped in shock.

"She can't do that," one of them said.

The other one shook her head. "She might be able to," she said in a haunted voice. Her mouth was covered with her hand, but her words were still audible.

"Doris will decode reports for us, and then I'll assign them," Paris said, leaving out the fact the old fairy couldn't do that until she'd napped and had a snack and done the crossword puzzle and told someone a story from her youth. Then Doris was really productive for roughly twenty to twenty-five minutes before she needed a bathroom break and another nap. She was helpful and did the work, just at her own turtle pace.

"Fine," one of the fairy godmothers said in a resigned voice. "Well, what do you want to know about the Practical Romance Department?"

Paris offered a smile. She wanted not to appear intimidating but definitely demand proper respect. "Let's start with introductions, followed by an overview of what you all do, what you'd like to be doing, ideas that you have, and how we can make this place more successful."

CHAPTER TWELVE

Refinement Department, Fifth Floor, FGA Tower, New York City, New York

"You'll do great," Penny offered when she escorted Paris up to the fifth floor where the Refinement Department was located. "People are going to see what a great manager you are, and then they'll be bending over backward to work for you."

"Well, I'd appreciate it if they didn't roll their eyes when I talk," Paris muttered as they stepped off the elevator to a very different floor than the one they'd come from.

"They are testing you, but you dealt with them great," Penny said. "I was surprised at how well you listened as the others went on with their complaints about the Practical Romance Department."

"I was too," Paris agreed.

"Yeah, I expected you to cut them off and tell them to suck it up, buttercup."

"Usually, I would have, but I'm under a listening spell." Paris pointed to her shiny boots. "We can thank Dwyer for my good behavior."

Penny grinned. "Well, I think it was smart to listen on your first day. If I know you, you'll go home and process everything you've learned and return with ways of making things better."

"Or a lot of duct tape," Paris joked. "Those girls do go on about their problems."

"Tell me about it." She waved as Christine Welsh, another of Paris' friends from Happily Ever After College walked over. Like Penny, she didn't wear the blue fairy godmother gown, so her red hair was visible. It had been Paris who started the trend of wearing her own clothes at Happily Ever After College, although the head professor, Mae Ling never did. She'd said she wasn't a trend setter like Paris and had encouraged her to be rebellious. She'd told Paris she was a change agent. If her friends were proof, Mae Ling was right.

"Oh, good, Paris is here," Christine gushed. "I can't wait for you to tell all the lame-o's in this department off. They really need to be straightened out with your no-nonsense approach. Get the insults ready to volley."

Paris scrunched up her nose and looked sideways at Penny. "Today might not be the one for me to be sassy."

Christine's smile faded. "Why? I was counting on you to whip all the fairy godmothers I work with into shape." She leaned forward and whispered, "Do you know that one of them buys her socks at Walmart? She says they are only socks, and it doesn't matter. There's another one who wears yoga pants and calls them slacks. No. Just no."

"Right, I realize the problems here are major," Paris said sarcastically.

"Paris is under a listening spell," Penny explained, helping her out. "She is compelled to mostly listen, which gives her the perfect opportunity to learn about what you do here before making any decisions or changes."

"What is it that you do here?" Paris asked, looking around and noticing many mannequins in the large open space. There were several bolts of fabric, dressers with jewelry and scarves, and tables that appeared set for tea service. The whole arrangement made it feel like something between a fashion runway and a department store.

"We refine," Christine said in a very dignified voice. "We take women and men and teach them how to dress, talk, eat and behave like classy members of society so that other people want to be around them."

"Yeah, like you've been helping us out with the guys from Sad Gaming Lion Company," Paris said.

Christine huffed. "No, usually we work with human beings, not chimpanzees, which is what those creatures are. I have to admit your employees in the Casual Romance department have a losing battle getting the guys dates, even with all that Penny and I have done to help."

"I appreciate it, and Isha's and Holly's jobs depend on them being successful, so let's hope your efforts pay off," Paris said with a wink.

"Wow, you're a tough manager, but it's good that we're friends, and you'll hold me to low expectations," Christine said and steered Paris around to guide her into the department space.

"Oh, I know what you're capable of, Christina, and I'm holding you to higher expectations than all the rest."

"My name is Christine, and you know that."

"I also know that you loathe when people mess up your name," Paris said with a sneaky grin.

Christine released her own sly expression. "Welcome to the Refinement Department. You're not going to fit in at all, but you're going to rock this place's foundation in the very best of ways."

CHAPTER THIRTEEN

Basic Love Conference Room, Twenty-Fifth Floor, FGA Tower, New York City, New York

Paris hoped the listening spell was wearing off. She'd spent an hour touring the Refinement Department and not saying half the things she wanted to. Her comments would have consisted of, "Why do you all waste so many resources buying fashion magazines?" "No one needs that many purses to sample. Or in general." Or maybe, "You all need to read an actual book and stop giving each other makeovers."

However, Paris couldn't say any of her usual snarky comments due to the spell Dwyer put on her shoes with magical listening polish. Maybe that was for the best because she now had a thorough knowledge of what happened in the Refinement Department. She saw its use and where it could trim up things and be more useful to the average Joe and Jane, and not by dressing women up to look like Kate Middleton in frilly hats like they were going to tea.

That thought reminded Paris of something important. "I can't stay long," Paris said to her boss as she waved bye to Christine and took a seat at the table in the Basic Love conference room.

"Why?" Agent Barney Jasper asked, lowering the file he was reading and regarding her with a disappointed look. "We have to conduct interviews soon to fill the IT and Operations Director positions, and that can't happen until we complete the grading process for applicants."

"Well, as I said before, I think we are spending too much time meeting about a meeting we're having about an interview," Paris said, earning contemptuous glares from the other agents around the table. "Also, I have a tea with Sherlock Holmes to get to."

Many of the men in the room laughed at her. Everyone in the room was a man, but thankfully for many of them, they didn't all laugh at Paris.

"Would you please stop interrupting the meeting with your made-up excuses about why you have to leave early?" Agent Jasper asked and slid his hand over his slicked-back hair. Not a strand was out of place.

"Were you late because you were meeting with Poirot?" one of the agents asked.

Paris shook her head. "No, I was late because no one told my new departments that I was in charge of them, making orientation a nightmare." She turned her glare on Barney.

"Oops, I knew I was forgetting something," he said, picking up his phone and scrolling through it.

"She got more departments?" an agent asked. "So, it's true then, is it? You're favoring her because she's a Beaufont?"

Paris really wished this listening spell would wear off because she had a lot of things she wanted to say, and they weren't coming out of her mouth, no matter how hard she tried.

"She is favored because she risked everything to fix the love meter several times, investigating when music was spelled, Josh was trying to kill us all, and more recently, Paris drew out the rat trying to bring FGA down." Barney didn't give her a look like he was proud of her but rather tolerating her. "Agent Beaufont, for all her faults, is proving to be a resource and will be treated as such. Saint Valentine is very interested in seeing what she'll do next."

Paris wanted to say something, but again, no words came out of her mouth, which meant her boss kept talking.

"I think it's a mixed bag," Barney continued. "She may be something great, or she'll get us in a lot of trouble. That's the thing about evolution. There's a fine line between thinking enough that you create good changes and too big that you blow a place up."

Wishing she knew sign language, Paris smiled.

"Really?" Barney asked, surprised, and looked at Paris. "You don't reply to that?"

"I guess not," Paris managed to say.

"Okay, well, then we'll get started," Barney said, filing through the stack of resumes. "I've reviewed your interview questions and grading matrixes for the applicants. Most sent me really good material." He shot a glance at Paris that seemed to say, "Where was your email?"

If Paris could have spoken, she would have said, "I was busy getting rid of Jackson Zelle while you were being a desk jockey." Instead, she shrugged in reply.

"Unfortunately, it appears we've lost many of the best applicants for the IT and Operations Director position," Barney continued. "We believe Jackson Zelle took them before he left, but the reasons for that are unclear."

Paris leaned forward. This was important information she needed to know more about. Thankfully her mouth started working again.

"Why would he take those resumes?"

Barney sighed, at a loss. "I really don't know. There's so much we don't know about the old Director of Finance. None of us, even Saint Valentine, were aware he was doing so many treacherous things to break the foundation of FGA. We're starting to understand how he financially had us tied to industries that hurt the love meter, but still, there's a lot to uncover."

"Do you think he was going to use the talent applying for the IT position for his own gain?" Paris asked.

"It's possible," Barney answered, not sounding sure.

"The resumes, they are just gone?" Paris asked.

"All traces were wiped clean from the Human Resources database. So no, there's no way to find out if Jackson contacted the applicants or about what." He thumped his hand down on the stack of files. "We have these, and that's our pool of candidates. So, we'll start interviews very soon."

"Sir, I hear there's a lot of corporate restructuring," an agent interjected. "Can we still afford a new director with what's happened to the Finance Department? There are rumors there is going to be some downsizing."

Paris could have sworn the agent cut his eyes at her, but she ignored the look. It wasn't like she could say anything anyway.

"We're not sure how the corporate restructuring will look," Barney said. "This is all very new. We will need an IT and Operations Director, so yes, the positions will get filled. It's our job to find the right person for the role. I'm counting on all of you for that. If we're going to turn FGA around, we need good people in place. Then we can repair what's happened."

Paris had to give it to him. Agent Barney Jasper might get under her skin and be superficial and obsessed with his reputation and appearance, but he also had the right motivations when it came to FGA. She sure hoped it was true because if she found another rat in that corporation, then she was stringing them up in the lobby as a lesson to the rest.

CHAPTER FOURTEEN

Elevator, FGA Tower, New York City, New York

Paris was in the elevator when she tried to summon Wilfred to her. She assumed he'd be available like he had been before. Paris was looking forward to more bad jokes delivered poorly by the magitech AI, so she was disappointed when he didn't pop up. Paris was even more disheartened when alone on the elevator, and the possessed compartment decided not to take her to the third floor like she'd told it but rather down.

She watched as the numbers lit up as the elevator descended. "Don't you dare take me to the basement…"

The second-floor button lit up as she passed it. Then the first floor. Finally, it stopped on B1, which was the first level for the basement out of a total of five. The elevator doors sprang open to reveal a darkness so black it felt like the pits of hell.

The frigid wind blasted Paris in the face and made her step back several inches. This time she didn't retreat like before when the sounds of whimpering echoed down the long dark corridor ahead of her. Instead, Paris stepped forward out of the compartment. If the elevator kept taking her to the basement, she might as well see what it wanted or if it was simply trying to kill her.

Pulling out Amantis, Paris made her way out into the hallway. It smelled moldy so badly it made her eyes water. Before, Paris had imagined that whatever was making the howling noise in the basement was a ghost. This time, it sounded like something was alive and hurt. It wasn't that far away; around the corner, she guessed.

Holding up her wand, she lit the tip and made a ball of light that cascaded around her, illuminating her surroundings. As she guessed, Paris was in a damp hallway with open doors along the walls. A cursory glance inside some of the rooms told her they were abandoned offices. The desks and chairs inside them appeared mostly unused, and they seemed in better condition than the stuff she had in her own office.

"Maybe the elevator is taking me down here because I need office furniture," Paris muttered to herself.

She remembered she wasn't alone when the whimpering happened again. It sounded like a small animal. Its calls sounded like it was afraid.

Turning in the direction of the sound, Paris started forward again, every muscle in her body at the ready. She reasoned that if something down here was hurt, then whatever had injured it could be down here too. Paris didn't call out to let the animal know she was approaching, and due to the listening spell, Paris' ears strained to hear what was around her.

A small cardboard box was vibrating, and the crying creature appeared to be inside it. Cautiously, Paris inched forward and leaned over to see what was inside the box, which was soaking wet.

Her heart nearly sank with panic and fear when she saw the animal and who she recognized at once.

CHAPTER FIFTEEN

Basement, FGA Tower, New York City, New York

"Faraday!" Paris gasped and reached down to pick up the squirrel. His eyes widened as the light from the wand reflected off them, but she spied the relief in his gaze.

He was soaking wet, and it made him look very small. He was shivering with cold as Paris lifted him out of the box and into her other arm.

"Are you okay?" Paris asked, looking him over the best she could. "What happened?"

"In-in-investigating tw-tw-twenty-sixth floor," he stuttered, his teeth chattering.

Paris wiggled out of her jacket the best she could with the wand in one hand and Faraday in the other. She wrapped him up, also careful to keep her attention on their surroundings. "Then what happened? How did you get down here?"

He shook his head. "I-I-I don't know. I blacked out as soon as I made it to the twenty-sixth floor."

Paris let out a breath of confusion. "You just ended up here?" She pointed to the drenched and empty filing box. "You woke up here?"

"Cold and wet and alone and so afraid. It was unlike anything I can explain."

"That's so strange," Paris said, turning and making for the elevator. She needed to get Faraday dry and warm before he caught something. "There must be a dark magic portal or something on the twenty-sixth floor. Maybe it's connected to the basement. I don't know, but no more going there until I'm with you."

"I promise, I won't go back there without you," he said, his voice still shaking.

Paris had never seen him like this. The squirrel didn't frighten easily, and she knew it was jarring to him to black out like that. He must have just woken, but she'd been there to find him. Maybe the elevator took her to the basement to find him. Maybe the elevator had a good reason to keep taking her down there. She'd have to find out later when she didn't have more pressing matters.

Stepping onto the elevator, Paris was grateful for the light, allowing her to put away Amantis and look Faraday over.

"Are you all right besides from being wet and cold?" she asked, holding him tightly, trying to warm him up.

"Yes, I'm not hurt," he said, nuzzling into her, exhausted from his adventures. "Thank you for finding me. I was lost without you."

Paris smiled at her best friend as the elevator took them up and away from the dark, cold basement.

CHAPTER SIXTEEN

Roya Lane, London

Although Paris had wanted Faraday to go with her to meet Sherlock Holmes, it was clear the little squirrel had been through an ordeal and needed to rest. He was told not to leave the third floor, and Doris was given strict orders to keep an eye on him. When Paris had left, the old woman was telling him about when electricity was invented.

Meanwhile, Faraday was hard at work on a new project. He said coming up with a remote love meter app that could be installed on Paris' phone would take his mind off things. Unfortunately, he really couldn't remember anything after arriving on the twenty-sixth floor. There was nothing for Paris to investigate until she ventured to the twenty-sixth floor too, which wasn't happening anytime soon since she didn't need a bath and nap. Well, she would have loved them, but not in the way Faraday got one.

Paris didn't know if it was teatime or not, but she was ready to meet the great Sherlock Holmes. He had left the farmhouse bright and early that morning, saying he'd start looking for a lead on Subfar so they could track down the Protector of Wealth.

Apparently, Subfar had intentionally left behind clues for the detective to find if anyone should ever want to locate him. It was all very convoluted why the man had gone into hiding but also left a way of finding him. One had to find Sherlock Holmes first, and that in itself had been a feat. The Englishman was now living with Paris at Little Pleasures, and her life had gotten stranger, which was saying a lot.

Sherlock had said to meet him on Roya Lane at teatime that afternoon. He hadn't said where to meet him, which was pretty much par for the course in Paris' strange life. She wasn't sure how she'd feel if the people in her life told her things directly instead of giving her as few details as possible and making everything into a riddle. According to Mama Jamba, it was more fun this way.

Paris was relieved to find after striding down the cobbled lane that finding the great detective wouldn't be a wild goose chase yet again. Sherlock Holmes, who looked as if he'd stepped out of one of Sir Conan Doyle's novels, was standing next to an old lamp post, fog hovering around in patches, although there wasn't any mist on the rest of Roya Lane.

He was wearing a pale green tweed suit and a flat cap. In one hand, he was holding a pipe, although Paris hadn't seen him smoke it. When his eyes connected with hers, he appeared to see right through her.

"Is the squirrel all right?" Sherlock Holmes asked in his deep voice, his English accent strong.

Paris paused and gave him a skeptical expression. "How do you know that something happened to Faraday?"

He waved at her with his pipe. "Your jacket is wet in places, and there are patches of the squirrel's hair on you. Also, you're late when you're usually punctual, and you appear somewhat disheveled by something I deduce pertains to unanswered questions and a lack of time to sort through them currently."

"Wow, you're good," Paris said and shook her head. "Yes,

Faraday is fine, and also, yes, I have a mystery to unravel, but it will have to wait."

"Well, I might be able to help when the time comes to untangle the mystery related to the curious squirrel, but I think our current mission must be top of the list. You found me to locate Subfar, and I'm supposing this is because your financial needs are pressing. The sooner we locate the Protector of Wealth, the sooner you can accomplish your goals."

"Okay, great," Paris said, liking the strange way the old detective talked. "Well, what have you learned so far, and how may I help?"

He held up a single finger, pausing her. "First, we have tea. Then we discuss the case. Teatime waits for no one."

"Okay, well, I grew up on Roya Lane, and I don't know where one goes to for tea," Paris said, looking around at the odd shops that sold strange magical items or were run by shady gnomes that stole unsuspecting elves' money.

"Well, to a tea shop, of course."

"Yeah, but I don't think there's one here."

"Certainly there is. It's right behind us."

Paris gave him a look of confusion before glancing at what she was pretty certain was a blank brick wall. To her amazement and surprise, the fog that had covered the light post and Sherlock Holmes drifted away to reveal a cute little tea parlor. Paris was confused about why she'd never noticed the place since it looked darling with frilly curtains in the large window, the bright pink door, and a sign in curvy letters that read Wonderland.

Sherlock Holmes offered his arm to her, a sly expression on his face. "Shall we, Agent Beaufont?"

She was curious about what they'd find in the whimsical-looking tea parlor.

CHAPTER SEVENTEEN

Wonderland Tea Shop, Roya Lane, London

The tea parlor was even more whimsical on the inside than the storefront suggested. The walls were painted with a mural of a garden with a windmill and a haunted woods in the distance. It was so lifelike that the branches of the trees moved and birds circled in the blue sky.

The dining room itself was full of various-sized tables covered with different colored cloths and frilly doilies. The chairs arranged around the tables didn't match either. Covering a long set of tables were assorted tea pots and saucers and cups, bowls of sugar and cream. There were also several towers of delicious-looking treats. The whole thing was so storybook that Paris realized she'd been speechless for a solid minute, staring at the sight. She hadn't even noticed the strange guests sitting around the long table and talking loudly.

Paris blinked at a man sitting in a tall chair and wearing a large hat. She thought she recognized him. The bunny-looking person beside him also appeared familiar, as was the white rabbit at the far end of the table who was very visibly fretting about something.

"Wait, we're in Wonderland," Paris said and turned to face Sherlock Holmes.

"Naturally. That is the name of the tea shop."

"We're in Wonderland," she repeated. She pointed to the man with the oversized top hat with an orange sash and wearing a floral velvet suit jacket. "That's the Mad Hatter."

Sherlock Holmes shook his head. "No, that's King Rudolf Sweetwater."

Paris blinked at the man who was pouring something from a flask into his teacup. He then threw the saucer and cup over his shoulder and took a drink from the flask. No one appeared to mind the crash of the cup when it broke on the floor behind the table. Sherlock was right. The man was Paris' uncle, the king of the fae.

Sitting beside him with bunny ears and teeth to match and wearing a suit was the assassin baker, Lee, the owner of the Crying Cat Bakery. She pulled out a watch, opened it, and emptied its contents, gears, and screws into the cup in front of her. Then she slid it down the table to the white rabbit, who wasn't a rabbit at all. Much like Lee, Ramy had floppy ears and bunny teeth, but he was wearing a white suit that made him appear like the rabbit from the classic tale.

"Here, drink this. It will make you feel better," Lee said, pushing the teacup over for Ramy.

He grabbed at his ears and tugged nervously. "Oh, my fur and whiskers! I'm late I'm late I'm late!"

"I have an excellent idea," Lee offered, grabbing another teacup and filling it with a steaming pot of dark liquid. "Let's change the subject."

"Yes!" Rudolf exclaimed, thrusting his hand with the flask into the air, a wide grin on his pale face, his eyes covered in bright eyeshadow. "Like, why is a raven like a writing desk?"

Paris giggled, not gaining their attention. Her friend's attention was all on their crazy tea party. "That's so funny they dressed up to have tea here."

Sherlock turned to her and gave her a curious expression. "They did not. One doesn't have to dress up when they come to Wonderland. One simply is immersed and becomes who they would be here."

Paris gave him a skeptical expression. "That's impossible. What are you saying? This is like a fully immersive, magical experience that transforms people into characters from Alice in Wonderland? That's crazy."

"It might be, but it's the case," Sherlock Holmes said.

"Yes, but I'm looking at you, and you look exactly like you always do," she argued.

He held up his pipe and grinned at her. "That's because I'm Sherlock Holmes."

"Right," Paris muttered. "No arguing with that logic. Well, how about the fact that I haven't been transformed?"

"Haven't you, though?" he challenged, standing back and looking at her.

Paris glanced down and nearly fell over as she took in her appearance, which was not at all what she remembered.

CHAPTER EIGHTEEN

So overwhelmed by the sights around her, Paris hadn't even realized her appearance had changed without her consent. She definitely hadn't signed on to be wearing a pale blue dress that fell off her shoulders or black shoes. She swung around until she caught her reflection in the front window.

Stunned, her hand went to the black bow in her hair, which now hung in long ringlets over her shoulder. She couldn't believe it, but somehow she'd been magically transformed to look exactly like a modern version of Alice in Wonderland. It was so amazing she didn't mind so much she was wearing a dress. It wasn't that uncomfortable. Even now, she was aware she was wearing it.

"Curiouser and curiouser," Paris said in awe.

"Another of the effects of dining here is that you speak in lines from your character."

"Wow, it would be so nice if something made sense for a change," Paris said and then clapped a hand over her mouth, wondering where that phrase came from.

"Shall we have tea then?" Sherlock asked as he waved at the mismatched table of lunacy.

"We're supposed to be discussing the case of finding Subfar," Paris argued, thoroughly bewildered. "I'm afraid that not much coherent talk will happen here."

A twinkle sparkled in Sherlock's eyes. "I'm all too aware of that. This meeting wasn't to discuss finding Subfar. Before that can begin, I realized that I needed an assistant. You see, I can work alone, but as I've told you before, I prefer not to. Even if they are dull and obtuse, I find having someone to bounce ideas off helps me to make breakthroughs in cases. The more unknowing my assistant is, the more likely they are to ask questions that lead me down new paths. I'm here to find someone to accompany me."

"Well, I can help you find Subfar," Paris offered, pressing her hands down on the puffy blue dress, surprised by how real it was for having magically appeared on her. "I am the one who wants you to find him."

"You are an agent presiding over three departments for FGA after a series of tumultuous events at the corporation," Sherlock said. "Furthermore, your squirrel has gone through trauma, and you have many a mystery of your own to unravel and a wedding to attend at the end of the week. I believe you're already spread thin enough, Agent Beaufont."

"Okay, so who do you want to be your assistant?" Paris asked.

Sherlock bobbed his head in the direction of the table full of raving mad people she knew who were in new forms. "I believe the candidates have arrived for their interview. It is unnecessary for them to know they are interviewing for my famed assistant role. However, I do require tea at this point."

Paris followed Sherlock Holmes over to the tea table with the Mad Hatter, March Hare, and the White Rabbit and realized she shouldn't have thought her life was a farce before. She should have known that only encouraged the universe to make it all the crazier.

"If I had a world of my own, everything would be nonsense," Paris said. She was about to have the strangest tea party, no doubt about it.

CHAPTER NINETEEN

"Oh! Alice is here!" King Rudolf exclaimed when Sherlock Holmes pulled out a chair covered in yellow upholstery for Paris and offered it to her.

She took the seat with a smile. "I'm still going by Paris."

"Of course you are," Rudolf said, tipping his large hat at her and grinning under the brim. "You must have a cup of tea!"

"She should have some wine," Lee said as she took out a large knife from the breast pocket of her suit jacket and stirred her tea with it.

Paris glanced around at the table full of broken teapots and full pots and dishes with various patterns and trays of food. "I don't see any wine."

"There isn't any," Lee said at once, putting down her knife and taking a sip of the tea.

"Then it wasn't very civil of you to offer it," Paris said. She was speaking from Lewis Carroll's book of Alice in Wonderland's adventures without meaning to or being able to stop.

"It wasn't very civil of you to sit down without being invited," Lee said, perfectly playing the part of the grumpy March Hare.

Paris harrumphed and looked down the table at Ramy, who was moving things around the table like he'd misplaced something. "Is everything all right?"

Ramy looked up, his white whiskers making him look mousey, but his floppy ears making him look the part of the White Rabbit. "I'm late! I'm late! For a very important date! No time to say 'Hello, goodbye.' I'm late I'm late I'm late!"

"Drink your tea," Lee said dryly. Taking the bowl of sugar, she poured her tea into it instead of putting a cube into her drink. She took a sip of the bowl of sugar cubes and smiled. "Perfect."

Ramy, wishing for the same enjoyment, took a sip of his tea and at once began to choke. His white-gloved hands flew to his throat as he spewed and coughed, but no one around the table bothered to help. Paris watched as Ramy's face flushed a violent shade of red. His mouth coughed and coughed until no air was able to pass through, and then he keeled over dead.

"Oh, he must have choked on the watch parts I put in his tea," Lee said casually and sipped on her sugar with a bit of tea.

"In the end, it's always time that kills us," Rudolf said and drank from his flask.

Sherlock Holmes leaned over and whispered into Paris' ear. "Ramy is out of the running. Now it's between the other two to see who becomes my assistant."

CHAPTER TWENTY

Paris, realizing she should embrace this craziness, snatched the closest teapot and inspected its contents before pouring some for Sherlock and then herself.

"So, what do you have to say for yourself?" King Rudolf asked her as he picked up his own teapot and filled a cup.

"I'm afraid I can't explain myself because I'm not myself, you know," she answered at once, unaccustomed to this strange Alice in Wonderland spell. Earlier she couldn't talk when she wanted to, and now she was saying things she didn't intend.

King Rudolf again threw the cup with tea and its saucer over his shoulder, then took a sip from his flask. "You used to be much more muchier. You've lost your muchness."

"Thanks," Paris said. "Is it because I smell like a wet squirrel? Take me as I am, I guess."

"You might as well say," Lee began, using her big knife to spread jam on a biscuit, "that 'I like what I get' is the same thing as 'I get what I like.'"

"That doesn't even make any sense," Paris said. She blinked at the assassin as red strawberry jam dripped off her knife in a very menacing fashion.

"Yes, but you're the one who is stark raving mad," Lee countered and took a bite of her biscuit.

"Aren't we all mad here?" Paris asked.

A cat appeared beside her, his fur was various bright colors, and there was a grin on his face. While Paris knew he was supposed to look like the famed Cheshire Cat, she recognized him as her mother's familiar, the even more famous Plato. "Hey, you stole my line. I've been waiting all this time to say it."

"Say another line," Paris encouraged.

Hovering in the air and curled up like he was on an invisible branch, Plato shook his head. "I can't be prompted into reciting lines."

"*Twinkle, twinkle little bat,*" Rudolf began singing, swaying back and forth. "*How I wonder what you're at. Up and above the world you fly, like a tea-tray in the sky.*"

Paris turned to Sherlock Holmes. "Any closer to narrowing down what we're working on? Is the lynx in the running?"

Sherlock glanced at Plato, whose eyes were glowing brightly. "The cat doesn't want to help, so no, and no to your other question."

"Yeah, and the cat isn't much help because he talks in riddles," Paris shared in a whisper.

"I love a good riddle!" King Rudolf exclaimed.

"I love a good killing," Lee yelled, finishing her cup of sugar.

"Maybe this isn't the right place to find someone," Paris imparted quietly to Sherlock Holmes. "They are all crazy."

"I'm not crazy," Plato said slyly, appearing between Sherlock and Paris. "My reality is just different than yours."

Paris pursed her lips. "Are you happy that you got your line?"

"Infinitely so," Plato answered, and with a pop, he disappeared.

"Are we going to have a merry unbirthday celebration before we run out of time?" Lee asked, then threw her bowl of sugar at the wall. It broke into pieces.

"What's the hurry?" Rudolf asked.

"Tomorrow is my actual birthday, and we are dangerously close to it being that wretched day."

"Oh, my!" Rudolf said with a gasp. "What do we do on birthdays? Do I have to take something from you? Should I? Maybe we should do a merry un-celebration?"

"Don't be absurd," Lee said and began picking her teeth with the knife. "I'm going on a crusade to defeat time. That's the only way to firmly win this war so that every day is a merry unbirthday."

Without another word, Lee, as the March Hare, stood and strode for the exit. At the door, she turned. Her floppy ears made her appear cute even though she was still brandishing the knife covered in red jam. "I wish you all a very merry unbirthday! Until tomorrow when I hope you all wish me a very unpleasant birthday."

"Until tomorrow." Rudolf picked up a teapot that sloshed with liquid and threw it across the room, nearly hitting Lee with it. The ceramic shattered against the wall, but the assassin didn't even flinch before she pivoted and exited the tea shop.

"I guess the choice for my assistant is clear," Sherlock Holmes said to Paris when things had settled down.

"You're going solo," she guessed.

He shook his head and indicated Rudolf with this pipe. "I know it doesn't make much sense, but his strangeness brings out my brilliance. We worked well together before. It's evident he doesn't have much going on."

"In his head or on his schedule?" Paris questioned and then shrugged. "Either way, the answer is probably yes."

"Are you two wondering how to defeat a Jabberwock?" Rudolf asked.

"We are not," Sherlock answered at once.

"We are considering giving you a job," Paris disclosed. "Sherlock needs an assistant when he goes to find Subfar. Are you interested?"

"Maybe, but have you guessed the riddle yet?"

"You didn't tell me a riddle," Paris said, blinking at her uncle.

"I don't know the answer, so we're even."

Paris glanced at Sherlock. "Are you sure you want him as your assistant?"

"I want a clean cup," Rudolf said, jumping up to his feet. "Let's all move one place."

Sherlock gave her a slight smile and nodded. "Yes, he'll be perfect."

Rudolf shoved at Paris, encouraging her to move down the table so he could take her spot.

She forced herself out of the chair but didn't move down to the next spot. "Well, I've had enough nonsense. I'm going home." With that, Paris left Wonderland. She hoped not to return anytime soon but knew she'd undoubtedly be back. Once someone visited Wonderland, they always returned.

CHAPTER TWENTY-ONE

Roya Lane, London

Paris was grateful that her appearance returned to normal when they exited the Wonderland Tea Shop. She and Sherlock Holmes had left as Rudolf jumped up onto the tea table to do a dance he said he'd invented.

The great detective told him to get it all out of his system, and they'd start the investigation first thing in the morning. King Rudolf didn't seem to know what he was signing on for but that was typical. Paris thought he would somehow end up being very helpful in the case of locating Subfar.

"So, what now?" Paris asked Sherlock Holmes when they stood on the cool streets of Roya Lane, the fog rolling in more than before. "Do you and Rudolf go looking for Subfar and you let me know when you've located him?"

"Not quite," Sherlock said as he led the way down the cobbled road. "First we need a lead, and for that, I think you should accompany me on one more trip."

"Oh?" Paris asked. "Are you taking me to the Leaky Cauldron for butterbeer?"

"I don't understand your reference, but I deduce it is a literary one," Sherlock said.

"Yeah, it was a joke."

"I need to question the person who saw Subfar last," Sherlock said. "That's always the best place to start when looking for a missing person."

Paris thought for a moment. "I'm guessing that's his brother, Subner."

"I believe you know the way to the Fantastical Armory."

"Oh, I do. Can't you get in there on your own? You are Sherlock Holmes."

"I think you underestimate all the places you have access to just by being you. Most can't simply walk into the Fantastical Armory where Father Time and Mother Nature often take tea."

"Oh, that would have been less of a headache, having tea with those two," Paris muttered. "Wish I'd thought of that before."

"Sadly, neither would make a good assistant to me," Sherlock argued.

"It would have still been a headache for me because they really talk in riddles," Paris supplied.

"As well, you have access to the House of Fourteen as a Royal, Happily Ever After College and FGA as a fairy godmother, and the Great Library. Never take for granted that you have many places and people at your disposal based on who you are, and more importantly, because of what you've done."

Paris was glad for the reminder. "So, you want me to take you to the Fantastical Armory to question Subner?"

"If you wouldn't mind," Sherlock Holmes said, holding out his arm again.

She took it and smiled up at the great detective. Working cases with Sherlock Holmes was on the list of the incredible access she had to people, all because she was Paris Beaufont.

CHAPTER TWENTY-TWO

Fantastical Armory, Roya Lane, London

Paris was surprised at who she found in the Fantastical Armory talking to Subner, the Protector of Weapons.

"Hey, Dad! What are you doing here?" Paris asked, giving Stefan Ludwig a peck on the cheek upon seeing him inside the shop full of weapons and artifacts.

"Annoying me with ridiculous requests," Subner muttered, pushing a stringy piece of black hair behind his big ears. He was wearing his usual sullen expression and pretending to read a book because sometimes some things didn't change.

"Hey, Pare," Stefan said, hugging his daughter into him. Like Subner, he was wearing all black and was in his usual long cloak that covered the many weapons the Warrior for the House of Fourteen was no doubt carrying. The demon hunter didn't so much as go to the grocery store without a knife strapped to each leg and more hidden all over his person.

His hair was also jet-black like Subner's but short and stuck straight up like he'd been blasted by a cold wind, which he probably had while out hunting down a demon in the Arctic. Most expected that demons preferred heat because they were hellish creatures, but Paris had learned after hunting demons alongside her father that they preferred extreme cold. They could often be found in frigid temperatures. Like the first time she'd been in the basement of FGA, but then it had good reason for feeling haunted, as it was being stalked by a demon leeching energy off fairy godmothers and agents.

"I see that you and Sherlock Holmes are working cases," Stefan said, waving at the detective. "What brings you two here?"

"Paris like you wants to annoy me," Subner said, turning the page of his book. "She does it by simply existing rather than demanding things I don't have."

"What's going on?" Paris asked as Sherlock slipped away to the front of the shop where Papa Creola and Mama Jamba appeared to be playing a game of chess. The pieces on the board didn't look like the usual king, queen, bishop, rook, and pawn. These appeared more lifelike and were moving on their own around the board.

"I was asking if Subner could make me a special weapon to kill a very powerful demon," Stefan explained. "None of my weapons have worked on this particular creature."

"I'm telling you; I don't have anything that will work on Tomár. He's too powerful." Subner didn't glance up to relate this as he did his usual, "This conversation isn't important enough to demand my full attention" act and continued to pretend to read his book.

"There has to be something," Stefan insisted, his face flushed with passion. "I've defeated strong demons."

"Tomár is different," Subner mumbled, turning another page of his old book.

"I know, which is why it's so important I find a weapon and stop him," Stefan said and banged his fist on the glass counter between him and the grumpy elf.

"Have you considered it won't be a weapon that takes Tomár down?" Mama Jamba asked casually from the front of the shop, where she sat in her pink armchair next to the large display window. She was wearing a blue velvet tracksuit that matched her big hair.

Stefan turned to Mother Nature. Sherlock Holmes watched the game with a furrowed brow. "Magic spells don't work on demons. In my experience, it's always a sword or an axe, but none of my usual blades work on Tomár."

"He's the oldest living demon," Papa Creola said as he moved a piece on the strange chessboard. Father Time was wearing a tie-dye shirt that said, If you're not barefoot, you're overdressed.

"Unlike most things that weaken with time, demons get stronger," Mama Jamba hummed, nodding at the board and making a piece move several places.

Too curious to resist, Paris strode over. "What are you playing?"

"It isn't chess," Sherlock Holmes said, combing his hand over his chin and staring down at the game board, studying it intently.

"No, chess is a game without consequences," Papa Creola said firmly and leaned forward to examine the board up close.

"This is All Gods Go To Heaven, which is a ridiculous name," Mama Jamba offered as she leaned back in her chair, a satisfied expression on her face.

"Since no gods go to Heaven," Papa Creola muttered, his nose inches from the piece closest to him.

"Wait, does what you're playing here affect the world out there?" Paris asked, pointing out the window.

"Oh good! She can figure out things that are obvious," Subner grumbled.

"It affects gods out there," Mama Jamba said.

"Gods?" Stefan asked and came over to join Sherlock and Paris. "There are other gods out there besides you two? I thought you two pretty much ran this show."

"We do," Mama Jamba said. "There are hundreds of smaller deities. Papa and I got careless in the beginning and thought we'd elect a bunch of demigods to do things for us. At one point, I had over a hundred gods working for me—everything from sun gods with the Greeks to wind gods in Native American culture."

"It got ugly fast because there's delegating, and then there's total chaos when no one minds their own territory."

"It's true," Mama Jamba affirmed, sipping her tea. "They weren't like us. Most of them were flawed and allowed their own stories to get in the way of their rule." She shrugged. "We created a lot of superhuman gods with too much power and way too many competing desires. So, we got rid of all of them and replaced the whole thing with different magical races. Everyone had power potential."

"Wait, you got rid of all of your gods?" Paris asked. "Like Zeus and Aphrodite? Are those the gods you mean?"

"As well as Osiris and Ra in Egypt and Shiv and Krishna in Hindu. It was a mess when they were all reigning. Took forever for us to clean things up."

"How did you get rid of them?" Sherlock asked. "You said they can't go to heaven. Does that mean they can't die?"

Mama Jamba smiled and put down her teacup. "They can't, but they can be contained for the most part."

"Is that what this game is about?" Stefan asked. "Is this how you keep tabs on your gods?"

"Papa and I don't like to simply do things. It's more fun if we get to play a game to run this universe." She tapped the table. "Papa, you're out of moves."

The hippie with stringy hair and wearing cut-off shorts looked up. "I realize that. You know what that means then?"

"I do," she sang.

"Someone is going to have to intervene," he continued darkly.

"I do," Mama Jamba sang again.

Papa Creola pushed away from the table, a deep scowl on his face. "I guess we can't always be the ones to keep the gods contained."

"You know that's always been the case," Mama Jamba said cheerfully, undeterred by her partner's sullen mood. "Things are too complex, and cracks in the foundation of this Earth are inevitable."

"Can someone tell me what's going on?" Paris asked, glancing between the pair.

"You were born, and since then, the world has been worse off," Subner explained in a monotone.

"Thanks, Sub," Paris chimed. "I meant regarding this game Papa and Mama are playing. Is something wrong with one of your gods?"

"Dear, there's always a problem with the gods," Mama Jamba said. "We tried to make our jobs turn-key, and instead, we ended up creating a lot more work for ourselves."

"It's true," Papa Creola related. "When you're a young god with a brand-new shiny world, you don't realize the small errors you make will go on to follow you around and give you a headache for centuries to come."

"So, it's like you got a bunch of sheepdogs to run the farm, known as 'Earth,'" Stefan began in a speculative voice. "These were really powerful sheepdogs that lived forever."

"That's right, dear," Mama Jamba said with a smile. "They were untrainable dogs, so we created a giant kennel, but sometimes one of the mutts gets out."

"What can we do to help?" Stefan asked.

"You can answer that message on your phone," Mamba Jamba answered, pointing at his pocket.

"Oh, I didn't realize I had one." Stefan dug into his cloak and retrieved his phone. After glancing at the screen, he looked up. "It's Paul in the Great Library. He thinks a demon broke into the place."

"Demons aren't allowed in the Great Library," Sherlock Holmes said, confusion on his face.

"No, they usually aren't," Papa Creola replied.

"Tomár," Stefan said quietly. "He's powerful enough to break the wards that keep him out. Why would a demon want to go into the Great Library?"

"Very curious," Mama Jamba said with a sneaky grin. She was definitely hiding something.

"Well, I'll have to pay Paul a visit to investigate," Stefan said with a sigh. "I wish I had a weapon to take that demon down with."

"Can't help you," Subner said from the back, not missing a beat.

"Take Paris with you," Mama Jamba said. "She can help."

"Paris?" Stefan asked and looked between Mother Nature and his daughter. "This is a demon case."

"It's a case of love," Mama Jamba said.

"Love?" Paris asked. "Demons are all about evil."

Mama Jamba pursed her lips at Papa Creola. "They really get so upset when we don't offer them any help. Then when we do, they question us."

"I want to have children, you said," he mumbled grumpily. "They won't be too much work, you said."

"I know," she said. "They're so cute when they're little."

"Okay, so I need to go on this demon case with my dad," Paris said. "Then what?"

"Then I'm going to take a nap, and Papa is going to fix me dinner," Mama Jamba said. "Sometimes you run the world, and sometimes you tuck in early and get a nourishing meal."

"I could use a bath and a nap," Paris remarked dryly.

Her father affectionately put his arm around her shoulder and hugged her. "Instead, you get a mystery case to work with me. Get ready for demon smell. You never grow used to it."

CHAPTER TWENTY-THREE

The Great Library, Timbuktu, Mali

Sherlock Holmes stayed behind to question Subner about his brother's potential whereabouts. Although the Protector of Weapons wanted Subfar dead, he was also the best lead for finding him since he knew him so well and had been the last known person to see him.

This was going to get tricky because not only did Paris need to find Subfar with Sherlock Holmes' help, but then she had to figure out how to keep the brothers from warring. It had been Mortimer, the leader of the brownies, who had told her that a long-needed balance could occur if the two got along.

Paris shoved this complex problem to the back of her mind, deciding to deal with it once Sherlock had a lead and when she wasn't randomly hunting down a demon in the Great Library when she expected to be running her new departments. When Mother Nature told you to do something, you dropped everything and did as you were told.

The Great Library was as Paris remembered, which was to say, it made her speechless for a solid minute upon entering. How could a place that held every single volume ever written not? For Paris, it held so much more magic because, from a young age, she'd been spelled not to want to read. That would lead to knowledge and questions and potentially put her in danger. Paris' upbringing had been beyond complicated, to say the least.

What wasn't complicated to Paris was standing in a place that had so many stories. It was beautiful with its tall ceilings and glass walls and rooftop and, more importantly, shelf upon shelf filled with volume upon volume. If one was watching, one could spot a book appearing on a shelf for the very first time. It was like watching a child being born, seeing a book appear in the world for the first time. Forever and ever, its mark would be made on the world, always changed by its inception.

"It's pretty cool, huh?" Stefan asked Paris as they walked down the main walkway through the Great Library that stretched on for miles.

"It takes my breath away," Paris answered. "It's so heavily guarded by so much magic because knowledge is power. How could a demon get in here? More importantly, why?"

"Why isn't as important to me as how," Stefan said. "Tomár, I've been suspecting for a while, has been growing restless and doing many diabolical things without reason. It's not hard to believe he'd do something like breaking into the Great Library, which holds truths on the greatest treasures in the world. How he accomplished getting in here is what worries me. If he was able to do so, that means he's beyond the power I originally suspected, which was pretty great. Even the biggest weapons I've used to slay the strongest demons don't work on him. If he can get into the Great Library, I'm at a loss for how powerful he could be at this point."

"Okay, then the investigation begins, it seems," Paris said, looking up and down the aisle for clues. There was a faint smell of rot in the air. She felt that remnant sensation that something evil had been there recently. There was no other sign that a horrible soulless being had been in the Great Library. What was clear based on her demon intuition was that Tomár was gone, but he had been there and very recently. The question was why and how.

They came to the area that had to be where the demon arrived and took his wrath out on the library. No one would question that evil had ransacked the space. Volumes were strewn all over the place like someone didn't just dislike books. Rather, they despised them.

"Wow, he really made his mark," Paris observed.

"They always do," Stefan said. He shook his head as they stepped over books rudely left all over the floor in crumpled heaps. "Demons love to leave destruction in their wake. It's how they sign their pieces, as it were."

"So, what is this piece?" Paris asked as they neared the epicenter of destruction. "Library in disarray?"

"I think what is important is what Tomár was after," Stefan said. "I don't know, but I highly suspect he's the one behind this one. It feels like something he'd do."

Paris turned. Something was tugging at her hip, or her heart, or her spirit. She glanced down and saw Amantis lit up in her holster. The wand was trying to tell her something. She allowed it to pull her forward until she came to a single book lying in the middle of an aisle, with nothing else around it.

Paris pointed to the book lying on its side. "My wand led me over here. Do you think what Tomár wanted had to do with this book?"

Stefan moved past her and picked up the thick volume. He read the title before looking up, a sober expression in his eyes. "This is what I think he was after, but we're going to need more information to know why."

CHAPTER TWENTY-FOUR

A creature that was neither an owl nor a cat flew up to the tallest shelf and slid a book into place. The assistant to the Great Librarian, Beatrix, returned to her master a moment later and picked up another tossed volume, continuing the work of reshelving.

The gryphowl's brown wings were strong as they flapped, taking her and the book she had clutched in her front claws up to the highest shelf again. The magical creature was the perfect assistant for Paul because she was excellent at finding things, something necessary in the Great Library.

Beatrix's cat-like tail swooshed in the air as she pivoted and dove back down for another book.

Paris watched the gryphowl work for a moment before glancing at Paul. His face was covered in stress as he looked around at the ransacked area.

"Did you see the demon?" Stefan asked, kneeling and running his finger over a pile of ash near where they'd found the book, *Magical Creatures*, written by the giantess Bermuda Laurens.

"Yes, but only from a distance." He pointed at the front of the Great Library. "I had gone to the portal that leads to the Gullington, hoping to get help from a dragonrider, when the chaos broke out. I couldn't find any Dragon Elite members in the Castle, so I returned, about to call the House of Fourteen. That's when I spotted the red creature stalking out the front of the library. He was huge and had long curved horns on the side of his head."

Stefan drew in a breath. "That sounds like Tomár."

A look of shame covered Paul's face. "I didn't do anything. I froze at the sight of the demon and just watched him leave. I should have shot a spell at him or done anything. Instead, I messaged you."

"You did the right thing." Stefan stood and wiped the ash from his hands onto his cloak. "A spell wouldn't have worked on Tomár. I'm not sure what will. Whatever he came for, I have a feeling it will only make him even more powerful. Was he carrying anything? Was anyone with him?"

"Not with him," Paul answered as Beatrix came to land on his shoulder, seeming to offer him comfort. "I spied three figures ahead of him as if they'd just left the Great Library as well. I should have rushed forward to get a better look, but honestly, I was afraid of the demon seeing me. The way it made me feel, even from that distance, was horrible. I've never felt anything like it."

"You followed your instinct, and that kept you alive," Stefan told him. "If Tomár had spotted you, you'd be nearly drained of all your life right now. If you saw what he was after, those three figures, then he wouldn't have left you alive. Tomár loves the element of surprise, so he won't want us to know what he was after."

"Do you think he used dark magic to pull *Magical Creatures* from this book?" Paris asked, tapping on the thick volume in her hand.

"I know he did. He's up to something incredibly dangerous, making him potentially even more lethal. Not only did that rotten demon figure out how to bypass the wards on the Great Library, but he's harnessed a magic we've only theorized before.

Many have speculated that a spell to pull things from the books in the Great Library is possible, turning that which should be fiction or documentation into something real."

"How do we figure out what *Magical Creatures* Tomár pulled from this book?" Paris asked, opening the huge volume and flipping through it. There were hundreds of pages, making it nearly impossible to know which three creatures were out there in the world—loose and doing who knows what.

"There's only one person who will be able to tell you what came out of that book," Paul offered, giving Stefan a pointed expression.

The demon hunter knew the answer immediately. "The author of the book."

"Bermuda Laurens," Paris remarked and shut the cover. She looked at the front, where the magical creature's name was printed in bright gold letters.

"She's purely connected with that volume since it's technically the original and organic in nature. If anyone knows what the demon did using that book, it will be her."

"Can we borrow this?" Stefan asked.

"You don't even have to ask," Paul answered.

"Thanks," Stefan said. Making for the portal door to the House of Fourteen, he glanced over his shoulder at Paris. "Let's go find out what we're dealing with. Hopefully, we can stop Tomár quickly."

Paris hurried after her father and wondered what *Magical Creatures* the demon released and what their connections to love would be.

CHAPTER TWENTY-FIVE

Inner Peristyle, Getty Villa Museum, Malibu, California

For Paris and Stefan, according to her son, Rory Laurens, Bermuda wasn't far from the House of Fourteen. Apparently, the giantess was working on a magical creature case at the place with shimmering blue pools and a huge collection of Greek, Roman, and Etruscan statues and artifacts.

Paris snickered with amusement when she and her father stepped through the large doors of the museum. They looked quite out of place. A group of Asian tourists gawked at them, their mouths hanging open in awe. They had cameras in hand and appeared to be wrestling with whether they should take pictures of the architecture in the open-air museum or the pair who looked like they'd just stepped out of a Marvel movie.

"I think they are staring at you," Paris said. She pulled her shades down on her nose and smirked at her father.

"You're the one who looks like a motorcycle cop with that jacket and shades," he teased, having gotten the joke from Faraday.

"I'm not a motorcycle cop and don't look like an uptight agent for FGA," Paris replied. "You look exactly like what you are, a deadly demon hunter."

"I don't even have my sword out," Stefan whispered from the corner of his mouth.

"Like you need to draw any more attention to yourself," Paris joked. She saw a group of girls nearby checking out her father. He didn't look old enough to be Paris' dad because he technically wasn't. For the fifteen years, her parents had been stuck in another dimension, only a single day had passed for them there, time moving differently in that universe. Paris had grown up during that time, and for Liv and Stefan, they hadn't aged at all.

A guard in a black suit with an earpiece and a stern expression pointed to the wand on Paris' hip. "We don't allow weapons in here. Didn't they search you at the ticketing office?"

"We don't have tickets," Stefan said, studying the large open area with beautiful concrete ponds, flowers, and statues.

"Without tickets, no entry," the guard said. "With tickets, you still can't have that wand in here."

"I'm guessing this will be a problem too, then." Stefan slid his black cloak back to reveal a long sword sheathed on his hip as well as holsters on either leg with huge knives. There were no doubt knives in his boots and a weapon strapped to his back.

The Warrior for the House of Fourteen didn't just hunt demons. They knew he was their greatest enemy, and so they regularly hunted him. Thanks to his demon blood, they didn't stand a chance of sneaking up on him. Stefan Ludwig, like Paris, could sense a demon a mile away. It didn't appear there were any in the vicinity, only a lot of curious tourists and now an angry security guard.

The mortal's eyes widened, and he waved at the doors they came through. "You're going to have to leave immediately. We don't allow swords in here."

"We need a ticket?" Paris asked, stepping between the guard

and her father. She pulled her agent badge from her jacket and flashed it for the man to see. "Does this work?"

He narrowed his eyes on the emblem for FGA, then glanced at Paris. "You're an FGA Agent." The man seemed surprised but also impressed. He pointed at Stefan. "What about him?"

"I don't have any identification because I prefer for no one to know who I am," Stefan said darkly.

"Well, without identification, you're not getting in here," the security guard said, "and definitely not armed the way you are."

Paris wanted to laugh at how ridiculous this mortal was being, trying to stop her father. She had to give it to him; he wasn't backing down. It would only take a snap of her father's fingers to break the man's neck. He would never do it, but not many could stop Stefan Ludwig even if he wasn't armed.

"Look, Mister," Paris began, hoping to reason with the guy and not give away her father's identity. It really was best if people didn't know who he was. Warriors for the House of Fourteen, even those who weren't demon hunters, had enemies lurking everywhere. "How about you—"

"Paris Beaufont and Stefan Ludwig!" a deep woman's voice called from the other side of the courtyard. "What is an FGA Agent and Warrior for the House of Fourteen doing here?"

Paris rolled her eyes as their cover was blown by none other than Bermuda Laurens. The giantess stood on the other side of the long rectangular pool, her hands on her hips and not at all happy to see them.

CHAPTER TWENTY-SIX

"I told the Getty Museum I could handle the infestation and didn't need outside help," Bermuda said, a furious look on her face. The giantess was earning even more attention than Paris and Stefan. The tourist group was unabashedly snapping pictures of the large woman wearing khakis, a white blouse, and a safari hat over her short brown curls.

Paris glanced sideways at her father, giving him a curious expression. "Infestation?"

The security guard cleared his throat. "Yes, Mrs. Laurens is here—"

"You don't know about the infestation?" Bermuda interrupted. "That's not why you two are here?"

Paris shook her head. "No, we're here to see you. Rory told us this was where you were currently working."

"We're making friends too," Stefan said and winked at the guard, who hadn't warmed to them.

"You're a Warrior for the House of Fourteen?" the guy asked. "Why didn't you say so?"

"Please don't believe anyone who goes around announcing they are a Warrior for the House of Fourteen," Stefan said. "The real ones don't announce ourselves, and when someone does it for them, it brings a whole host of unwanted attention."

"I apologize," Bermuda said, sounding like she meant it. "I thought you two were here to encroach on my job."

"We wouldn't dream of it," Paris said and smiled at her. She held up the book, *Magical Creatures*. "We're here because we need something, and only you can help."

Bermuda considered this, her gaze bouncing between Stefan and Paris. Finally, she waved them toward the stairs that led to another area with an even larger shimmering blue pool. She gave the security guard a very stern expression. "We'll be in the outer peristyle. While there, it's closed to the public."

He looked around like he was worried someone was about to jump off the roof and attack Stefan now that his identity had been revealed.

There was no one ready to attack, and if there was, the security guard wouldn't stand a chance against one of Stefan's enemies.

CHAPTER TWENTY-SEVEN

Outer Peristyle, Getty Villa Museum, Malibu, California

The few tourists idling around the outer peristyle were told to leave by Bermuda Laurens and didn't question the giantess. When the mortals left, Bermuda closed and locked the large doors that led to the Inner Peristyle and the rest of the Getty Villa Museum.

Drawn in by the beautiful Greek and Roman sculptures, Paris walked down the stairs to the long rectangular pool that stretched the length of the garden. Grapevines and climbing roses lined both sides of the fountain and were surrounded by perfectly manicured shrubs.

Stopping in front of a bronze sculpture, Paris studied the strange bust of a Roman man with a beard wearing a serious expression. It was his eyes that creeped Paris out. The statue was dark, but his eyes were white with irises and pupils and made to look real as if he was peeping out of the stone.

"Why are his eyes all weird-looking?" Paris asked, noticing the other statues in the fountain and around the garden. Some had painted eyes, and others were blank.

"You have your mother's lack of decorum," Bermuda said as she thundered down the steps and joined them by the pool.

"She also has her mother's smile," Stefan said affectionately, giving Paris a fond expression.

"It's art, Paris," Bermuda said, ignoring the demon hunter. "The statues have all been done in the style of the Greeks and Romans dating from 650 BC to 400 AD."

"Before modern art, then," Stefan began. "When a yellow shoe sitting on a coke can was considered art."

"It's not up to me to decide what is art," Bermuda said stiffly but then resigned her seriousness. "However, I agree that modern art is a waste of space."

"Yeah, and it's pretty cool, these old statues," Paris said, reaching out and running her finger over the head of the statue. It felt cold even though the Malibu sun was shining overhead.

"So, what is this infestation?" Stefan asked Bermuda.

"It's in the statues," the giantess answered at once.

Paris yanked her hand back. "That seems like a problem. Shouldn't this place be closed? What type of infestation?"

Bermuda leaned over and studied the bust of the man closely. "This one is fine. There's no danger to the public. It's a few loose golems who like to play tricks. They sneak into museums and impersonate statues. I've tracked them here."

"They are just standing around pretending to be a part of the actual exhibit?" Stefan asked. "Where's the harm in that?"

"The harm," Bermuda began in a tone of disapproval, "is their intent is to deceive. These statues are all a part of history, representing real people and the styles of the Romans and the Greeks. I'm certain when I find the golems, they'll have Mickey Mouse ears on Hercules or something."

Paris laughed. "I'd check out that exhibit."

"If the exhibit is all cataloged here, then how hard is it to find out which statue doesn't belong, narrowing down which one is the golem?"

"Mr. Ludwig, there are over forty-four thousand pieces in this museum," Bermuda said harshly. "Finding the golems isn't as easy as playing a game of 'what doesn't belong here.'"

"Right," Stefan said, not deterred by Bermuda's usual no-nonsense manner.

"Furthermore, these golems know that we're looking for them and shift to appear normal when I come around," Bermuda said. "I'm the only one who can spot them, so it means I have to study them closely." She pointed to the bust Paris had been regarding. "This one I cleared earlier. Now I have the afternoon to inspect most of the rest in this part of the museum."

Stefan whistled as he looked at all the statues all over the garden. "That's a big job."

"It is," Bermuda said flatly. "Which is why your interruption is poorly timed. So, the sooner I help you with what you've come for, the sooner I can get back to work. What is it that you need?"

Paris held up the thick volume in her hands. "We need you to tell us which *Magical Creatures* were pulled from your book."

A look of confusion fell over Bermuda's face. "*Magical Creatures*? Pulled from a book? You mean, made into real creatures?"

Both Stefan and Paris nodded in reply.

Bermuda's eyes widened. "The only way that someone could do that is if that's…"

"This is the version of *Magical Creatures* from the Great Library," Paris supplied.

"That's incredibly advanced magic. Who would do such a thing?" Bermuda asked, shocked.

"A demon by the name of Tomár," Stefan answered. "I suspect we're not going to like the creatures he has brought alive from the pages of your book. Still, please go ahead and tell us, so we know what we're looking for."

CHAPTER TWENTY-EIGHT

"Three creatures, you say." Bermuda sounded overwhelmed by what Stefan and Paris had shared about the events at the Great Library.

"That's how many Paul saw," Stefan said. "There could be more. I mean, you have everything in there from lophos to celcidas. Tomár could have pulled a ton of creatures from the book that weren't seen."

Bermuda shook her head in reply to this notion. "There's no reason a demon would want to pull celcidas from my book. The forest creatures can be found out in the world, and much easier than using that advanced and dark magic. As for lophos, although they are rare in the world, I see no reason a demon would want a snake that guards things."

"Good point," Paris remarked. "So, we can give up on the hope that Tomár only brought through a mermaid or centaur then."

"That's right, Agent Beaufont," Bermuda affirmed, holding her book in her large hands. "I suspect this demon didn't bring through just any magical creature, rather a unique and individual one. That would be the only reason to go to such great lengths, breaking into the Great Library and then using a very complex spell. No, Tomár would want to bring someone back who was gone."

Paris spied the heavy look in her father's usually light eyes. The giantess was affirming what they both knew but hadn't voiced yet.

"Okay, so can you tell us who Tomár brought back to life?" the demon hunter asked.

"I should be able to." Bermuda lay the large leather-bound book down on the surface of a bench. She closed her eyes and ran her fingers over the closed book but without touching it. The cover flew open on its own, and the pages flicked as if a breeze had riffled through them.

When the book fell still, Bermuda opened her eyes and glanced down at the open page. She nodded as if what she found made sense. "The first magical creature Tomár brought through the book and back is Cupid."

Paris' face screwed up in confusion. Her father shared her reaction to this news.

"Cupid?" Stefan questioned. "You mean the fat little cherub with wings who goes around and shoots people with love arrows?"

Bermuda sighed, not appreciating this description. "No, I mean Cupid, as in the Roman god of love, whose arrows could either spread desire or aversion to someone. His youthful appearance caused the other gods to treat him as lesser. Often Cupid was used by the other gods to do their bidding or play out their schemes to bring each other down."

"Wow, no wonder Mama Jamba and Papa Creola banished all their gods," Paris remarked. She knew why Mother Nature and Papa Creola were playing that chess-like game. They must have known one of their gods was loose.

"Yeah, but poor Cupid," Stefan said. "Why would Tomár want to bring back a god of love?"

"That I can't tell you," Bermuda said. "I can tell you that Cupid didn't put up with the abuse well. He fell in love with Psyche, but it was a forbidden romance. Venus, the goddess of love, sent Cupid after her, enraged by the woman's fame and beauty. He fell in love with her but knowing Venus would never allow it, he abandoned Psyche. The history books, which like happy endings over the truth, say that after serving Venus, Psyche was allowed to become immortal and marry Cupid."

She pointed to the page of her book. "I unearthed and recorded the truth, which is that after learning of Cupid's affections, Venus did require Psyche to serve her. She was sent on several missions. One was to steal a dose of Proserpina's beauty. Knowing Psyche wouldn't be able to resist, Venus tricked her and had her steal something that would make someone ugly. Psyche, as Venus guessed, took a drink of the potion, taking away all of her beauty."

Bermuda sighed. "Venus believed that with Psyche's beauty gone, Cupid would not love her anymore. This is the foundation of the story of true love because Cupid loved Psyche even more after laying eyes on her new form. Enraged, Venus took Psyche from the god of love and imprisoned her until she died from a broken heart."

"Oh, for the love of the angels," Paris said with a gasp. "That's dark. No wonder the history books were rewritten."

"The history books don't get to decide what happened based on events being too dark," Bermuda said. "That's very dangerous. Because history was remembered wrong, most think Cupid would spread love. That's why he's associated with Valentine's Day. The opposite would be true in this world. If Cupid has been brought back, I will guarantee he's not spreading love. He will be trying to destroy it."

CHAPTER TWENTY-NINE

"This is making more sense," Stefan said, beginning to pace as he thought. "It explains why Mama Jamba and Papa Creola were playing that board game."

"All gods Go to Heaven," Bermuda guessed. "It's not a game as much as a way to keep track of the gods. If they were using the board, they would have known one of the gods broke free from banishment."

"Yeah, they seemed upset about something," Paris remarked. "Well, at least Papa Creola did. They explained to us how they had to banish the gods because they made things worse, warring and not getting along. Now I understand specifically why. It sounds like they were a bunch of immature jerks who abused their powers."

"That's exactly what they were," Bermuda agreed. "The idea of creating the demigods had merit, but in the end, they had too much power and too much ego, which is a deadly combination. If allowed to stay on Earth, they would have created a world war that destroyed everyone."

"So, what did Mama Jamba and Papa Creola do?" Stefan questioned. "Send them to the underworld?"

"That's exactly right," Bermuda answered. "A prison for gods where they couldn't hurt anyone or each other. A purgatory of sorts for those who can't die."

"Using your book, which tells the accurate history, Tomár was able to bring Cupid back," Paris guessed.

"Yes, and in that way, the accurate accounts of my book are the culprit here," Bermuda said. "Cupid could only be brought back from a text that told what really happened to him. Otherwise, it wouldn't be the real Cupid who was pulled through."

"Now it makes sense why Mama Jamba thought you should accompany me," Stefan said to Paris as he continued to pace.

"Yes, she said this wasn't a case of evil as much as about love. It sounds like Cupid will be out there destroying romance instead of creating it, seeking revenge for what happened to him."

"He has arrows that make people averse to love?" Stefan questioned Bermuda.

"He does," she affirmed. "I suspect that loose once more, he will want to destroy the love he once spread, sickened by what happened to him."

"Okay, well, one down, two to go." Paris pointed to the book. "Let's find out who else Tomár brought back."

CHAPTER THIRTY

Bermuda looked up, alarm on her face as she yanked her hand back from the book.

"What is it?" Stefan asked, reading the worry on the giantess' face.

"Who is it?" Paris questioned. She had been holding her breath, waiting to hear who else was pulled from *Magical Creatures.*

"It's another god," Bermuda said and clutched her chest, breathing heavily.

"Of course, it is," Stefan muttered. "I'm sensing a theme."

"Are you okay, Mrs. Laurens? Who is it?"

"The Norse goddess of love," Bermuda began after catching her breath. "She's very powerful and is most commonly referred to as Freyja."

"Freyja," Paris said, testing out the name. "I haven't heard of her."

"She doesn't have a reputation like Cupid and isn't associated with a holiday of love. Don't underestimate her. She was associated with love, fertility, beauty, gold, magic, and war."

"Wow, I didn't expect that last one," Stefan said.

"Love and war are really very closely aligned," Bermuda explained. "Freyja was much revered but also feared. She taught magic to mortals, which was a sin. The other gods feared and hated her. Loki, for instance, terrorized her, trying to steal her power which she held in a necklace called Brisingamen. Freyja was quite the legend, flying around on a chariot pulled by two cats."

"Wow, I'd like to see that," Paris remarked.

"What's the part of her story that's not in the history books but is in yours?" Stefan asked.

"Right you are. Freyja was loved by the giants but only in love with one man. In the reported myths, she scoured the globe looking for Odin, who constantly went missing, always crying tears of gold for him. However, the real story has no happy ending."

"I'm sensing more of a theme," Paris repeated from before.

"Giants, desperate for the goddess' affections, hunted down her husband, Odin," Bermuda explained. "They cornered him and savagely overpowered him, although he was guarded by Freyja's magic. In the end, I'm sorry to say, my very own murdered the goddess' one true love."

Paris gulped, at a loss for words after hearing this story.

"The goddess of love will want revenge," Stefan finally said.

"She will be the goddess of war now. Yes, she'll come after giants and any who she thinks deserves her wrath."

"I'm not sure I entirely blame her," Paris said. "These gods and goddesses of love were tortured individuals."

"Yes, that's true," Bermuda affirmed. "That's the reason they were all banished. The stakes were too high and their power too great. It's like if everyone in the world had your power, Paris, but none of your conscience and reasonability. Soon everyone would be in battle, and it wouldn't take long before the demigods of the world flattened the planet."

"I'm glad that Paris is a rarity," Stefan said, smiling at his daughter. "She has her mother's thoughtfulness and my taste for justice."

"For gods, it was always about their own desires," Bermuda continued. "So, there will be no justice for Freyja until she's avenged her husband."

"Which will require wiping out the giants and all else she felt were against her," Paris said.

Bermuda gave her a heavy expression. "Which is why you two must find the goddess as soon as possible before she does too much harm."

"We will," Stefan said with conviction. "Tell us who the third person is that Tomár brought through, and we'll know exactly what we're dealing with."

CHAPTER THIRTY-ONE

The look of stress deepened on Bermuda's face when she opened her eyes. Her hand was shaking over the book, *Magical Creatures*.

"It can't possibly get any worse," Stefan said, sounding defeated.

"I wouldn't think it possible, but Tomár has brought out the most dangerous goddess of love that I can think of," Bermuda said, her voice shaking.

Paris braced herself for what she'd hear next.

"Of course, it's another god of love," Stefan said with a heavy sigh. "That demon is playing a game with us, trying to use those who once protected love to destroy it."

"I think what he intends to do is destroy the planet," Bermuda said darkly.

"Can this goddess of love do that?" Paris asked.

"Not only can she, but she once tried and nearly succeeded," Bermuda answered. "If fueled to full power, it will be no problem for Hathor to finish what she started, ending all of mankind."

"Hathor," Stefan said, drawing out the name. "You mean the Egyptian goddess?"

"That's exactly who I mean," Bermuda said, looking chilled to the bone. "She was the goddess of love and beauty and also of war."

"Again, this is in line with the theme," Paris muttered, not liking all the symmetry but having to give Tomár credit for the expert planning.

"So, what is the history that wasn't told in Hathor's story?" Stefan asked the expert on *Magical Creatures*.

"That's the thing," Bermuda began. "That history was accurately recorded. Hathor took many different roles and forms, usually at her father Ra's insistence. That's how she became the goddess of war. Once she was, there was no controlling her. She was bloodthirsty. So much so that even Ra couldn't control her. She vowed to destroy the Earth and was almost successful, but her father subdued her at the eleventh hour, making her unconscious. She's been that way ever since."

"Now she's back…" Paris left the statement hanging.

The look on Bermuda's and her father's faces told her the answer.

"If Tomár has brought her back, then he believes she'll return to her evil ways, trying to destroy mankind," Stefan said, shaking his head, his eyes full of anger.

"She's the one you have to fear most," Bermuda warned. "The others, they will be a force to control, but only Ra could contain Hathor. She is too powerful when at full strength for any others."

"You said something earlier about how she'd have to be fueled to full power," Paris said. "What does that mean?"

"Gods' powers, like yours as magicians, aren't absolute," Bermuda explained. "They ebb and flow, based on their condition. Hathor has been in the underworld for a long time. She won't be strong enough to do what she did before. With the help of others, she could regain her strength."

"Others?" Stefan asked, a hint of frustration in his voice.

"One of the reasons all the gods had to be banished together at the same time is they fuel each other when on Earth," Bermuda said. "In the underworld, it doesn't work. Up here, what one does supplies energy for another. This was how they began to work together and also how they could take each other down."

"So that's why Tomár brought back three gods of love," Paris exclaimed, putting it all together in a sudden rush.

"Yeah, Cupid and Freyja are a part of the fueling system. They are supposed to take their wrath out on the world, and as they do, that will build Hathor up to full strength."

"Would that work?" asked Paris.

"Yes, it would. Their acts of destruction and abolishing love would be exactly what the goddess of war craves. They thrive on energy. The same way the Earth thrives on love, so do those who want its demise profit on the loss of good."

Stefan closed his eyes and put his hands to his head. When he opened his icy blue eyes, there was a sobering look in them. "Now I see what Tomár really wants. Of course. I should have seen this coming all along."

"The destruction of the planet?" Paris asked.

"The end of love?" Bermuda asked.

Stefan shook his head. "No, he wants to die, and he wants to take us all down with him."

CHAPTER THIRTY-TWO

When her father explained the demon's plan, it sounded horrible and convoluted and also made sense. Paris realized then that a demon who had existed for as long as Tomár couldn't give up, but he was tired of existing. So, he'd figured out the perfect way to destroy the planet. Take out love. Fuel the goddess of war. Bring her back to finish what she started. When the planet burned and died, so would the demon, going out on his terms.

"The stakes for this just got a lot bigger," Paris remarked, looking between her father and Bermuda.

They both nodded.

"As big as I can ever remember," Stefan replied.

"Maybe the House of Fourteen and the Dragon Elite will want to intervene," Paris said. "Maybe we should take this case to them."

"Mama Jamba and Papa Creola wanted you on this case," Bermuda interrupted. "They are right. This is a case of evil. Your father is right to be on it too."

"This feels so big," Paris said, her voice haunted.

"Then take it to Saint Valentine," Bermuda offered, "but this feels like something that has your name written all over it."

"Me!" Paris exclaimed. "I don't know how to take down three gods of love."

"You shouldn't," the giantess said firmly. "You can't kill gods, as we've discussed. You can only contain them."

"Well, I don't know how to contain three gods," Paris said.

"You might be the only one I'm aware of with the power to do so," Bermuda told her, a hint of mischief in her voice.

Paris and Stefan's eyes met, both perplexed by this statement.

"Please explain," the demon hunter urged.

"Well, the gods of love were unleashed by a demon," Bermuda began. "Meaning complex magic only a demon can use has to be the counterspell."

"That makes sense," Stefan said, not appearing convinced.

"The gods being contained are in the realm of love," Bermuda continued. "So that means you'll need someone who has that elemental force at their disposal."

"Like an agent for FGA," Stefan answered.

"Finally, the person who contains the gods must have a magical instrument strong enough to hold all of them in before they are forced back into my book and sealed away for good once more."

Paris, Stefan, and Bermuda all looked at Amantis in the holster on the halfling's hip.

"You think that my wand is the key to containing the gods?" Paris asked, her chest tight with tension.

"I believe so," the giantess said. "That sapphire is from the queen of the fae. It's strong enough to hold gods. It will only work if you're bonded to the weapon."

"I don't know if I am," Paris said.

"You'll only know if you try," Bermuda countered.

"Okay, so I need to risk it all to try to suck all these gods of love into the sapphire on Amantis, but I won't know if it worked until when?" Paris asked uncertainly.

"Until you put them in my book and try to seal it back."

Bermuda pointed to *Magical Creatures* still sitting on the bench. "The spell has to be reversed exactly as Tomár did it. That's the only way."

"If Paris hasn't bonded to Amantis?" Stefan questioned.

"Then the gods won't be locked away and will be free once more, but angrier than ever," Bermuda answered.

"Is there a way to know that I'm bonded to the wand?" Paris asked.

Bermuda gave her a heavy expression. "In life and definitely in the world of magic, faith is a part of the spell. If you know, then it takes away from the power. Not knowing, but simply believing. Hoping. Having that element of faith is the fuel. If you have an ounce of doubt, that will be the downfall, and none of this will work."

"Then the world will be more at risk than ever before," Stefan said.

Paris bit her lip. "It really feels like this is more than a two-person job. I feel like we should have everyone on this case. All forces together."

"I think less is more," Bermuda said.

"I agree. I'll take it to the Council for the House of Fourteen to get their input. You take it to Saint Valentine. Then we can decide how to proceed. I have a feeling that whatever happens, it needs to happen fast. Those angry gods are out there, and they won't be wasting time."

"They'll be fueling Hathor," Bermuda added. "When she's at full strength, the world will meet a very dark day."

CHAPTER THIRTY-THREE

Little Pleasures Farmhouse, Outskirts of Boulder, Colorado

"We have a problem," Faraday said from across the breakfast table. The morning sunlight streamed through the window, but Paris' eyes were too tired to adjust to the bright light.

"There's not enough coffee in the world to wake me up," she said.

The squirrel, who had recovered from his ordeal on the twenty-sixth floor at FGA, shook his head. "No, remember I was trying to create an app on your phone that links to the love meter so that you could keep an eye on it remotely?"

"Yes, since the board doesn't want its recording public knowledge, and I never get to see how it fluctuates."

"Well, I've got good news and bad news," Faraday began, flicking his tail.

"Start with the good news, then pour me another cup of coffee and take a break while I drink it before supplying the bad news."

"The love meter has plummeted," Faraday said in a rush.

Paris' mouth dropped open. "That's the good news? Wow, I don't want to hear the bad news."

He shook his head. "No, that was the bad news. I switched it up to help you digest it better."

"You just gave me acid reflux, so that approach didn't work," Paris said, taking a sip of her coffee.

"The good news is the app works." Faraday scooted her phone over to her to see a picture of the love meter. It was very low. Really low. Too low.

"Maybe the app doesn't work," Paris offered. "Maybe it isn't linked to the actual one, and the readings are wrong."

He shook his head. "It works. I know it does. A significant decrease like this must mean that…"

"Gods of love with vendettas are on the loose and creating destruction and fueling a bigger, badder god who wants to destroy the planet," Paris finished.

"I was going to say something a whole lot less specific, but yeah, sure. You're probably right."

"Dad and I hoped they were having fun first with their newfound freedom," Paris said with a yawn. "It appears these gods don't waste any time and hit the ground running."

"Well, once we get to FGA Tower," Faraday began, "I can use Wilfred to start monitoring world events. I'll search for activities related to the demigods. I'm sure I'll be able to track them down."

"Okay, and I'll go to Saint Valentine first thing and see how he wants to handle this. I'm sure he'll have lots of experienced agents he'll want to assign to this. Then I can go back to reviewing cases involving silly flings, and the world will continue to revolve on its axis."

"What about the House of Fourteen?" Faraday asked.

"They want my father to go after Tomár," Paris said, having gotten the message from her Uncle Clark that morning about the Council's decision. "That's House business and definitely something my dad is best at, having already been tracking the mega demon. They say the gods of love are definitely FGA territory, and they shouldn't be involved. They are afraid too much involvement will cause problems."

"It's true. There's a reason there are jurisdictions. The Dragon Elite handles nations. The House of Fourteen, magical affairs. FGA, matters of love. The fae, well, they've got Hollywood and Las Vegas."

"Don't forget the elves handle hemp and CBD regulations," Paris joked.

"Then Mama Jamba and Papa Creola have an eye on everything," Faraday said.

"Yeah, so I'll take this to Saint Valentine, and you can hand over what you find," Paris said, standing from the table and throwing back the rest of her coffee in one gulp. It wasn't enough, but she wasn't sure there was enough coffee to fuel her at this point. She hoped it wouldn't be a very taxing day and she could put her feet up on her desk and relax, reviewing cases for the rest of the day. She had to turn this "angry gods of love on the loose" business over to someone better equipped to deal with it.

CHAPTER THIRTY-FOUR

Fiftieth Floor, Saint Valentine's Office, Matters of the Heart, FGA Tower, New York City, New York

"This case is all yours all the way," Saint Valentine said, giving Paris an intense expression.

It had been a while since Paris had been to the Fiftieth floor to the Matters of the Heart office, and that had only been once when hunting demons. The carpet under her feet was bright red with black lining along the walls. Textured striped wallpaper covered the walls to the ceiling. The décor was mostly modern paintings that revolved around a theme of love. The design was both loud and refined, as if it was teetering on a line, trying to decide whether to be rebellious or conservative.

"Bu-but..." Paris stammered, looking between her boss, Agent Barney Jasper, and Saint Valentine. "I'm so new that I don't know where the fire exits are in this building. I have no experience. This is the biggest case ever. How are you handing it to me? The world is at stake. We need a task force and people in suits and ones who say fancy things and—"

Saint Valentine held up a hand, interrupting her. His office was a giant heart. There was a large desk where the leader of

FGA sat in front of the bank of windows that formed the top of the heart of the office. Thick red velvet curtains framed the glass where sunlight streamed in, illuminating the space.

Saint Valentine leaned forward across his large, shiny, and mostly empty desk. He stared at Paris, seeming to see her soul. "This case needs you."

"Bu-but—" Paris protested.

"Agent Beaufont, I'm a very good listener," Saint Valentine interrupted. "I listened while you told Agent Jasper and me a very informative and detail-rich story about your conversation at the Fantastical Armory with Mother Nature and Father Time."

"I didn't want to leave out any details," she argued, throwing up her hands. Staring at the elaborately decorated ceiling, she saw it was made of three large tiles. Each of the three-by-three tiles was a painting of scenes from various famous love stories. Paris recognized Romeo and Juliet, Orpheus and Eurydice, and Napoleon and Josephine.

"I appreciate that," he said with a smile. The old man's expression was slow but genuine. "You said Mother Nature encouraged you to accompany your father on the case to track the demon, Tomár, at the Great Library."

"Yes, because it was a case involving gods of love," Paris said. "I did, and I got all this information, and now I'm turning it over to you. So go ahead and assign it to your best agents and fairy godmothers and have them track down these loose and diabolical gods before they destroy the planet because, as I've seen with my love meter, they are already doing damage."

"Your love meter?" Agent Jasper asked, raising an eyebrow at her.

She scooched down in her chair. "Oh, yeah, I might have gotten the scientist squirrel to hack the love meter and create an app that links it to my phone so that I can monitor it."

Paris was ready to be reprimanded. Instead, Agent Jasper and Saint Valentine exchanged a look.

After a long silence, Saint Valentine said to the other man, "Do you agree?"

"Absolutely."

"Agree to what?" Paris asked. "Am I fired? I shouldn't have hacked the love meter. Sorry. I should have called for backup when Mama Jamba told me this was a case of love at the Great Library. I should have phoned in all this last night, but I was tired and hadn't eaten, and the squirrel had an ordeal on the twenty-sixth floor, which we should discuss. There's a weird portal problem there. Please don't fire me."

"Do you know how many agents have access to looking at the love meter?" Agent Jasper asked.

Paris shrugged, wondering why the strange question when she should be having her exit interview. "A dozen."

"Currently one," Agent Jasper answered, "and it's me. Usually, it's only directors. Although other higher-level managers can have access, most don't care. They care about their department's performance and budgets and bottom lines. Most don't care if the love meter is up or down."

"That's mostly because the board has conditioned it out of them. They've told them not to pay attention to it. Its fluctuations are unpredictable, but I've always believed it tells us global truths, which are important. The fact you cared enough to put an app on your phone so you could monitor it says a lot."

"Oh," Paris chirped, louder than she intended. "Well, at Happily Ever After College, Headmistress Willow Starr and Mae Ling always paid attention to it, so I thought it was important."

"It is," Saint Valentine said. "Do you know how many people call Mother Nature by the name 'Mama Jamba?'"

Paris thought that was a trick question. She held up her hand and started counting, running through her family members. "I don't know, a dozen or so."

"Only those who she trusts are allowed to call her that," Agent Jasper answered.

"She sent you to the Great Library," Saint Valentine imparted. "She knows what she's doing and plays a very strategic game. You were there when the call came in, and therefore you were supposed to go on the case with your father. You're supposed to take the lead on this case to find the demigods."

"But—"

"Oh, enough with the buts," Agent Jasper cut her off. "You're the right person for this case. You have to know that."

"I'm new, and I'm inexperienced." Paris held up her hands, pleading.

Saint Valentine's eyes sparkled when he smiled at her. "Your hands, they are so very small. This problem is so very big. Sometimes the biggest problems do best in the smallest of hands."

"Although I appreciate the poetry, I don't think the logic works," Paris said, earning an eye roll from Agent Jasper.

Saint Valentine chuckled. "Maybe not. Excuse an old man and his ways. Again, I heard what you said, and Bermuda Laurens is right. You have Amantis. You have demon blood and can perform the counterspell. No one here at FGA has a magical instrument that can hold demigods that I'm aware of." He cut his eyes to Barney, who nodded in agreement.

"Furthermore," Saint Valentine continued, "you are untested with that magical instrument, and we will need faith when trying to contain gods. Of all the options at FGA, you're the only one who makes sense, and I think you know it."

Paris wasn't ready to admit anything yet. "Mama Jamba knows about her gods being loose. Maybe, I use my contact with her and make her go and round up her naughty creations. Then we're back to being happy and defeating whatever evil on the internet is disrupting love."

Saint Valentine gave her a patient expression but suddenly looked old and tired, all his youthful charm having receded even though it was still early in the day. "Do you think Mother Nature would simply fix these problems for us? Has she ever?"

"Well, no," Paris admitted. "From what I understand, she doesn't like to enable her children. Maybe because this is her fault."

"Is it a parent's fault when a grown adult runs a traffic light?" Saint Valentine asked, his face serious.

"Well, no," Paris repeated. "They are grown at that point and should know better."

"Is it the parent's responsibility to go after that grown adult when they run that traffic light?" Saint Valentine continued his questioning.

"Of course not. That's the police's job."

Saint Valentine smirked. "You're the police. This is your job."

Paris felt like the weight of the world was sitting on her shoulders, and in a way, it totally was. She had a hard time breathing, knowing what a huge adventure she had before her. Paris had to track down three demigods, use a complex spell to contain them in her wand, and then have faith she was bonded to Amantis to seal them into the book they came from. It was a lot. A whole lot. Like the weight of the world a lot.

"You aren't alone, though," Agent Jasper offered. "You have resources. Whatever you need, we will get you. Funding won't be a problem on this mission."

"No, but we also aren't as wealthy as we once were," Saint Valentine amended. "Agent Jasper is right. You aren't on your own. We want you to head up this case. It's a lot, and I realize it. After everything you've told us, we'd be fools to think we're better equipped to handle something of this nature. I hate to say it, but a case involving gods of love and a demon and complex magic. Well, it almost seems like it was made for you, Agent Beaufont."

Paris gulped, trying to breathe. Finally, she bolstered her spirit and brought some confidence to her eyes. "Okay, then, I'll do it. I'll get straight to work, tracking down these demigods and capturing them before they do too much damage to the world."

CHAPTER THIRTY-FIVE

Bazaar, Marrakesh, Morocco, Maghreb, North Africa

The brightly colored spices piled high in baskets in the outdoor market in Marrakesh, Morocco, were both pleasing to the eye as well as the nose. It had been a few hundred years since King Rudolfus Sweetwater had been in the bustling city rich with culture, history, and also bootleggers of every sort. The king of the fae was still outlawed in most of Morocco, but he was in disguise and also with the great Sherlock Holmes. He hoped no one would notice.

For starters, the detective went unnoticed by most, even dressed as an Englishman in one of the Imperial cities of Morocco. His bland tweed suit and flat cap weren't begging for any stares. Also, according to the detective himself, he'd mastered the art of going undetected by blending in and being inconspicuous. Rudolf enjoyed the idea that the person who was the best at detecting went undetected.

Rudolf, on the other hand, wasn't drab in appearance and therefore invisible to most passing by them in the busy bazaar. As always, Rudolf looked fabulous, wearing a traditional Moroccan burgundy and gold silk kaftan. He liked the airy feel of the gown-like clothing and the pointy leather slippers. It felt like he was getting ready for bed in the ensemble, but the bright African sun reminded the fae it was nowhere near bedtime. Besides, he and Sherlock were there on an important mission.

This bazaar in Marrakesh was the very last place Subfar, the Protector of Wealth, was found.

"So, what are you shopping for?" Rudolf casually asked his companion, who was studying every stall they passed with the keen focus unique to Sherlock Holmes. "Maybe a hookah, since we know how much you love your pipe, or maybe a rug?" He waved at a large stall where hand-knotted rugs of various colors and patterns hung around the makeshift walls or were rolled up, lining the space.

Unhurried, Sherlock brought his gaze away from a lantern where the shiny objects twinkled with firelight. "We're not here to shop."

"I know," Rudolf replied, waving at a vendor who was trying to get them to come into his stall full of mosaic artwork and ceramic ware covered in bright colors and Moroccan style patterns. "I'm good, buddy. I can't tell you how many Moroccan dinner plates I have."

"How many?" Sherlock asked as if he was curious.

"Well, a lot less than I did after that party last week," Rudolf answered. "My wife Serena thought it would be funny to smash a bunch of plates like the Greeks."

"What were you celebrating?" Sherlock questioned, not missing a beat.

Rudolf blinked at the detective in confusion. "Celebrating? I thought the Greeks broke plates because they were the angry type. Anyway, it didn't make me feel better, and the noise gave me an awful headache. Or that could have been from all the Ouzo we drank."

"You really had a Greek night," Sherlock said, watching a

transaction between an old woman and a vendor in a stall that sold beads.

"Why? Because we pretended we were in the Olympics and tried to pole vault over the couch and race through the mansion?"

Sherlock gave him a confused look. "I think we are better ending this conversation since it never leads to a logical path, and explaining myself doesn't have the effect that leads to positive notions for me."

"I thought you picked me as your assistant because I asked dumb questions that made you figure out other things," Rudolf said, well aware that his ideocracy led to genius moments for others.

Sherlock narrowed his eyes at him. "That's true. Sometimes you do, and sometimes you surprisingly figure out clues. I think, of my options, you made the most sense as an assistant, but how you'll aid me on this case is unclear."

"Makes sense to me," Rudolf said as they came to an open area where the stalls selling wares fell away and the bustle of the city could be felt as it stretched out in front of them for miles.

Unencumbered by the walls of the bazaar, the winds from the foothills of the Atlas Mountains were a welcome relief splashing against their faces.

Rudolf drank in the fresh air, careful not to swallow too much sand with it. He then noticed Sherlock looking speculatively over his shoulder.

"What's got your attention?" the king asked.

The great detective turned back, shaking his head. "Nothing."

"Okay, so this is where Subfar was last seen all that time ago," Rudolf began, wanting to be of help and ask the questions that would lead to epiphanies. "If it was so long ago, how can you be sure you'll find a clue to the Protector of Wealth now?"

"Because that was the arrangement," Sherlock said, looking around as the sun made its descent over the desert in the distance. "If someone wanted to find Subfar, they had to locate me first. Then I was obligated to search for the Protector of Wealth, and therefore, I'm sure he left clues that only I could find."

"Not at all complicated and there are not a hundred ways that this plan could be foiled."

"Elementary, my dear Wa…Rudolf. Subfar knew to leave me a clue that only I would find. That would then send me on a hunt for him."

The fae shrugged. He was way overdue for a drink. He wondered what kind of wine Morocco was known for. The last time he'd been there, he'd spent all his time in an underground jail until he escaped, and he hadn't been back since.

"Do you want to get some dinner?" Rudolf asked, striding down the stone path, taking in the sights of the city.

He had walked several paces before he realized Sherlock wasn't beside him. Stopping, he turned and looked over his shoulder to find the great detective also looking over his shoulder as though he sensed or saw something.

"Everything all right?" Rudolf asked.

Sherlock let out a long breath and then turned back, walking in his direction. "It's fine, and yes, dinner would be fine."

Rudolf smiled, starting forward again before something shiny on the edge of the wall bordering the path caught his attention. He paused to retrieve a coin. "Hey, it looks like I'll be paying for dinner. Look at what I found."

Sherlock grabbed the piece of money in his hand and inspected it. "This isn't Moroccan money."

"Okay, well, then you can pay for dinner," Rudolf muttered. "I did get us here on my private jet."

"You opened a portal," Sherlock corrected, still studying the thick piece of gold.

"I call my portals private jets," Rudolf said.

"I'll pay for dinner because you're already paying for yourself."

Sherlock Holmes slipped the coin into the breast pocket of his jacket, looking satisfied.

"Oh?" Rudolf said, curious.

"Yes, as I suspected, you bring a spontaneity to this investigation," Sherlock disclosed. "The worst thing a detective can do is get complacent, which I'd be prone to do if not for the likes of people like you."

"Well, I'll be sure to keep you on your toes," Rudolf cheered. "Expect no relaxation when I'm around."

CHAPTER THIRTY-SIX

Team-Building Conference Space, Casual Romance Department, Third Floor, FGA Tower, New York City, New York

"I don't mean to be offensive," Holly began. She was filing her nails, her boots propped up on the conference room table in the corner of the team-building space for the Casual Romance department.

"Then don't say anything," Paris cut in, aware that everyone around the table was staring at her. Well, not Doris. She was napping, but Paris would wake her up when it was time for her to take notes.

"As I was saying," Holly continued, pretending not to hear Paris. "We're the ones who are supposed to stop three gods from destroying the planet." She glanced around at Isha, next to her, then Christine from the Refinement Department, Penny from Practical Love, and then Faraday sitting next to Wilfred. "We should cut our losses and just go and max out our credit cards."

"I'm the one who is supposed to stop the three gods," Paris corrected. "You all, you're all I got."

"Hey!" Christine complained, throwing up her hands. "I'm missing *Bridgerton* for this."

"It's streaming," Paris said. "You aren't missing anything."

"This is the night I catch up and binge-watch it," Christine argued.

"Well, good news, if we all die, you won't miss the show," Paris told her.

Christine sat back in her seat, crossing her arms. "Because I'll be dead. Yeah, I get it, but don't think that excuses you from your ungrateful remark."

"I'm not ungrateful," Paris amended, softening her tone. "I'm saying that when I was given all the resources the FGA had to offer, you all are who I chose to help. We're up against something huge. If I have anyone at my back, then I need it to be people I trust. I need it to be fierce warriors who will take risks and not pansy fairy godmothers or wimpy agents who are afraid to get their hands dirty. So, on the long list of choices, you're it."

Holly glanced sideways at Isha. "It was a nice attempt at recovery, but I think she's still settling for us because no one is stupid enough to sign on to this mission."

"Why would anyone turn down this opportunity?" Isha argued. "We get to do something incredible. If we're successful—"

"When you're successful," Faraday corrected.

"When we're successful, we get to know we saved the planet from something huge."

"It's going to be scary," Paris offered. "It's going to be dangerous. We might get hurt or die trying to contain these gods."

"If we don't try," Penny began, "then everyone dies. I'd rather fight than sit back and put this in someone else's hands. This case was given to Paris and put in her small hands because she's more than capable of handling it. I think she's smart to keep the team small.

"If you go in there, trying to fight these demigods with huge leagues of armies, the collateral damage would be massive. Instead, we'll work strategically. We'll be one step ahead of the gods. We'll figure out how to lure them and trap them. Before they know it, they'll be back in the book and locked in the underworld."

"Are we getting awards for giving speeches?" Holly asked, still filing her nails like she didn't have a care in the world. "Because if so, then I have to work on mine, but I'll have something that makes all of you cry."

"I think you talk enough," Paris said. "You get a shiny sticker if you're quiet for more than a minute."

"Faraday is right," Penny continued. "What we have to do is figure out these gods and goddesses. Figure out where they are, what will lure them, and how to trap them. If we outthink them, then Paris can do her job."

"I haven't really figured out what that is or how to do it."

Christine pointed to Amantis on her hip. "You point that and do the opposite of shoot. I guess you suck."

Giving her friend an annoyed look, Paris lowered her chin. "How do I do that?"

"Hey, I can only help you so much," Christine said with a shrug.

"Yeah, I think I'm going to have to talk to the maker of my wand to figure out how it can be used to absorb gods," Paris said, having considered this part of the mission. "My father is working on finding the demon counterspell to seal the gods back into the book, so I've got my work cut out for me."

"Okay, and while you're doing that, we all need to put our heads together to research these gods," Penny said, indicating the other women. "I'm certain that if we learn as much about them as possible from reading Bermuda Lauren's real account of them, we can figure out their weakness or a way to trap them."

"Good idea," Paris remarked, grateful to her friend.

"Wilfred and I are reviewing the news reports worldwide," Faraday said. "I think if those gods are out there causing problems, as the love meter indicates, we'll be able to locate them."

"Good," Paris said with a sigh, backing up and preparing to take her leave. "You all get to work on your tasks."

"Where do you think you're going while we save the world?" Holly challenged.

"I thought I'd take a bathroom break," Paris said. "I might be a lot of things, but I'm not a god who can go without peeing."

"Okay, fine, you get a hall pass," Christine said graciously. "Be sure to wash your hands and don't splash water on the counters and make a mess."

Paris groaned as she trudged for the bathroom. "I wonder if others who attempted to save the planet had to deal with such attitude from their so-called friends."

CHAPTER THIRTY-SEVEN

"I've read so much that I think my head is going to explode," Holly said, leaning back in her seat and rubbing her temples.

"How much did that take? Two paragraphs?" Paris asked. She was chewing on a protein bar and looking out the window at 5th Avenue, impatiently waiting for a lead to come in on how to trap the gods with her wand and counterspell.

"Ha-ha," Holly replied. "This stuff isn't that easy to understand. I mean, Cupid's life was messed up. His mom, Venus, got jealous of Psyche's beauty and so sent him after her to make her fall in love with a double bagger."

"Double bagger?" Penny asked, looking up from the copy of *Magical Creatures* she was reading.

"You don't want to know," Isha said. "Holly's karma is her own."

"You're right. Cupid had it rough. It's not surprising he went against his mother and fell in love with Psyche."

"Then the soulless goddess killed his lady," Christine said, shaking her head. "All because they were able to love each other for more than appearances. I mean, I could never do that, but props to Cupid. That takes a lot of heart."

"Heart!" Faraday chirped, laughing. "Cupid has heart."

"Maybe we need a break," Paris offered. She glanced at her phone, but there was still no message from her dad or from Subner, who was her best bet for telling her how the wand could contain the gods. "You all have been at this for a while."

"Hey, we're looking for a way to lure Cupid, right?" Penny began.

"Yeah," Paris replied.

"So far, all I can tell is that a winged creature is attacking from the sky in various locations globally, but by the time the reports come in, there are no traces," Wilfred related robotically. "There are no eyewitnesses."

"Because he swoops in and shoots people from the sky," Faraday explained. "He makes people have an aversion to love and then flees before he can be spotted. It's always outdoor areas, concerts, parks, and beaches. Places where he has cloud coverage or trees or something."

"What about Freyja?" Paris asked. "She has to be up to something with how much the love meter is down. If Bermuda's hunch is right, these two gods have to do enough damage to fuel Hathor back to life."

"Again, it appears to be a case of stealth," Wilfred said. "There are several reports of a string of attacks, but they happen so fast no one sees enough to pursue."

"What is she doing to people?" Christine asked.

"As far as I can tell, it's all magic spells that cast doom and hatred over people," Faraday said, combing through several reports. "Some people are hurt, but they don't know by what. They say it feels like they've been whipped or slashed by something, and then afterward, they fall into a depression. The mental hospitals are overflowing."

"Whips?" Paris breathed, thinking. "Like what someone driving a chariot would have."

"Wow, so we've got Cupid with evil arrows and Freyja with a

mean whip," Holly remarked. "They are gods and therefore fast and can go unseen, which will make stopping them really tough."

"That's the thing," Penny disagreed. "They aren't gods. They are demigods, and that means they have flaws from their human side. If their stories tell us anything, it's that."

"What are you saying?" Paris turned to face her team directly, putting her back to the window.

"I think if we construct the right playing field, we can lure both Cupid and Freyja out," Penny answered.

"Okay, so let's think about what we're working with. Cupid's mother has to be his biggest source of anger. He wants to take love away from the world, but really it's because of his mother, Venus de Milo."

"She's trapped in the underworld, I'm guessing," Christine muttered, pushing away her copy of *Magical Creatures*, defeated.

Faraday flicked his tail. "Yeah, and I'm guessing they were all sequestered to different areas, so they didn't kill each other or at least try over and over again to do so."

"Too bad that we don't have a pretend Venus we could use to lure Cupid to a place," Isha said.

"I could pretend to be the goddess of love," Holly offered.

Paris shook her head. "No one would believe that."

Holly rolled her eyes in response.

"That's it, though," Penny exclaimed.

Holly pointed at her chest. "I should be the goddess of love? I knew I liked you."

Penny shook her head. "No, but all we have to do is create an event centered around Venus that would draw Cupid's attention. Something he couldn't ignore. Something like a celebration of his mother and possibly love. Like a huge romance convention of sorts."

"That's called a party," Christine teased.

"Yeah, a party," Penny said in an excited rush. "It'll be the Venus de Milo Celebration, a huge affair with lots of couples.

Cupid will have to show up, but it would be on our turf. We'd be ready, and then Paris could trap him in the wand."

"That's a fantastic idea," Paris said, shaking Doris' shoulders to wake her. The old woman startled and looked around dazedly. "Hey, I need you taking notes. We have a plan."

"Oh, okay," Doris said, pulling a pad and pen to her. "What are we doing?"

"Having a party," Christine said.

"How many paper cups will we need?" Doris asked.

"First, we need a location," Paris said. She started to pace, her heart suddenly racing with excitement. This felt right, like a plan forming, but they needed more.

"How about at the place that has the most famous Venus statue in the world?" Faraday asked, a sneaky grin on his face.

Paris halted and looked at her friend. She grinned back. "Do you think we can get away with that?"

"We were told we could have anything at our disposal," Faraday said. "The world is at stake, so why not?"

The others were looking between Paris and the squirrel anxiously.

"Would you two tell us what you're talking about?" Holly demanded.

"The Louvre," Faraday supplied. "That's where the most famous Venus de Milo is located."

"It's a fantastic location for a romantic party," Christine cheered.

"It's in Paris," Penny added. "Which has to be good luck."

"It's contained enough that we could set traps," Paris affirmed.

"Isha and I throw a fantastic party," Holly said, motioning to her friend. "We should start spreading the news fast."

"Yes, because this needs to happen right away. We don't have much time. The love meter is plummeting, which means they are working rapidly, and that means Hathor is getting stronger. Can you put this on tomorrow night?"

Holly glanced at Isha, and they both nodded.

"So, how many paper cups?" Doris asked, confused.

"We'll get caterers," Christine said. "Leave that and the decorations up to the Refinement Department."

"The Practical Love Department will be in charge of setting traps," Penny offered. "We are very crafty like that. Since we know we're working with a winged creature, we can work on something like nets that Cupid won't see. I'll figure it out."

"Okay, this could work," Paris said. "A huge romantic party celebrating Venus at the Louvre. How could Cupid not want to show up and shoot everyone present?"

"Well, that's morbid," Holly muttered.

"Shoot them with despair," Paris corrected.

"It's a good plan," Faraday said. "Now, if only we could kill two birds with one stone. Or rather, take down two gods with one event."

Penny shot forward and began flipping through her copy of *Magical Creatures* at a breakneck speed, obviously having thought of something. "I read something. It could work out perfectly."

Paris rushed to Penny's side and looked over her shoulder. "What is it?"

"Freyja had a necklace. It was called Brisingamen," Penny said, her voice vibrating. "It was very important to her and very powerful. Of course, Loki, trying to torment her, took it. According to Bermuda Laurens, he buried it, never for it to be found again."

"Wow, that's a fantastic story with another horrible ending," Holly mumbled.

"No, but that's the thing," Penny continued. "While we're setting up this party for Venus, we can also have another ceremony, and we can have it at the Louvre."

"You're a genius!" Paris exclaimed, patting her friend on the back.

Holly looked between the two, confused. "Okay, go ahead and fill in the rest of us who aren't following."

Paris smiled, looking around at the group. "We do a press release and say Brisingamen has been discovered by some archeologist and is going to be on display at the Louvre. The exhibit will kick off on the night of Venus de Milo's celebration."

"Wow, that is genius!" Faraday said. "Freyja won't be able to resist either. She'll rush in there on her chariots pulled by cats to try to take what belongs to her."

"What if she learns there isn't a necklace there?" Isha said. "I mean, there's a lot of security at the Louvre. She might not risk it until there's a less busy night."

"Good point," Christine said. "So, we craft a look alike necklace of Brisingamen in the Refinement Department. Then we put pictures of that in the press release and blast it everywhere. She's getting around. She'll hear about it."

"Great idea," Paris said. "The necklace is amber and was gnome-made, so ensure you get all the details right. We can't have anything clueing her in that it's a fake."

"For sure," Penny said. "Then she'll be lured to the Louvre on the same night as Cupid, and you can trap them both. Again, the Practical Love Department can help with setting traps."

"I can set up security alarms that will also slow down the gods," Faraday offered. "I just need to get inside the Louvre."

"I'll have Saint Valentine and Agent Jasper arrange for us to get in there immediately."

"Then you'll just have to find Hathor," Holly said. "After throwing a party at the Louvre, taking her down will be a piece of cake."

"It might be a bit more difficult than that," Wilfred said, sparking to life like he'd been in research mode before.

Everyone looked up at him.

"What did you find?" Paris asked.

"Hathor," he answered. "Or so I believe." The AI pointed to the screen in front of the conference table and projected an image up onto it. It was of a huge Egyptian temple with four large statues guarding the entrance.

"These are two temples known as Abu Simbel," Wilfred began. "They're in Egypt and are from the thirteenth century BC. The smaller of the temples is for Hathor and Nefertari. She's the one there."

"That's a small temple?" Christine gawked.

"It's called the Small Temple, but it's the same size as the king's," Wilfred explained.

"Which is huge," Faraday said. "How big is that statue of Hathor?"

"Thirty-three feet tall," Wilfred answered.

Paris squinted at the image, noticing that the one of Hathor appeared different from the others. "Why is she a different color in places?"

"From what I've been able to deduce," Wilfred began, "this statue of Hathor is slowly coming to life."

CHAPTER THIRTY-EIGHT

"That's one big goddess of love," Holly observed.

"Yeah, and if she comes all the way to life, her wrath is going to be absolute," Isha added.

"So, we have to catch Cupid and Freyja quickly," Paris said, suddenly not excited but nervous. "Tomorrow night. Can you all pull this event together in time?"

Everyone nodded in unison.

"Throwing parties is what I'm best at," Holly gushed.

"We'll make sure it's full of lovers," Isha said.

"Traps will be set," Penny offered.

"It will look like a real party, even if it is thrown together at the last minute," Christine told them proudly.

"How many paper cups will you be needing?" Doris asked.

"Even once you capture the gods," Faraday began, ignoring the senile old receptionist, "Paris, you're going to have to go after Hathor. She may not be at full strength, but she'll still be a formidable force."

"Yeah, and I fear that going after her will involve entering that temple where she's coming to life."

Faraday's nose twitched with stress. "Yes, I'm guessing that's where her spirit is housed. As she is fueled, it's converting her statue into her real form, which will be able to stomp over cities and destroy buildings and…"

"Be the destruction of mankind," Paris completed for him. "That's what she set out to do, and I'm guessing bringing her statue to life is only the beginning of her power. With more destruction, I'm betting she gets even more dangerous, possibly able to split continents."

Holly shook her head. "That's the thing. Of all the gods of love we've read about, she didn't have it so bad. No mom telling her who she could love. No giants taking out her husband. She had a rich dad and a lot of power, but some people are just never happy."

Paris wanted to laugh, but the severity of the moment prevented it. The giants had been warned about Freyja's return and they'd all gone into hiding, knowing they'd be one of her first targets. Paris had considered using them as bait, but since relations with the giants were fragile, she didn't think it was the most diplomatic move.

No, luring the goddess to the Louvre with her necklace was a good plan. It was a good way to get Cupid there too. Paris just had to do her part, which started right then. She needed to find out how to contain the god and goddess of love when the time came. More importantly, she needed to know how to banish them back to where they belonged.

CHAPTER THIRTY-NINE

"I don't get it," King Rudolf said, looking at the stalls full of colorful fruit and nuts and dried herbs. "Did the market in Morocco not have enough stinky fish for you?" He pinched his nose and pointed at an area filled with boxes of ice and piled high with whole fish.

Sherlock Holmes shook his head, looking around. "I'm following Subfar's trail."

"So, he was a shopper, then?" Rudolf asked. "He would get along with Serena. She lives to shop. Come to think of it, maybe we shouldn't find this guy. The one person my wife would dump me for is the Protector of Wealth."

"I don't think he's available in that regard," Sherlock said matter-of-factly, his eyes taking in the many sights as people haggled and shopped.

The busyness of the outdoor bazaar in Istanbul was similar to that in Morocco, although the climate was different. The smells were rich, and the air was mixed with many different aromas wafting from the food vendor area.

"So, how do you know this is Subfar's trail?" Rudolf asked, his attention pulled in by a stall that wasn't gross with eel guts or useless things like dried fruit. Instead, artfully arranged around the small area were hundreds of bottles of Turkish wine.

"I know," Sherlock Holmes said in reply, following Rudolf over to the booth as he inspected one of the bottles.

"Do you think the Turks are better known for their white or red varieties?" Rudolf asked, ignoring Sherlock's sullen nature as he looked all around like a paranoid freak.

"I really couldn't say," Sherlock Holmes said, looking over his shoulder. When he glanced back, there was a serious expression in his eyes.

Rudolf grinned and held up two dusty bottles. "Then we'll try one of each. Don't drink all my wine again like last time."

"I don't think we have time for such things," Sherlock protested.

Rudolf waved him off and put one bottle under his arm while he retrieved his money. He always carried every currency, just in case. "There's always time for wine. Don't be absurd."

"It's just that…" Sherlock's voice trailed off as he peered over his shoulder the other way this time.

"Here you go," Rudolf said, to the vendor, handing him the money. "Keep the change."

The old man shook his head, not accustomed to taking tips. He handed Rudolf back his change, which was a shiny gold coin.

Rudolf strode out of the stall and handed one of the bottles to Sherlock, who followed him down the lane. "Well, that was nice of the chap. He didn't want to take my change. So here you go. Have some wine and a coin. You can buy yourself a trinket with it."

Sherlock took the coin, showing a lot more interest than Rudolf thought was necessary. He stopped in his tracks, looking at the coin.

This was fine by Rudolf because it gave him a chance to use

magic to uncork his wine and take a swig. Sherlock was still studying the coin when Rudolf lowered the wine bottle.

"I don't think you can get much with that." He pointed to the coin.

"I don't think I can get anything," Sherlock said. "It's our clue about where to go next."

Rudolf's eyes widened. "The clues are on the coins! Clever Subfar. I get it, Protector of Wealth. Of course, he'd put it on the coins."

"Yes, and you're just happening to find them, proving helpful."

Rudolf happily took a drink. "What can I say? I always save the day even when I don't try. So where are we supposed to go next? To a flea market in Texas? I do need a new dune buggy or a knock-off watch. I'm not allowed real ones because I keep breaking them, thinking that will somehow stop time."

Sherlock blinked at him. "Are you by chance drunk when you do this?"

Rudolf nodded and took another a sip.

"We're not going to the next place the clue leads to." Sherlock uncorked the wine bottle Rudolf had given him and took a swig.

"Because we're getting drunk in Istanbul?"

"Because we're being followed. Let's wander the streets and lose them."

CHAPTER FORTY

Fantastical Armory, Roya Lane, London

"Where's Subner?" Paris asked upon entering the Fantastical Armory and finding the spot usually occupied by the Protector of Weapons empty. She looked around and saw Mama Jamba and Papa Creola in their usual place.

"He's gone," Papa Creola answered, taking a sip of tea.

Paris sighed. "Thanks. I can see that. He's never gone. Where did he go?"

"Out," Papa Creola replied.

Paris knew there was no point in pushing Father Time. He wasn't supplying information. That was clear enough.

"So, you both know the three demigods of love are loose."

Mama Jamba looked up from her tea, an expression of shock on her face. "Oh, no. Really? What? How? When?"

Papa Creola's expression was suddenly flat, then it cracked, and he chuckled. Mama Jamba joined him, slapping her knee.

"How was that?" she asked her partner. "Was it believable?"

He shook his head. "Not in the least. It was kind of cute."

"Thanks. I think you're cute when you lie too."

"I don't lie," he said, sounding offended. "I just withhold the truth."

"The other day, I asked you if the cookies I made were okay, and you said yes," she said flatly.

"So? They were okay."

"They were burned, and you know it."

"Burned is still okay," he countered.

She giggled, taking a sip of tea. "I always burn the cookies."

"I know," he chirped. "I'd worry if you didn't."

"Well, who has time to watch clocks when there's so much to be done?"

"I do," Papa Creola said.

"That you do," she agreed.

Paris held up her hand. "Hey, I'm still here."

"Of course you are, dear," Mama Jamba said with a sweet smile. "You'll be on this planet for a bit longer."

"A bit," Papa Creola repeated, a hint of mischief to his tone.

"You two are…"

"The rulers of this planet and your world, and therefore, you'll choose your words carefully," Mama Jamba said sweetly.

"Of course," Paris amended suddenly. "I wasn't going to say anything."

The pair erupted into laughter again.

"Oh, it really is too much fun playing with her."

"Right, I guess you two wouldn't really care if someone said something bad about you," Paris said.

"We've got thick skin," Mama Jamba said, setting her tea down. "Go on and ask your questions. We won't answer them."

"Seems like a waste of time, but whatever," Paris said, blowing out a breath. "So, you know that your demigods are on the loose, and you're just sitting here having tea."

"You're going to catch them," Mama Jamba said.

"Or die trying," Papa Creola added.

"Yes, the jury is still out on that."

"Can't you use that game of yours, All Gods Go To Heaven, to put them back in the underworld or do something like you did before?"

Mama Jamba glanced at her partner with a serious expression. "What do you say?"

"I've got a wedding this weekend and really need to get measured for a suit."

Mama Jamba clapped. "I'm going too. I need to get a hat. I love a spring wedding."

"I'm going to that wedding too," Paris interrupted. "That's my Uncle John's wedding."

"Then you better go and round up the demigods so you can make the festive affair," Mama Jamba ordered.

Paris groaned, wanting to stomp her feet. "So, like Saint Valentine and Bermuda, you two think I need to be the one to go after these angry love gods?"

"You've got the wand," Mama Jamba said.

"Don't forget the demon blood," Papa Creola added.

"You also have a plan," Mama Jamba said. "I always wanted to go to a party at the Louvre."

"You're Mother Nature," Paris argued. "Just go. Throw one. Hell, you can come to the one we're throwing tomorrow night."

The old woman shook her head. "Oh no. I haven't got a thing to wear. Which is why I need to go shopping for a hat for the wedding this weekend."

"Okay, well, since Subner is missing or gone or whatever, and you two want me to round up your demigods, can one of you tell me how I'm supposed to contain them using Amantis?"

Papa Creola pointed to the wand on her hip. "It's the sapphire that will contain them."

"Okay, well, how does that work?"

"I have no clue," he mumbled at once.

Paris glanced at Mama Jamba. She shrugged. "I don't even know how to work one of those fire sticks that turn on the television. Do you really think I know how your fancy wand could capture a bunch of misbehaving demigods?"

Paris sighed. "Yeah, I guess not."

"Oh, perk up, dear." Mama Jamba waved a hand at Paris' jacket pocket, where her phone was located. "Your mother has good news for you, but it's not about your wand and how to contain the gods."

Paris did perk up at this news and hastily retrieved her phone from her jacket. She had a message from her mother. It read:

I have someone who can teach you the counterspell to banish the demons.

Meet me in five minutes.

Paris looked up, smiling victoriously. Papa Creola was wearing an annoyed expression as he handed her a cup of tea he'd just poured.

"What's this for?" she asked, taking the tea.

"She's going to be late," he said. "Your mother is always late."

CHAPTER FORTY-ONE

Lithia Park, Ashland, Oregon

"I was six minutes late," Liv Beaufont said when they stepped through the portal onto a grassy field in a wooded part. "That man is always so particular about time."

Paris laughed, enjoying the cool breeze. "He is the father of time."

"Which means he should be more relaxed about the whole thing, but if you do the smallest thing, he's all like, 'Oh, you're going to sever the fabric of time.' He really is so melodramatic."

Paris shook her head at her mother, but she was grateful to be there with her. Apparently, when Liv and Stefan had to find the antidote to heal her father from the demon who bit him before he turned into one himself, they met a man by the name of Renswick Shoshawnawalla. He was a dark elf who lived in an old Victorian house in a hippie town in Southern Oregon.

After tracking down and slaying the demon who bit Stefan, they were able to give his blood to Renswick. He then was able to make an antidote that kept Stefan from turning into a demon. However, the change had started, and Stefan gained all the strengths of the demons without becoming one of them. Instead, he could sense them and had a thirst to stamp out evil, and he passed all of that to Paris.

The expert on demons, Renswick, suffered a worse fate than Liv when his wife was bitten by the same demon who bit Stefan—Sabatore. Unable to track down the demon who enjoyed turning magicians into monsters like him, Renswick had to watch his wife become what he hated. Before she turned fully into a demon, he killed her, nearly breaking his own mind. Even so, he'd been there to help Liv and Stefan but ever since, the man was very reclusive.

"So, you talked to this Renswick?" Paris asked. "He's agreed to help?"

"Yeah, but he said the counterspell would be really complicated and take a lot of power, even if you have the demon blood. That's why he needed us to come and see him. It wasn't something he could simply pass along."

Paris gulped, feeling that overwhelming weight on her chest again. She then felt a warm arm around her shoulders as her mother pressed her in close. "Hey, this is big. You're bigger. You're going to conquer this, and we'll be there to help you."

"Really?" Paris asked, looking up with hope. "You really will? You'll go to the Louvre and help me with containing the demigods?"

Her mother's blue eyes were sparkling. "Of course, my love."

"Okay. Then let's get this counterspell, and we'll be that much closer to putting the demigods where they belong," Paris said.

"Don't forget, we still have to find Tomár, who is the big baddie behind all this," Liv added.

Paris pointed to a group of teenagers with long hair and baggy pants. The field around them was filled with strange types like them, playing guitars or doing cartwheels like school children. This group was playing a strange game with a small sack they were bouncing back and forth off their ankles as they jumped around.

"Real quick, though. What are they doing?" Paris asked, indicating the group.

"Oh, those are hippies, and they are playing hacky sack," Liv answered. "Please promise me that you'll let your demon blood take over and go for world domination before you become a hippie or play a dumb game of 'the floor is lava, don't let the sack of rice touch the ground.'"

"Is that a serious request?" Paris asked, chuckling.

"Spend an hour with a hippie, and you'll realize there are some things worse in this world than evil demons," Liv said. "There are people who drink hemp milk and tell you all about it."

CHAPTER FORTY-TWO

Renswick Shoshawnawalla's Residence, Lithia Park, Ashland, Oregon

The Gothic Victorian house belonging to Renswick stood out like a sore thumb among the hippie houses lining the cheerful park. The mansion had several spires and unique attention to detail. Gargoyles perched on various places of the roof, which was covered with spikes. The house was painted in varying shades of grays and blacks. There was only one light on in the entire building, on the third floor at the top of the tallest tower.

Before they saw the front door to the demon expert's house, Paris knew something was wrong. She could feel it. At her core, she knew a demon had been on the property. The same instinct told her the demon was no longer there.

In a flash, Paris pulled Amantis from her hip as the view of the front door, now split in two, came into view. Liv stiffened and turned to Paris. Her hand was on the hilt of her sword, and given where she was looking, Paris guessed she was going to tell her to pull her weapon. Paris was one step ahead of her.

"Someone has been here," Liv said.

"Recently. A demon."

Liv sniffed the air. "Yeah, I'm getting it now. They're gone?"

Paris reached out with her demon senses to be sure. "Yes, they are gone."

With a heavy look in her eyes, Liv glanced up at the broken door. "Which means we're either going to find something really bad in there or nothing at all."

"Tomár," Paris guessed.

"He would have known that Renswick would know the counterspell. He's always been one step ahead of your father. He won't want you putting the demigods back or sealing them away," her mother agreed.

"Do you think he's dead in there?"

The cold look in Liv's eyes said yes, but her words contradicted them. "I don't think so. Renswick is smart. His place is full of traps. He would have been alerted as soon as Tomár stepped foot on his property. I'm going to hope he got away somehow. That means that not only do we not have the demon expert to teach you the counterspell, but now we've got to go track him down."

Paris glanced up at the tall gothic house and drew in a steadying breath. "Okay, well, let's go and find some clues. Hopefully, we'll be able to reconstruct what happened and go from there."

Liv smiled at her daughter. "Spoken like a real detective. If I didn't know any better, I'd say you must be roommates with Sherlock Holmes."

CHAPTER FORTY-THREE

Although Paris was on guard as they entered Renswick's house, stepping through the broken door, she didn't think the danger that had broken in was still there. Paris guessed that no one was in the mansion or worse, that Renswick didn't get away and was somewhere in the house, dead.

The foyer of the place would have been overwhelming if it hadn't been ransacked with splintered pieces of the front door everywhere. It was full of distracting elements with so many strange items in the small space. Without having met Renswick, Paris knew the elf had to be eccentric.

A stuffed crow sat on the banister of the staircase in front of the entrance. Hanging on the walls were several large oil paintings, all of them in black and white, as if the painter didn't have any colors on their palette. There were gothic-inspired items, such as a grandfather clock with detailed carvings around the face, a coat rack with no coats, and an umbrella stand without any umbrellas.

Besides the damage caused when the front door had been kicked in, there didn't appear to be any other struggle here. Paris glanced up the stairs and then down the long corridor and saw muddy footprints from a very large boot. She pointed ahead. Tomár went that way first. She knew because the muddy prints dissipated down the corridor, and the white runner on the stairs wasn't covered in much dirt, although there was some.

Liv took the lead. "Then we go that way first."

The corridor was filled with more black and white paintings of an elfin woman in Victorian dress or horseback riding across a pasture. In one, she was standing beside a man who Paris guessed was Renswick. He looked like he'd just stepped out of a silent film, dressed in a black and white suit. His black hair was cropped tightly to his head, and his mustache looked like a tiny pencil sitting below his nose. In his eyes was brooding mischief that was both curious and disconcerting. It was as if he was planning a trick.

"Renswick could be trusted?" Paris had to ask. Elves usually weren't dark like this man in the photos. They gravitated toward the hippie lifestyle. Sometimes a rare elf was born who was on the darker side, much like how Subner was in his current incarnation as Father Time's assistant.

"Oh, yes. He only studied demons to try to help his wife. When that didn't happen, then he started a crusade, albeit from the confines of his home, to try to rid the world of them through science and research. Your father often relied on Renswick's advice and expertise when hunting demons."

Catching Paris' line of vision, studying the black and white pictures on the wall, Liv understood. "Yes, he is of the darker nature. I think it's inevitable when one spends all their time studying evil creatures. I would trust Renswick with my life, though. It is because of that man your father survived and didn't become a demon. He would also advise me on you, knowing that you'd become part-demon even though your father was cured. That was why I sought out the djinn's lamp to try to balance things out."

Paris nodded, having only recently learned her personal

history. "That's why I'm half-fairy, to balance out the demon aspect of me."

Liv smiled. "Yes, you're the best of everything. Some people thought having a child with demon blood was a curse, but you turned it into something that is immeasurably wonderful."

Paris' face flushed with warmth, but she shook off the sentimental feelings. She needed to stay focused. She pointed ahead at an elegantly appointed sitting room. "It looks like big feet went that way."

Liv glanced in that direction. "Yeah, I mean, not only did Tomár break down the door, but he didn't even wipe his feet before barging in. So rude. I'm starting a school that teaches etiquette to demons."

Paris laughed. "Good luck with that."

Turning and continuing down the hallway, Liv said, "I always have overly ambitious goals. Those produced you."

As in the entryway, the sitting room was devoid of color. The chairs were black, the marble floors white, and the walls a mixture of both. There was an ornate coffee table with a decanter and crystal glasses. Even here, there were no signs of struggle.

"Thoughts?" Paris asked.

"Well, I wished the poltergeist was still here," Liv muttered.

"Say what?" Paris asked. "There was a poltergeist? I haven't had the greatest experiences with poltergeists."

"Most don't," Liv replied. "Todd was like Renswick's security dog. He'd bark and alert him of intruders. He's not here, or he'd be licking at my feet and wagging his tail, or so that's what I imagine that weird assortment of light does when I've visited. It's hard to tell."

"If Todd isn't here?" Paris asked.

"Then either Tomár destroyed him, or he could be hiding somewhere, frightened by the events that unfolded here," Liv said.

"You think the poltergeist got scared?"

"I think most would be afraid of Tomár. Todd was a puppy dog once you got to know him. Well, a puppy dog who threw objects at your face and screamed so loud it could burst your eardrums. He and I made a truce."

"This is very strange," Paris remarked, looking around for clues but not seeing anything that told the story of what happened during the break-in.

Liv came to the same conclusion. She pointed up to the ceiling, indicating the second floor. "I think we better venture up the stairs. Remember, a scared poltergeist could be hiding in a closet, and if he doesn't know and like you, he's extremely volatile and dangerous."

Paris held out her hand to her mother. "Then, by all means, lead the way since that guard dog apparently likes you."

CHAPTER FORTY-FOUR

Following her mother up to the second floor, Paris braced herself for what they might find next. She was surprised when Liv led her to a room that had actual color. It was comprised of black, white, and too much red. After taking in the sight, Paris froze, tense. She nearly shot a spell at demons when she entered the room but soon realized they weren't moving. They were all taxidermies.

"What in the world," Paris said. The room was a library with dozens of shelves, all filled with thick volumes.

There were many demons, complete with horns, stationed around the room, as well as cases displaying different artifacts. With her mouth hanging open, Paris stared at the strangeness and waited for her mother to speak. Liv was enjoying Paris' reaction.

"It took Renswick the better part of a century to construct this," Liv said proudly, as if she knew the space well.

"Why?" Paris asked.

Her mother shrugged. "Why does anyone study the devil? That's what Renswick said to me when I asked the same question."

"What did he say in reply?"

Liv smiled thoughtfully. "That studying evil was how to heal the world of that corruption."

Paris thought this made surprisingly good sense.

"When I first met Renswick," Liv continued, "he told me, 'When you ignore evil, you open yourself to it.' He'd spent an entire lifetime cataloging demons because he didn't want to be susceptible to them. That's what he called constant vigilance."

"Are you sure it didn't just make him paranoid?" Paris asked. "He had a poltergeist guarding the place."

Liv sighed. "As we saw by the break-in, he was right to. Renswick always knew the demons would come after him. He knows too much about them. He knows their strengths better than anyone else. More importantly, he knows their weakness, and they know this. Like they know your father is their greatest enemy, the demons know that Renswick is the start of their greatest demise."

"Wow, so what do you think happened to Renswick?" Paris asked. The orderly room had no footprints or new impressions on the carpet despite their boots.

"I think he went up to the third floor where Renswick made his elixirs," Liv answered. "I'm guessing that's either where we'll find clues, the place that Renswick got away, or the man himself."

CHAPTER FORTY-FIVE

Paris knew as soon as they made it to the third floor that this was where the drama had gone down. For starters, there was debris from pictures on the walls and vases on stands broken everywhere in the hallway. A fight or a race went on there.

As they strode down the long hallway, similar to the others, Paris braced herself for what they'd find at the end. There was only one door on this floor, and under it, a light could be seen peeking out. Paris realized it must have been the light she'd spied from the outside at the top of the house.

Liv had Bellator out and in her hands as she stepped to the side of the cracked door. Paris had Amantis. She didn't expect to find Tomár, a perk of being attuned to the demons, but still felt it was prudent to brace herself for whatever they'd find.

Liv glanced at Paris over her shoulder, a question in her eyes.

Paris nodded minutely at her mother, and it was enough.

Liv shot forward so fast that Paris hardly registered the movement. Her mother pushed open the door and revealed the room. It wasn't what Paris expected to see. There was no dead body. There was no more chaos. There were two singular objects of importance, and they told a story all their own.

CHAPTER FORTY-SIX

In the small room that would have been the last place Renswick resided were two things of importance. The first was sitting on top of a small table. It was a bowl of thick liquid in what looked like a washing basin from back in the day. A demon wouldn't know what it was because as Paris glanced sideways while looking at the large bowl, she recognized the glamour as it became a simple piece of pottery. The demon wouldn't have seen the scrying bowl for what it was. He would have most likely been fooled into thinking it was nothing of importance.

Next to the scrying bowl was a large pile of ashes. One might have thought this marked Renswick's demise, but they'd be wrong.

Liv bent and touched the pyramid of ashes, then sniffed. "He nearly burned down his house and himself."

Paris gawked at her mother. "How so?"

Liv stood, wiping her hand on her black cloak. "Renswick created a portal in his house, which is a no portal zone. To do so, he would have had to hastily bring down the wards, then open the portal, and then hope it all worked as he stepped through. It almost didn't, but the burned remains of his portal make me think it did."

"Fascinating," Paris said. She wasn't acquainted with this type or level of magic. "You know all this as a Warrior for the House of Fourteen? That is so cool."

"I do," Liv replied. "You have a very cool job too. I haven't ever had to track down and contain demigods. You're at the beginning of a very long and cool career."

Paris smiled at her mom. "As long as it means our paths always intertwine, then I'm happy."

"We're Beaufonts, fighting for justice. Our paths will always intersect."

Paris wanted to hug her mom, which she always felt she hadn't embraced enough. Instead, she focused on the pile of ash sitting in the room. "So, you think Renswick got away, then?"

"I do because I don't see any more signs of struggle. My best guess is he created all the destruction in the hallway, trying to slow Tomár down from following him. Then he got up here, sent a message, took down the wards, and portaled away."

"Sent a message?" Paris asked. "Did you get one from Renswick?"

Liv shook her head and then pointed to the scrying bowl. "No, but I'm guessing he left one there. It won't have much information in case Tomár could spot the scrying bowl for what it was and reveal its contents, but we will be able to tell soon enough."

CHAPTER FORTY-SEVEN

"How do we reveal the contents of a scrying bowl?" Paris asked.

"There's a spell," Liv replied, circling her finger over the stone bowl sitting on a plain pedestal and intently watching the contents, which remained placid. "First, we have to see if anyone has tried to read the messages left to know if Tomár found out what Renswick said."

"So, a scrying bowl is like a voice message of sorts?"

Liv glanced up, thinking for a moment. "Yeah, a good way of putting it. Back in the day, magicians and elves and such would leave messages in puddles of water for allies. You'd have to know what you were looking for to find one. Then, if you knew the time to look at a scrying bowl or body of water, you could talk in real-time to someone."

"Like Facetime back in the day," Paris supplied.

"Yes, but Renswick is old-school, and he wouldn't rely on technology for a message of this caliber. He would be right too. Demons are masters at hacking into technology. Remember, use old-school methods as much as possible. Evil guys like demons have forgotten the old ways. Also, they can be glamoured to go unnoticed, unlike technology that is always on everyone's radar."

"Ha-ha. Radar. Technology," Paris joked.

Liv glanced at the surface of the bowl of liquid which was like the surface of a mirror. Her mother smiled victoriously. "Good news. It appears that again, the demon had ignored the old-school ways and didn't tamper with the scrying bowl, maybe never having seen it due to the glamour. Or having forgotten how to decode it."

"You know how to decode the message?" Paris asked, realizing at once this was a stupid question. Her mother was Olivia Beaufont, the best Warrior the House of Fourteen had ever had and that was saying a lot.

Liv continued to circle her fingers over the surface of the liquid and chant indistinguishable words.

A moment later and the surface rippled with activity, and the image of a man appeared as though the scrying bowl had turned into a television screen.

"Liv… Stefan… Whoever gets this…" the man who looked like Renswick from the photos downstairs said from the surface of the rippling liquid. His face was frantic as he looked toward the door, standing in the same room where they were now, looking into the bowl the same as them. "I have to tell you a series of important messages before it's too late. Then I have to get away. I hope you can help in more ways than one. First, I know you need to save something bigger than me. You need to stop what Tomár has done."

Paris gulped. She was on the cusp of something big. If she didn't already feel that way, then the way her mother gripped her hand made her tense with apprehension. Renswick had left them a message, and Paris sorely hoped it was the information on how to do the counterspell to seal the demigods. She hoped the expert on demons was okay because he'd definitely risked everything to leave this information for them.

"Look, I can't tell you how to do the counterspell to seal the demigods away," Renswick said in a rush on the heels of Paris' thoughts, making her instantly deflate. He glanced back over his shoulder as a loud noise erupted below him. "I simply don't have the time. I can tell you where to go to find the counterspell. It may not work, but it's all I can do. You have to do what Tomár did. You have to find the demonic witch who gave him the spell. She's the one who will know how to reverse it. Her name is Elvira. I can also tell you that defeating Tomár isn't impossible, as Stefan described when he called me for the counterspell. I did some checking, and I found the weapon that can defeat him."

Another crash from Renswick's world inside the scrying bowl shook the foundation of the mansion, stealing his attention briefly. He glanced back at the scrying bowl with a new intensity. "I don't know *where* the weapon is. I know *what* it is. I can't tell you here because it's too dangerous in case this gets into the wrong hands. I'm going to be running from Tomár. So, get one step ahead of him and find me, and I'll help you. I'll always help you, Liv and Stefan. For now, I have to run. I'm so sorry. I'll leave you clues. Ones only you'll understand. Follow them. Find me. Please. Then we'll bring him down, once and for all."

The surface of the scrying bowl went still and black as though Renswick was never there.

CHAPTER FORTY-EIGHT

Morning Glory Café, Ashland, Oregon

"This is insane," Stefan said, over-stirring his cup of black coffee, which didn't need stirring. "There's zero way Paris can go undercover at Elvira's."

The cutesy restaurant's yellow walls and mismatched tables and chairs were full of whimsy, like the tea shop called Wonderland. Paris didn't think there was any magic at play in this much-loved restaurant for locals. It had an empty table around the corner when she and her parents walked in, and they didn't have to wait because Liv had saved the owner from peril or a piranha or something similar.

"I hear you, babe," Liv said in her calm voice, taking a sip of her own black coffee. "It was Renswick's advice. Elvira has the counterspell. The way to get it is to go to the source. Can you do it?"

Stefan shook his head. "No, I can't get close to that safe house. I've been trying. As far as going undercover, even with a glamoured appearance, they'd spot me a mile away. Well, smell me. I mean, I can pass for a demon if I'm glamoured and they're bad at seeing past that. They have been tracking me long enough that they know my smell, though. For demons, it's always about the smell."

Liv pointed to Paris. "What about her?"

Stefan shook his head adamantly. "She's not going into Elvira's halfway house for demons to get a counterspell. That's like sending our daughter…well, into a house of demons."

"That's exactly what it is, but it may be the only way," Liv argued. "Renswick is on the run, and he knows the weapon that you need to defeat Tomár."

"Which means I have to find Renswick," Stefan said.

"I can help you because I know how to track Renswick," Liv said. "He said he was leaving clues that we'd recognize."

"Yeah, but she can't go to Elvira's. It's full of demons, and if they realize who she is? It's a bunch of lowly demons who will eat her alive."

"They are just that," Liv argued. "They are low-level demons who don't know their tongue from their toe. They won't spot her if she's disguised. She goes in there and gives that demonic witch what she wants for the counterspell."

"It's always money with that woman," Stefan said with a disgruntled sigh. "She can be bought easily."

"So, she gives her what she wants, and then we can contain the demigods," Liv said. "Meanwhile, you and I go after Renswick before Tomár gets to him. He knows how to kill him, and we can't leave Renswick on his own."

"Liv, even if that all sounds good in theory, we're sending our daughter into a halfway house of demons," Stefan argued. "They are disgusting. The worst of the worst. They will eat her alive if they find out who she is."

"I am the only real person of moral aptitude who could get in there, right?" Paris argued, cutting into the conversation.

Her parents both looked up at her like they'd forgotten she was there.

"Well, yes," Stefan answered. "They'd sense anyone who

wasn't demonic in there. You'd pass because technically, you're demon enough to pass. If you were glamoured..."

"It could work, Stefan," Liv encouraged.

"Okay, I admit it could work." Stefan shook his head, obviously not convinced but caving gradually. "It might be our only solution now that Renswick is on the run. We do need to track him down, both to save him and also to find out what he knows about this weapon to stop Tomár."

"We're running out of time," Paris urged. "The party is tomorrow, and I need to know how to contain the demigods. That's not even the biggest problem. I have to know how to seal the gods back into the book."

"How are you going to figure that out?" Liv asked. "Elvira knows the counterspell, not the way to contain."

Paris shrugged. "I don't know. Maybe I can find something along the way. Right now, I've got to keep moving forward. We're running out of time. Soon Hathor will be fueled to full power, and then she'll be too strong to stop. I don't want to see the type of destruction she'd do before we banded together and stopped her with all our forces. It wouldn't be worth it to do things that way. If I can stop Cupid and Freyja, then I'll halt Hathor's progress too."

Stefan and Liv gave each other looks of affection.

"She's got your practical sense," Stefan said to his wife.

"She's got your tenacity," she countered.

"She has your bravery to want to do this."

"Then you'll let her do it?" Liv asked.

"Only if she has the best disguise possible. I'm not putting anything to chance when it comes to my daughter entering the belly of the beast. She has to look like a demon to pass as one."

CHAPTER FORTY-NINE

Rogue Riders Mansion, Beverly Hills, Los Angeles, California

"Hold still. I'm trying to get your nose right," Sophia Beaufont said. She was pointing at Paris' nose as they stood on the grassy knoll in front of the large mansion that belonged to the Rogue Riders in Beverly Hills.

"By 'right,' she means really, really wrong," Lunis said, flapping his wings before settling them into place along his large body.

"No, I mean right," Sophia corrected. "It just needs to match the rest of her face."

"Which means be really ugly," the blue dragon said.

Paris dared to peek open one eye. "Are you sure this disguise isn't going to stick? I can't be looking like a red-faced demon for the rest of my life."

Lunis waved his clawed hand and shook his snout. "Or smelling like one. There's no way you'll be invited to Thanksgiving dinner. Your invitation will be lost in the mail."

"No, it wouldn't," Sophia argued, glancing over her shoulder at her dragon. "We'd still love Paris even if she smelled and looked like a demon."

"Sure, we'd love her. We just wouldn't want to sit next to her and eat turkey and mashed potatoes," Lunis countered. "I mean, smelling like that, we wouldn't want to sit next to her and die."

"The rotting smell is part of the disguise," Sophia explained. "Paris has demon blood, which will help her pass, but she's got to have that smell as well as the look, or she won't be believable as a demon."

"Don't forget the demon attitude," Lunis said. "Can you act like you don't care about anything except for sucking all the good emotions out of the world?"

"Where's the closest Jamba Juice? I'm thirsty and not for a smoothie," Paris said dryly.

Lunis nodded proudly. "She's ready."

Sophia laughed. "Yeah, and before your father turned part-demon, we didn't know as much about them as we do now. The House of Fourteen thought demons sucked negativity from the world, but what we learned is they siphon good emotions. When good is taken from people, the result is a bunch of depressed individuals, hence the sign a demon has been leaching you."

"Do you think that's your boyfriend's problem?" Lunis asked Sophia quite seriously. "Do you think Wilder is being visited by a demon, and that's why he's always so crabby in the morning?"

"No, I think it's because you think it's cute to chew up his slippers every morning like you're a misbehaving Labrador retriever," Sophia replied.

The dragon laughed. "It's hilarious when he gets up and I hear him yell, 'Seriously, not again!' It's like he thinks after a hundred days in a row that I would give up and not chew his slippers."

"What surprises me is that you care so much to sneak into our bedroom and steal the slippers and chew them up every single night," Sophia remarked.

"What surprises me is that Wilder keeps replacing the slippers," Paris added.

"The dragonriders got him a year's supply for his birthday,"

Sophia explained. "It was after the first week of chewed-up slippers. It was supposed to be a joke because no one thought the prank would keep going on and on."

"That's why it's so funny," Lunis said proudly. "It's cute the lengths Wilder goes to hide his slippers from me."

Paris shook her head at the dragon. "You're very strange."

"You have a big nose!" Lunis exclaimed.

"It's not her nose," Sophia explained. "What do you think of the horns?"

Lunis tilted his head to the side and regarded Paris. "They are hideous."

"That's what I was going for," Sophia said smugly.

"She definitely looks like a demon," Lunis said, looking Paris up and down.

Paris glanced down at her figure and took in the sight of her red muscly arms and body. Since most demons were male, that was what Sophia made her. Being in the body of a man wasn't so weird after all the disguises Paris had used, but having horns on the sides of her head was strange.

"It's so weird having these things on the side of my head," Paris said, reaching up and touching the horns. "How am I supposed to walk straight with them?"

"Try flying with them on your head," Lunis said, his eyes rolling up to spy his own horns.

"Well, I'd have to try flying first, but yeah, I'm guessing they take some getting used to in that regard," Paris agreed. "Really, it's pulling off this whole demon vibe that I need to master."

"Have you tried hanging out with Wilder?" Lunis asked. "He's the worst."

Sophia snorted. "No, he's not. You're just mad because he accidentally spoiled the Wordle for you today."

The blue dragon growled. "He knows I don't do the Wordle until I've had my coffee, and he walks into the kitchen this morning and goes, you're taking it black today like the Wordle, huh?"

Sophia laughed. "He forgot."

Lunis gave Paris a long look of disgust. "The word was black."

"I figured as much," she replied.

"He spoiled it," Lunis said.

"Again, I'm drawing the appropriate conclusions."

"I'm going to tell you everything you need to know about being a demon," Lunis began, an air of authority in his tone. "I used to date one, so I know."

Sophia rolled her eyes. "Here we go."

"I dumped her, of course," Lunis continued, ignoring his rider. "She was too possessive."

Sophia sighed loudly. "We all saw that coming a mile away, right?"

"I feel like I'm only seeing red." Paris looked at her hands, mesmerized by how different her skin was.

"You really look like a demon," Sophia said, smiling at her niece.

"You smell like one too," Lunis said.

"You need to act the part, which I'm sure in the moment, you can do." Sophia looked serious. "I know, talking to Liv, that Stefan is worried about you going undercover. I agree this is the only way to get the counterspell, and I have faith in you that you can do it. You're the right person for the job. Turn on the demon part of you that loves evil, and you'll be fine."

"I am acquainted with that part of myself," Paris admitted. "Usually, it clues me into evil and is repulsed by it. I know how it works, and I'm just…"

"You're afraid that once that part of you is activated that you won't be able to turn it off," Sophia said, finishing Paris' thought.

She nodded shamefully.

"Pare, you're part-demon because you inherited your father's blood, but you're not a demon. You're the best of all worlds.

You're a Beaufont, and we know how to spot evil because we were born to stamp it out. There's no way you can become it. That's impossible for you."

"What if once I activate the demon side of me in this way, it does take over?" Paris said. "Before, it's always been a moral compass. For my father, it's helped him to find evil. He also has told me it could be our very undoing if we weren't careful. It can burn us alive from the inside out."

"That's why you have the fairy aspect. It balances it out. You're never going to let it take over. It's like when you banished the Deathly Shadow, you had the demon part of you come out to overpower that evil spirit, but then you shut it back away as soon as it had done its job. You're always in control. Remember that."

Paris felt the pressure in her chest again.

"If you do become a demon," Lunis began, "I'll throw holy water all over you. I did that to a demon and banished them to hell. Of course, Wilder came right back after he'd gone to the bathroom."

Paris laughed, but Sophia just shook her head.

"Do Wilder and Lunis really not get along?" Paris asked her aunt.

"They like each other more than I like them," Sophia answered. "That's why they love to prank each other."

"Okay, I'm ready to see what I look like. Do you have a mirror?"

"You're going to break it," Lunis muttered.

Sophia ignored her dragon and conjured a full-length mirror in front of Paris.

She gasped at her appearance. She was hideous. The horns on the side of her head were short, and her eyes were black. She had rippling muscles under the red skin and a look about her like she was ready to kill. Her teeth were all pointed, and her lips thin. "Wow, this is the best disguise I've ever had."

"It is pretty good, but Sophia's costume beats yours," Lunis said. "She's scary as hell."

Sophia fluttered her eyes with annoyance. "I'm not wearing a disguise."

He pretended to be shocked. "Oh, wow. Oh…I'm sorry."

"Maybe you want to take the dragon with you to the demon halfway house and drop him off as a peace offering," Sophia said to Paris. "They could feast on him for days."

"They could not," Lunis argued. "I'm not full of good emotions. I'm a wickedly dangerous dragon full of terror."

Sophia gave her dragon a straight face. "Sure. So what are you thinking for dinner tonight?"

"Can I get curly fries with my kid's meals?" he asked. "I like to drape them on my face and pretend they're my mustache."

"Sure, but why don't you get a regular adult meal instead of a dozen kid meals?"

"Because I like it when you order them over the phone and say, 'I need twenty-four dozen kid's mac and cheeses with curly fries,' and then order your adult cheeseburger. I can picture the person on the other side of the line thinking you're really bad at family planning."

Sophia turned to Paris. "Maybe take me to the demon halfway house and leave me there."

Paris smiled at her aunt and dragon. "You two enjoy your night and curly fries. I'm going to go and make friends with a demonic witch."

Lunis waved as she backed up, taking her leave. "Don't bring her to the wedding though. Those types always make a scene with their curses and black veils. No one should wear a veil to a wedding."

"What about the bride?" Sophia asked.

"Oh, for angel's sake, this is the twenty-first century, Sophia. Please get a clue. Women don't wear veils to get married."

"What do they wear?"

"Whatever is trending," Lunis said.

"That's not veils?" Paris asked.

Lunis shook his head. "Unless you're Madonna, don't wear a veil when you get married."

"What should I wear?" Sophia asked.

Lunis groaned. "If it's Wilder, an apology."

CHAPTER FIFTY

Minneapolis, Minnesota

Finding the demon safe house was the first part of the challenge Paris faced. She had a few clues to help her get started. According to her father, Elvira's safehouse was in downtown Minneapolis, located somewhere along the river. To find it, one had to look for crosses on rosaries draped in trees, bushes, or other landmarks. If one followed the crosses in the right direction, it would lead to a door of a residence with a crucifix hanging crookedly next to it.

Paris just had to find one of the necklaces and then follow the trail, hoping she went in the right direction and didn't miss any signs. It was nighttime in the city of Minneapolis, and that was when demons were out, so it made sense for her to make the visit then. The dark streets also made it easier for Paris to hide in the shadows, so she didn't scare any mortals with her hideous appearance.

Of course, most demons went unnoticed due to their strange brand of magic. Many times, when mortals saw them, they saw nothing at all or something less sinister than the horned creature. Although Paris had demon blood, she didn't have that type of magic, so she was sneaking through the streets, hoping not to be seen by anyone.

For a long hour, Paris made slow progress, lurking between trees and scouring the downtown area for signs of the rosary beads with crosses. Since she had to hide from cars or pedestrians, she was especially hindered while searching.

She was about ready to glamour herself to help her search more freely when she caught sight of something shiny in a bush. When Paris got close enough to the thorny bush, she discovered the shiny object was a silver cross on a rosary beaded necklace.

Glancing around, Paris tried to decide if she should go north or south on the path where the bush was located. Since more residences were located to the north, Paris chose that direction, hoping her instinct was right. It wasn't a decision based only on logic. Her ability to tune into evil and track it told her there was something evil to the north.

Of course, in that rundown area of the city, she could have been picking up on drug dealers, homeless camps, or other criminals who weren't demons. Luckily, as she progressed down the path, not only did Paris spy two more crosses on necklaces in trees and draped on the corner of a park bench, but she felt a stronger draw toward a nest of evil.

It was strange how she could home in on evil. Paris was worried that when she was in a safe house full of demons, it would be overwhelming. She'd have to clap a strong hand down on her desire to fight the evil. Her father had coached her on practices that would help her to stay objective when surrounded by a bunch of wicked demons.

It was also bizarre to Paris that she'd walk into a house full of demons and then stroll out without ending them all. Her mission was to get the demon counterspell to seal the demigods away only. Stefan would later try to swoop into the safehouse and take out the population of demons. As he'd told her, it wasn't easy for him to get close. The demons sensed when the warrior was getting near to them and usually fled. The safehouse often moved, so finding it wasn't as easy as giving him directions.

Paris wondered how many crosses she'd run across before she found the house when she rounded the corner and saw a row of apartment buildings. Most were fairly neat, with potted plants on the doorsteps or welcome mats. There was one with an over-flowing trashcan out front, graffiti on the walls, broken blinds in the windows, and a sideways cross beside the door.

Paris knew she'd found Elvira's halfway house for demons. Now all she had to do was act the part, make the payment, and get the counterspell. It was the acting part Paris worried about. She could act tough, but she didn't know if she could pull off the evilness that was unique to demons.

CHAPTER FIFTY-ONE

Elvira's Demonic Safehouse, Minneapolis, Minnesota

Paris had made it to the supposed place she was looking for, and she was suddenly filled with doubt. Should she knock on the door? Did demons knock, or did they kick the door, or did they just barge in? Since it was a safehouse for demons, Paris guessed everyone inside was on edge, and barging in unannounced was unwise.

As Paris stood on the front step, she listened to the noises coming from the other side of the door. There was a television blaring something, the sounds of two men arguing, something being sawed. The smell would have been overwhelming if she hadn't already gotten used to her own revolting smell.

Looking at the other nearby residences, Paris felt bad for the neighbors who lived close and had no idea there were demons next door. They no doubt felt low all the time and had no idea why. Most who were leeched by demons never knew.

Deciding knocking was the best option, Paris raised her hand, still surprised by her red skin. She rapped at the door several times, a firm, hard knock like she thought a demon would give. The voices on the other side paused. So did the sawing. There were thunderous footsteps in her direction, and Paris suddenly hoped a password wasn't required. She thought her appearance was password enough for demons.

When the door pulled back, Paris was surprised at the face that peeked around. She'd expected a demon to answer. Paris worried she'd knocked at the wrong door as she looked into the eyes of a mortal.

CHAPTER FIFTY-TWO

The doubt didn't last long because when the man set eyes on Paris, he pulled open the door, welcoming her in without a word. The man was huge both in height and weight, and he didn't look particularly friendly, but he wasn't questioning Paris and seemed to know she was a demon who needed shelter. Unlike most who visited the safe house, Paris needed more.

"I'm looking for Elvira," Paris said, stepping into the cramped hallway and shutting the door behind her. The place was filthy with dirty walls, the floor covered in mud and trash littering the space. Ahead in the main living area, Paris spied several demons lying on the floor. A few were sitting in front of an old television. One was staring at her, a strange intensity in his red eyes.

Paris was vibrating with adrenaline being shut in a house with so many evil, soul-sucking creatures. It was against her instincts to just stand there. Her insides were raging with anxiety, overcome by all the horrible feelings she was being accosted with. She shoved down the panic and growled at the staring demon before returning her focus to the strange mortal.

"Elvira doesn't see drifters," the man said, showing a mouthful of blackened teeth.

"I'm not here for a place to stay," Paris said, her voice strange to her ears. It was deep and gravelly and she spoke in a series of hisses, all part of the disguise Sophia had put on her.

"Then what do you want?" the demon who had been eyeing her said, rising to his feet and coming over. He was large and menacing, his face tattooed and a single horn protruding from the top of his head.

Paris stood taller and tried not to allow any fear to show. The demon would sense it, and then her cover would be blown. "That's between me and Elvira."

"She doesn't see anyone without an appointment and especially not anyone who just stops by," the demon said with authority. "Who are you?"

"No one to you," Paris countered. "I don't need an appointment."

The demon pressed his fist into his hand, his knuckles making a loud cracking noise. "I asked who you were."

"I told you, no one to you," Paris replied, her voice growing louder, waking up one of the demons sleeping in the corner.

A snarl and a growl escaped the demon's mouth, and Paris noticed the vein in his neck bulge. She was fairly certain he was about to lunge at her, but she held his gaze, knowing she couldn't back down. Paris growled back, feeling like an untrained dog.

The demon's hand flew up and was about to come down on her head, but she reached up at lightning speed and halted his strike. He was strong. His skin felt like cold steel in her hand, but she was holding him, keeping his hand blocked. With her free arm, she threw back his other hand as he swung it at her, and then with a force she didn't know she possessed, Paris threw the demon into the group lounging on the floor.

Ungracefully the demons rolled on top of each other. They were making a ton of noise, hisses, growls, and more commotion. Fists flew as a fight broke out, the demons offended by being assaulted when they were lying idly by.

Paris braced herself to be yanked into the fight, but everyone halted when a door at the back of the large room opened. They all looked in that direction, straightening as a tiny woman appeared, her black eyes little slits.

She had dark stringy hair, and her gaunt face was ashen gray. She wore baggy, dirty robes, and when she looked around the room, all of the demons and the mortals looked down at the floor as if ashamed.

"Are you fighting?" the woman asked, disapproval heavy in her voice. "I told you there will not be any fighting here."

The demon who had tried to hit Paris pointed in her direction. "It was him. He started this."

The old demonic witch glanced at Paris. For a moment, she worried the witch could see past her disguise by the way her eyes flared with hostility. "Who are you?"

"I have come to see you," Paris answered. "I need something."

"A place to stay," the woman supplied.

Paris shook her head, the horns feeling strange. "No, I need something from you."

"I only meet with those I know and only with an appointment."

Paris reached into her jeans and withdrew a wad of cash. "Do you know who I am now?"

The woman didn't reply but just stared at Paris.

She reached into her other pocket and pulled out another set of folded-up cash. "How is this for an appointment?"

The strange expression in the witch's eyes was unreadable. Paris braced herself to be attacked or cursed. Everyone in the room stood frozen, all eyes on her. If they attacked, she'd be outnumbered and dead instantly.

Finally, the old witch took a step backward to the door she'd come through. As she turned and walked away, her movement seemed to say, "Follow me if you dare."

CHAPTER FIFTY-THREE

Paris didn't glance back at the demons. Instead, as though she owned the place and wasn't at all afraid, she stalked after the old witch to follow her through the door.

A witch was different from a magician or elf or fairy or other magical creature. They didn't have any magic. They were mortals who used spells to cast magic. Usually, the energy they drew from was dark, so most witches were considered of the evil variety. Elvira fit that bill.

The room through the door wasn't any cleaner than the one she'd just come from. If anything, it was more cluttered with shelves piled high with dusty books and mostly burned-out candles and strange artifacts.

Even though Paris' senses were mostly overwhelmed by the smell of demons, she caught a strange odor of herbs. The space was dark. All the windows were covered and only one light on a desk was lit, but even that had a shawl over it.

Elvira hobbled over and took a seat at the desk before looking up at Paris, her gaze full of darkness. "We'll start with your name."

"It's Saul," Paris said.

"I haven't heard of you," the woman growled, putting her withered hands on the desk.

"I don't get around, and I don't make myself known," she said, repeating the words her father had said to the security guard at the Getty Villa Museum.

"What did you come for?"

"You gave Tomár the spell to pull *Magical Creatures* from books," Paris said with authority, watching as the witch's expression shifted to surprise and then offense.

"How do you know that?"

"I have connections," Paris replied. "I want the counterspell."

"Why?" the woman asked.

"Because Tomár wants to take all the love from the world—"

"Tomár wants to die," she corrected, interrupting.

"I'm aware. I for one don't want to die when he depletes our power source and then gets this planet destroyed. How could you?"

The witch shrugged noncommittally. "I care about money, not about this world. Tomár paid me a lot more than you've flashed at me for that spell."

"I've got more," Paris said, having loaded up on cash thanks to her parents, who were now funding this operation. FGA was pretty much broke, and most of its resources were going to the party the next night at the Louvre.

"You want the counterspell why?" Elvira asked.

"I'm going to stop Tomár," Paris replied. "Already, the gods he unleashed are taking love from the world, giving us fewer emotions to leech. Soon he'll have the power he needs to destroy this place."

The woman leaned forward. "How do you know so much about his plan?"

Paris leaned forward. "You may not have heard of me, but I make it my business to know things."

"To put the gods back, you're going to need a container, or it won't work."

"I have one."

"Do you know how to put them into it?" the witch asked.

Paris shrugged this time. "I'll figure that out if you'll sell me the counterspell."

The witch considered for a long moment. Then she pulled out a drawer next to her and withdrew a piece of parchment. "This is going to cost you double what Tomár paid."

Paris threw the money in her hands on the desk and then retrieved the rest from her pocket and tossed it down too. "So, this spell. It will seal the gods back in the book they came from?"

"Yes, but do you have the book?" the witch asked.

"That's not your concern."

Elvira paused, studying Paris. "Tomár is very powerful and figured out how to get into the Great Library. I'm not sure you have that same type of power."

"Again, that's not your concern."

This was the right answer because the witch held out the parchment, offering it to Paris. "This is the spell. If you don't know how to work it, that's not my problem."

Paris snatched the parchment from the woman, trying to hide her excitement. She had almost gotten away with this, walking into a demon safehouse and taking exactly what she needed so easily. Without another word, Paris spun around, stalking for the door, thinking a demon wouldn't exchange goodbyes.

The witch cleared her throat at Paris' back. "Oh, and before you go, there is something you should know, halfling..."

CHAPTER FIFTY-FOUR

Paris froze and ran through her options. She could use magic to fight the demonic witch. Paris knew she was much stronger than the evil woman. However, there was a slew of demons in the other room and Paris couldn't fight all of them. No, she had to remain calm. She had to talk her way out of this.

Turning to face the witch, Paris made to smile, the action feeling so wrong on her face. "So, you know who I am?"

"I know what you are. Did you really think that you could disguise yourself as a demon and I wouldn't see through it?"

"I *am* a demon," Paris argued, trying to act casual but feeling anything but.

"You are so much more than a demon," the old witch argued. "You are that. Unlike that trash out there." She motioned to the door. "You have magic and whimsy. You must be the famed halfling with demon blood. I believe your name is Guinevere Beaufont, although you go by Paris."

Paris considered hitting the witch with a stunning spell. She had what she came for. By the time the demons figured out what happened, she could be long gone, but something told her not to.

She decided to try and put her at ease and keep talking to the woman.

"Did you really think that because I'm only a witch, I wouldn't see you for what you are?"

"Most wouldn't see me for what I am," Paris countered, not thinking she should play into the witch's hand.

"You know magicians think they are better than me. So do elves and gnomes and just about every magical race. I wasn't born with your powers. I had to earn them by learning and sacrifice. All my life as a witch, your kind has looked down on me because I'm a witch, mortal born, but not by choice," Elvira said.

"There is no one like me, so I don't know what you mean by my kind," Paris said.

Elvira smiled, and the expression looked wrong on her face as if a creepy doll was smiling. "You're smart, Paris. You're respectful. You're brave. You came in here, a place no magician would dare to enter, knowing what those demons would do if they knew what you were. They don't because your disguise is that good. Not enough to fool me, but I have the gift of sight. I might have nearly burned up my soul to earn my magic, but it gave me the ability to see things for what they are. When I saw you, a beautiful young halfling, out there in my living area making demons fight, I realized I had a gift."

"How so?" Paris asked, tensing. "Because I gave you money?"

"Because I knew exactly why you were here," Elvira said. "I don't want Tomár to succeed. I'm a businesswoman. He wanted the spell, and I sold it to him. Secretly I was hoping a do-gooder like you would come along and stop him, and here you are." She pointed at the parchment in Paris' hand. "I would have given that to you without paying."

"Why did you sell it to him, though?" Paris asked. "Some things aren't worth the money."

The dark witch shook her head. "You say that because you have what you want. You were born incredible, whereas I was born a mortal and had to go to extremes to have a tiny bit of the power you were born with. You are a Beaufont and have money and family and everything."

"I was born hunted and lost my parents for most of my life," Paris argued.

"You wouldn't understand why people like me do the things we do," Elvira said. "When you've been reduced like I have, you sell out easily and then with regrets. At first, I didn't think Tomár would succeed. I knew he had to get into the Great Library, and I thought that was impossible, but he must have. Then I got word about the gods loose and realized the spell had worked. It's only a matter of time before Hathor is successful."

"Why are you telling me this?" Paris asked, not fooled by the corrupt witch.

"I know you won't trust me. I'm not asking for that. I'm giving you something after taking your money."

Paris held up the counterspell. "This. Yeah, I'll figure it out."

Elvira shook her head. "No, I'm telling you what you don't know. You haven't figured out how to contain the gods in your wand."

Paris was silent, wondering how the witch knew so much. She shouldn't be underestimated.

Elvira laughed, a sharp, cold sound. "Yes, I know you carry a wand. I make it my business to know things as well as you."

"You know how to contain the gods?" Paris asked, her heart suddenly racing.

"Yes, you must do an absorbing spell, which you can find on your own. Dozens will work."

"That's not very helpful," Paris muttered.

"To contain the gods, you have to chant their real names."

"Real names?" Paris asked. "Like Cupid?"

"No, that's what they are called, but each god at the time of origin was given a godly name. It holds power, and if you speak it, they'll be trapped in your wand until you put them back in the book."

Paris thought for a moment. "Do you know what these gods' real names are?"

The witch shook her head. "No, but you could find it. Or you can ask someone."

"Someone?" Paris asked.

"The ones who created the gods. They are the ones who named them, after all."

Paris backed slowly for the door. She hadn't underestimated the demonic witch, but now she was impressed by her. Elvira knew much more than she should have, and Paris could only fathom how powerful she was as a mortal witch. She was grateful for her help but also hoped their paths didn't cross again. Someone who knew so much but consorted with demons definitely couldn't be trusted. She could do a lot of damage if she ever intended to.

CHAPTER FIFTY-FIVE

Outdoor Bazaar, Marché aux Puces, Paris, France

King Rudolf Sweetwater didn't look over his shoulder as he and Sherlock Holmes walked down the flea market alleyways. He didn't know if they were still being followed, but he knew the man beside him would know. After strolling through Istanbul for a whole night, Sherlock and he had finally gone to the place indicated on the coin Rudolf had been given at the outdoor bazaar. This was the third location Subfar had led them to. With over 1700 dealers and fourteen distinct markets, it was also a place to find great deals.

"I wonder if I can find another Picasso," Rudolf said as they snaked down the path between stalls.

"Another?" Sherlock Holmes asked. "You bought one here before?"

"I bought one at a TJ Maxx," Rudolf explained. "Those places get the best stuff, but you have to know what you're looking for."

"I'm not certain you got an original."

The king of the fae laughed. "Like I'd want one. They don't age well. The original is never as good as a copy. The one I got is nice and framed and without that gross authentic oil painting odor."

Sherlock Holmes went over to a vendor selling old books. He picked up one and read the title aloud. "The Hound of the Baskervilles."

"Do you want it?" Rudolf asked. "I'll buy it for you."

Sherlock shook his head. "I think I have an inkling of how it ends."

"It's dreadfully boring. The main character is totally pompous, and it takes him forever to solve the case. In the end—"

"He kills his assistant," Sherlock finished, interrupting.

Rudolf pressed his lips together, considering Sherlock. "No, in the end, he unmasks the identity of the one he's searching for."

Sherlock turned around suddenly, doing a complete circle.

"So, are you like the detective in that novel?" Rudolf pointed to the book in his hand.

Sherlock shook his head. "No, not quite yet. I'm close."

"Oh. You know what we should do?" Rudolf said, taking the book from Sherlock and throwing it on the stack on the table, then continuing down the aisle of vendors selling their wares.

"Keep our eyes open, search for clues and find out everything pertinent we need to know," Sherlock supplied.

Rudolf shook his head as they came to a courtyard with food vendors and tables. There was a large fountain in the middle with three tiers and cascading water that fell into a large pool at the bottom. "We should make a wish. I sometimes find that when I've thought and thought and investigated and researched, the best thing to do is to wish for a resolution to my problems."

"That is a fool's solution," Sherlock said disapprovingly.

Rudolf tipped the imaginary cap he was wearing and bowed in the detective's direction. "You can call me King Fool."

"That's not something you should ask someone to call you," Sherlock said sternly.

"Well, I'm going to wish for answers to our mysteries and

solutions to our problems while you approach things the boring way."

"By looking at the facts and for concrete evidence?" Sherlock asked.

Rudolf dug into his pants for a coin. He retrieved one and held it up above the fountain they'd come to. Then he closed his eyes and sang, "I wish for—"

He was interrupted by someone taking the coin from his hands.

Rudolf opened his eyes to find it was Sherlock Holmes who'd stolen his money and was now closely inspecting the coin.

He looked up at him curiously. "Where did you get this coin from?"

"My pocket," Rudolf answered. "You were right here when I did."

Sherlock shook his head. "No, before that?"

Rudolf shrugged. "Who knows. I hardly ever know where my money comes from. Is it another clue? Where are we going next?"

"Nowhere," the great detective answered. "We're still being followed, so we're off the case until someone stops the man who won't stop following us."

"Oh well," Rudolf hummed, snapping his fingers. "Hey, since we're in Paris, what do you say we go to a party here? I'm on the list, and you can be my plus-one."

"Like a date?" Sherlock Holmes asked.

Rudolf shrugged. "Call it what you want. I do think it's supposed to be very romantic. How could a soiree at the Louvre in Paris not be?"

CHAPTER FIFTY-SIX

Stretching over seventy-two thousand square meters, the Louvre Museum in France was no small venue to throw a giant party of love. Saint Valentine had come through for Paris Beaufont, pulling strings so she could lure Cupid and Freyja to the location and absorb them into the sapphire on her wand.

Mama Jamba had also promised to send over the real names of the gods of love. Apparently, Mother Nature and Father Time had to jog their memory to remember what they had originally named Cupid, Freyja, and Hathor. Their real names would hold power over the gods, making them submit when Paris went to absorb them and trap them in her wand.

It wasn't as easy as just pointing Amantis at the gods and using an absorbing spell. The gods would be fast and armed and they wouldn't want to be caged once more, knowing banishment was the next step after they'd been caught. Therefore, Paris and her team had to come up with elaborate plans to disarm the three different gods, lure them to certain places, and then bind them. Then and only then could Paris use the absorbing spell combined with the god's true name to trap them in the sapphire.

The Louvre was located on the Right Bank of the Seine River and once was the home of Louis XIV before he relocated to the Palace of Versailles. Since 1793, the museum had been open to the public, displaying over thirty-five thousand works of art, although it contains a staggering three-hundred and eighty thousand.

Maybe on another day, Paris would be interested in seeing the larger part of the collection not open to the public. Although she had full run of the entire museum, that night, she would be too distracted to browse the artwork.

For the festivities, the party being called Venus de Milo Gala of Love, only the Sully and the Denon wing would be open to the guests. The Sully wing was where the Venus de Milo statue was on exhibit. The Denon wing was where the forged necklace, Brisingamen, that Freyja would come for was being displayed. It was also where the most famous pieces of art were on display, such as the Mona Lisa.

Guests would enter through the pyramid in the Louvre Palace and then be allowed to browse the main collection while listening to a live jazz orchestra and sipping champagne. Christine's team in the Refinement Department had come together to decorate and set up the details for the party. Holly and Isha in the Casual Romance department had handled the media and guest list. Penny and her team in the Practical Love Department were handling security and traps to catch both Cupid and Freyja. It was up to Paris, with Faraday's help, to corner the gods and trap them.

Pulling out her phone, Paris checked it for the tenth time in the last few minutes. She still hadn't heard back from Mama Jamba. The party was starting soon, and hopefully, the two most important guests would be arriving—Cupid and Freyja. Both would be armed, enraged, and totally dangerous. It was crucial that everything went to plan, or this could quickly go very wrong.

The gods' wrath was fueling Hathor, and she was growing stronger. As soon as they were subdued, that would help to stop the Egyptian goddess of love and war. Paris planned to deal with that big baddie after she'd trapped the lower gods.

First things first, she thought, seeing no new messages and putting down her phone only to find Agent Barney Jasper in front of her, a serious expression on his face.

"Is that what you're wearing to this party?" he asked. She was in her usual get-up, leather jacket, black pants, shirt, and boots.

Paris laughed at Agent Pompous, who was wearing a tuxedo and a smug look. "Well, some of us are working tonight. Hey, I took off the demon disguise, if that helps."

He grimaced. "It does. Are you ready?"

"Well, the caviar is on ice," Paris supplied.

Agent Jasper shook his head. "No, I meant, are you ready to catch these gods?"

"The nets are set," Penny said, moving across the marble floor and pointing to the high ceiling at something unseen in Venus de Milo's gallery.

"We're ready to disarm that baby," Holly said as she sidled up next to Paris, Isha beside her.

"We set the track for Freyja," Christine offered, coming in from the opposite side from Penny, a proud look on her face.

Paris smiled at her team. "The necklace is in place in the Denon wing. We can spread out the gods so I can get to them easily enough, but they won't be together to gang up on us."

"This was a big ask, using the Louvre," Agent Barney said, looking around at the group.

"Well, you and Saint Valentine also asked for something big, having us go after demigods," Christine said boldly.

"I realize that," Barney said. "Although there's a lot of security in place, please be careful." He motioned to the statue of the Venus de Milo, which was white stone and somewhat unassuming, standing in the middle of the gallery. It had no arms, having lost them long ago. "These priceless artworks can't be replaced, so protect them with your life."

"If the gods are successful, love will be destroyed and the planet too," Paris reminded him. "That can't be replaced."

Barney lowered his chin with a look of warning. "Be extremely careful. You have traps set up all over this place."

"The Louvre security team checked them out and approved," Penny said.

"I realize that, but once things get started, chaos could break out," Barney replied. "We have a god with a bow and arrows and a goddess on a chariot pulled by cats. Everyone's on edge. If it wasn't for the extreme circumstances, the Louvre would have been off-limits."

"Just wait until I have to go after Hathor at the ancient Abu Simbel temple in Egypt," Paris said. "Imagine all the damage I'll have to keep from happening when facing a thirty-three-foot statue that wants to destroy the Earth."

"Don't allow the temple to get ruined," Barney warned.

"That's acceptable if you save the planet," Holly corrected.

"If it can be avoided, let's do that," Barney said.

"You could go and face the angry goddess of war instead of Paris," Isha suggested.

"I can't," he said. "This all relies on Paris since she has Amantis and the demonic counterspell."

Paris felt that now familiar weighty sensation on her chest. "Yeah, let's hope I get the gods' names in time, or we're screwed."

If anyone was going to offer any words of encouragement to her, they would have been drowned out by the sounds of the orchestra starting in the distance and excited guests as the doors to the Pyramid opened. It was officially party time.

CHAPTER FIFTY-SEVEN

After facing demons and witches and throwing a ruse of a party in the Louvre, Paris thought her adrenal glands were close to exploding. She took a deep breath and looked around at her team.

"Okay, take your places," she said in a clear and determined voice. "Communicate over the comms. Do what we've planned for and always expect that things can change and we'll have to as well."

"You got it, boss," Christine said with conviction, running for the Denon wing where the traps would be set for Freyja.

Holly and Isha both set off for the pyramid to be in place to disarm Cupid.

Faraday slid down an unseen wire next to Paris and landed gracefully on the marble floor. "The nets are all set."

"Great," Penny affirmed. "I'm going to go get into place."

Paris pulled Amantis from her holster and held it up, feigning a look of confidence.

Barney looked around and then gave Paris a sturdy expression. "I know this is a lot to ask you to take the lead on, but you're the only choice. After everything you've pulled together, I think Saint Valentine made the right one."

"Thank you, sir," Paris said sheepishly, not used to her boss complimenting her.

He pivoted and made his way for the Tuileries Garden. "Don't screw this up."

Paris gulped.

"Don't worry," Faraday offered as the first of the guests began to spill into the hallways. It was dangerous to have people there with two gods lured to the location, but it was all part of the ruse. If there weren't couples there, Cupid wouldn't buy the whole thing. Everyone on the guest list had signed a waiver and knew the level of danger.

Paris expected to see elegantly dressed couples at the front of the party guests, so she was surprised by two familiar faces coming in her direction down the long corridor. She wasn't sure if it was a good thing or a curse who had decided to show up.

Running forward, Paris didn't halt until she was in front of the two men. "What are you doing here?"

King Rudolf Sweetwater smiled beside Sherlock Holmes. "We're here to help save the day and the planet. Put us to work."

CHAPTER FIFTY-EIGHT

"Hey, I think we're good," Paris said, looking between Rudolf and Sherlock, surprised they came. "I appreciate you offering to help."

"If I'm honest, I had an ulterior motive," the king of the fae admitted.

Paris lowered her chin, distracted by the mingling guests spilling into the area and the band playing in the distance. "Do tell?"

"Well, the thing is, Cupid and I met once," King Rudolf said. "He's gotten out of banishment one other time before. That little naked god, and I do mean little, shot me with an arrow. He made me fall for this barmaid. The fact she was poor wasn't the worst part."

Paris sighed. She didn't have time for King Rudolf's antics or stories. She retrieved her phone from her pocket and was disappointed to find no message from Mama Jamba yet. This was cutting it dangerously close on time, which Papa Creola should know and be all over.

"What was the worst part?" Paris asked, pulling her attention away from her phone and surprised by her own question. There was really nothing to be done until the gods showed up. They'd put out the word all over the world on various media sites. This had to work, or Paris would fail, ruin her reputation, and possibly bankrupt FGA from the investment. Oh, and have Hathor destroy the planet. She was using Uncle Rudolf as a distraction, so she didn't overly worry.

"Well, this barmaid was like a six," Rudolf said. "I mean a six back in the day, which now would be like a four."

"I don't understand," Sherlock said speculatively. "What do the numbers represent?"

"They are a rating system for a woman's attractiveness," Paris explained. "Rudolf is rating this woman's looks on a scale from one to ten."

"So, six isn't passing, then," Sherlock replied. "I see the dilemma."

"You do?" Paris asked, surprised. "Wow, hang out with the king for long, and his superficial ways infect you."

Rudolf indicated the detective. "He gets me. Yeah, I have a beef with Cupid. I was with that barmaid for a whole year, and we were blissfully in love and poor, but we didn't care."

"What's the problem, then?" Paris questioned.

"The problem is that his arrow wore off at exactly the one-year mark," Rudolf said. "I woke up, expecting to wrap myself around the love of my life. Imagine my surprise when I thought a barn animal had crawled into my bed. She was very upset when I kicked her out, but what was I supposed to do? Poke out my eyes and pretend our incredible compatibility was enough to sustain us?"

"Well, it wouldn't have killed you to try to see past the surface," Paris argued. "That's what Cupid did when Psyche lost her beauty, and their love was epic."

Rudolf shook his head. "Their love got Psyche killed."

"He's right."

Paris threw up her hands. "Really, guys. You've both lost your mind. What happened to searching for Subfar? What are you doing here?"

"About that," Sherlock said, trailing away as he looked around suddenly.

Penny cut in over the comm. "Hey boss, good news. Cupid is here."

Paris held up her hand, pausing Sherlock from continuing. She indicated the comm in her ear, so they knew she was talking over that and not to them. "Great news. I'm not ready to trap him yet. I'm waiting on Mother Nature to give me his real name."

"That works," Penny said, an edge of tension to her voice.

"Why?" Paris wanted to know.

"Because he didn't come through the entrance that we were expecting," she answered. "Cupid came through the opposite side to where you are in Venus de Milo's gallery."

"Oh, the Carrousel entrance," Paris said, having memorized the map for the Louvre. "That might work, but what if we don't get him over here to where the nets are set? Or by Holly and Isha, who need to disarm him first?"

Rudolf grinned, pausing her this time by holding up his hand. "No worries. Sherlock and I are on the case. We will go and get Cupid, lead him by the disarming twins, and then to his mother where you can trap him and then *really* trap him."

Paris smiled at her uncle, surprisingly grateful he showed up to save the day. He might at this point.

CHAPTER FIFTY-NINE

Richelieu Wing, Louvre Museum, Paris, France

"Come to Papa, you little conniving jerk," King Rudolf said, hurrying down past the Near Eastern Antiquities and toward the Carrousel entrance. The fae had spent a couple of years trapped in the Louvre in the underground medieval portion by an evil cult of magicians during World War II when the Museum was closed and much of the artwork removed. It was only after promising to do some espionage work that Rudolf was set free, and unironically, the French liberation happened. The fae had a thankless job and had been ignored in the history books.

"What is your plan for leading Cupid?" Sherlock asked, hastening up beside him and keeping up quite well even after so many years of smoking that pipe.

"I'm planning on taunting the child-like man," Rudolf answered. This wing of the Louvre was much quieter. There were only the ugly artifacts and security guards with comms, relaying information to their various supervisors for the night.

"You remember Cupid is armed with a bow and arrows that give us an aversion to good feelings," Sherlock Holmes reminded him.

Rudolf arched an eyebrow at the great detective. "Is that really a problem for you?"

"I don't see how it would affect me in the slightest," Sherlock answered. "The injury could be an inconvenience."

"Let's plan on not getting hit. Even if you don't have any emotions for him to mess with, it could slow us down. Instead, we'll lead him to the area where Holly and Isha are planning on disarming him. I believe it's the statue area with Hermaphrodite, who, by the way, was a bit of a diva. Then we'll go get drunk and avoid Freyja. If that grumpy goose gets her sights on me, she'll be nagging me through the next century."

"Have you angered all of the demigods?" Sherlock asked.

"Pretty much." Rudolf paused, picking up on the sounds of wings flapping in the distance. "I think our feathered friend is up ahead."

The pair halted and hid behind the statue of a naked figure. They caught sight of another nude on the far side of the gallery, but this one was flesh and not stone.

CHAPTER SIXTY

King Rudolf wasn't surprised when he realized what statue Cupid was hanging out next to. It was one James Pradier had done of Psyche in 1824. The mostly naked figure of the woman had her bottom half covered in draped fabric and her arms over her chest, but otherwise, she was pretty much revealed.

Rudolf shook his head at the room full of sculptures. "I swear, there are more bare butts here than at a hippies' house."

"Yes, it appears the Greeks hated clothes."

Rudolf pointed to Sherlock's side. "You go out that way and get Cupid's attention. I'm going to sneak down back the way we came in and taunt him in that direction."

Sherlock gave an efficient response in the form of a nod, and then he popped out into view, immediately earning the god of love's attention.

Rudolf glanced over his shoulder in time to get mooned by Cupid before he swung around brandishing a new weapon. Cupid didn't have the same bow and arrow as before with different tips. Instead, he was carrying a crossbow, and by the looks of it, the weapon could do a lot more damage than simply make people sullen. It could possibly harm someone physically, and an angry Cupid was pointing the weapon straight at Sherlock Holmes.

"Not on my watch, you nude little fairy man," Rudolf said, swinging around as Cupid was about to release the trigger. "Hey, remember me, you giggly cherub?" Rudolf exclaimed, earning Cupid's attention as he released the arrow. It flew past Sherlock Holmes and hit another mostly naked statue.

"You!" Cupid growled, his wings fluttering as he flew after Rudolf.

Not wasting any time, Rudolf sprinted back the way they'd come, leading Cupid toward the gallery of Venus de Milo where the traps were set. First, the little man with wings and a temper had to be led through the sculpture room with Hermaphrodite, where he'd be disarmed.

Rudolf glanced over his shoulder, sad to see that Cupid was faster than he remembered. Or maybe the fae had slowed down. He had to work for a living where the god of love had been hanging out in the underworld, probably working on his six-pack abs.

Many pictured Cupid as a child, and although his appearance was deceivingly quite young, he was still a man. He was smaller in stature, but by the look of everything he was carrying, he was a full-grown man. Still, Rudolf thought he could announce that fact rather than show it.

Racing around the corner, Rudolf slid as though getting to home base just as he heard an arrow whizzing over his shoulder. He narrowly avoided being hit and jumped to his feet. As he continued, the sounds of beating wings could be heard.

As Rudolf ducked behind a large vase, he glanced over his shoulder, seeing Cupid catching sight of guests coming in from the Sully entrance. They were couples, hand in hand, invited to enjoy the festivities of the night and celebrate the Venus de Milo.

Cupid had given up on Rudolf and was hovering in mid-air, taking aim at one of the guests.

Jumping out into full view, Rudolf waved his hands over his head. "Hey, is there a reason you go commando? Is it because your mom refused to wash your whitey tighties and they all have stains?"

That did it based on the way the little man's face flushed red. Rudolf had found the trigger, and it was definitely mom.

Barreling in his direction headfirst was an angry god of love, and he was flying fast. Rudolf decided he needed to employ something to slow down his pursuer. He threw out a hand as he ran and shot a combusting spell at a series of glass cases with figurines.

The glass exploded all over the huge gallery, making Cupid dart backward to avoid being hit.

Rudolf took the opportunity to pull ahead, clearing that room and darting straight into the next one. He threw his back up against the wall. He knew he might have destroyed a bunch of artifacts, but also that they were just objects at the end of the day. This battle was about love and people and this planet and was way more important than protecting some silly stuff no one but art historians cared about.

In the next room, Rudolf caught sight of the statue of Hermaphrodite and then stationed around the room Isha and Holly. They were ready for their part of the mission. By the sounds of it, Cupid was on his way and had no idea he was about to be disarmed. Rudolf opened a portal escaping to safety, having done his job and leaving the rest for the fairy godmothers to complete.

CHAPTER SIXTY-ONE

Sully Wing, Louvre Museum, Paris, France

Holly was telling herself she could have become a medical doctor when the naked winged man with a crossbow flew into the room where she and Isha were stationed. She also knew she wasn't fooling herself. Not only would Holly have flunked out of medical school, but even if she hadn't, she had the bedside manner of a cactus.

Holly had gone to Happily Ever After College because it seemed like an easy career path, one which would allow her to work on her base tan and her blog. Then Paris Beaufont came along and demanded Holly actually work. The new agent for the Casual Romance department had unreasonable demands like Holly had to show up to work every single day, usually in the morning, and work cases.

Holly wasn't going to tell Paris that since she started as an agent for FGA, everything at the corporation of fairy godmothers had gotten better. Things had gotten crazy, no doubt, with Agent Josh Emerald and Agent Jackson Zelle's real identities being revealed. In that way, things were starting to get better. It was like the evil ghosts were being cleared out so real change could happen.

On the long list of things Holly wasn't admitting, especially to her boss Paris, was she liked going on cases and knowing at the end of the day she'd made a difference. It was much more rewarding than listening to podcasts and marathoning *Real Housewives of Beverly Hills*. Lately, at night, when Holly laid down to fall asleep, she felt a sense of completion and pride. She fell asleep easier, knowing she was making the world better, and she awoke more energized and excited to be a part of something that mattered.

If Holly had become a medical doctor, ironically, she thought she'd be making a lot less of an impact on the world than the role she had right then. Cupid was on the loose and trying to harm the world, and it was part of her job to stop him. On top of being cool and brave, Holly got to throw a huge party at the freaking Louvre. Before that, the best place she'd ever thrown a party was at a Dave and Busters.

Not only did Holly get to plan a fabulous party in a prime location, but due to the genius who was her boss, she was disguised as a caryatid in a room full of ancient Greek statues. A faux balcony sat on top of Holly's head along with three more statues of women holding up the structure as they could often be seen doing in architecture. Holly was only magicked to look like a statue.

Across the room, also disguised as a Greek statue, was Isha. The idea was they'd confuse and distract Cupid. When he was wrestling with his bewilderment, Holly would magically yank the crossbow from him before he knew what hit him and before he hit them or anyone else with an arrow.

As the bare-butt man flew into the room, Holly waited until he hovered in the center of the area, trying to decide which way Rudolf Sweetwater had gone. Before he could make up his mind, Holly made a small squeaking noise at his back.

The god of love spun around, holding the crossbow at the ready, menace in his eyes. All he saw were four stone statues of caryatids. Narrowing his gaze, Cupid studied the space, scrutinizing every detail. He might have spotted Holly for what she was, but then, Isha squeaked on the far side of the room, once more making Cupid spin in the air, his wings flapping as he turned toward the noise, crossbow cocked and ready.

CHAPTER SIXTY-TWO

All Paris could do was wait to hear from her team. She didn't have Rudolf hooked into the comm, so she had no idea whether he and Sherlock had been successful at luring Cupid to the right room. Experience had taught Paris she could rely on the fae. She was curious what they were doing at the Louvre instead of hunting down Subfar for her. After all the money FGA was spending on this event, they'd soon need funding desperately.

Paris reminded herself the most important thing that night was stopping Cupid and Freyja from fueling Hathor. As soon as that was accomplished, the bigger task needed to happen of stopping the Egyptian goddess. Paris didn't want to wrap her brain around that just yet.

Pacing in front of the Venus de Milo, Paris was growing anxious. She knew she should be hiding for when Cupid showed up, but since she hadn't heard from her team, she didn't know where he was, whether close or still chasing after Rudolf and Sherlock. Getting his bow and arrow away from him was key, or he'd be especially difficult to subdue.

Paris glanced at her phone and deflated. Even if Cupid

showed up right then, she wouldn't be ready to trap him since she didn't know what his name was. She needed his real name, and there was no way of getting around it.

Paris was growing angry at Mama Jamba and Papa Creola for keeping her waiting. Sure, they named the gods long ago, but they should be able to come up with their names together or by researching them. Mama Jamba was probably taking a nap, and Papa Creola was most likely complaining about something to Subner. She hoped they sent her the names before they lost their opportunity.

She was consoled by the fact that only Cupid had shown up, and she wasn't under the time crunch to trap both gods at once.

It was possible Freyja hadn't gotten the news about Brisingamen being found. Maybe the goddess of love knew it was a hoax and the necklace in the case was fake. Maybe they wouldn't lure Freyja out. Then what? Paris wondered. Taking Hathor down depended on taking down the other gods.

Paris heard a crashing sound in the distance toward the Denon wing. She tensed and bit her lip. That definitely sounded like something breaking. Paris hoped it was a champagne flute. It was quickly followed by more crashing and the sounds of damage.

"Hey, boss," Christine said over the comm.

"I'm here," Paris replied, continuing to pace.

"Freyja has just shown up, and she's making a beeline for where the necklace is located."

Paris drew in a breath. "Okay, then that means she's going to run right into our trap, right?"

"Her and her cats," Christine said. "Just as you planned."

"Good," Paris said, relieved the goddess of love had arrived. Now things would get even more intense.

"Oh, but one thing," Christine began over the comm.

Paris held her breath. "What's that?"

"The cats, they're huge."

Paris gulped. "Okay, well, separate them from the goddess. We need her on her own."

CHAPTER SIXTY-THREE

Denon Wing, Louvre Museum, Paris, France

Before Paris Beaufont was Christine's boss in the Refinement Department, she had mostly been giving Cinderellas makeovers and fixing fashion faux pas. It wasn't important work. If Christine did anything meaningful with her life, she wanted to stop grown women from dressing like toddlers. Seriously, Christine thought to herself, if she ran across another adult wearing a onesie, she was going to scream. The only thing worse was overalls, which farmers thought were okay. They also had dirt under their fingernails.

Since working for Paris, Christine's job had gotten even better. She wasn't only helping with things she had expertise with, like throwing parties and being fabulous, but she was doing something that felt meaningful. Before with her old boss, there were zero chances Christine would be about to throw a track of spikes in front of a chariot to slow a goddess of love down.

Paris' plan didn't involve hurting the cats that pulled the chariot, nor the goddess riding in it. The idea was to disconnect them. On her own, Freyja was enough of a force. If they could slow them down and break them up, Paris stood a chance of containing the goddess. Christine firmly believed that if anyone could trap three gods, it was her old college friend.

It felt surreal to stand at the top of marble stairs in the Denon Wing of the Louvre Museum in Paris and watch as a chariot rode into the building on the ground floor. Of course, the security could have attempted to keep the goddess out, but they would have tried and failed. On this night, they'd been instructed to allow the ancient goddess to enter. Unless she was lured to the right spot, weakened and tricked, trapping her would be impossible.

Freyja had been all over the world terrorizing people and not getting caught. The only way to stop her and Cupid was to pretend to let them play at their own game. The playing field had been set, and now, they had to hope that everything went to plan.

So far, it was. Christine spoke into the comm. "She's coming to the second floor where the necklace is located."

"Good," Paris breathed.

Freyja must have known where her necklace was on exhibit. The goddess was wasting no time getting there.

Christine watched from the second story, hidden behind a large column at the top of the stair as the goddess rode up the long stairs, pulled by her cats. They weren't really cats but were akin to giant leopards. The animals were beautiful, with their lustrous orange fur covered in black spots. They were hooked into leather bridles and pulled a lightweight chariot.

More beautiful than the giant creatures was the warrior being towed behind them. Freyja's long black hair flew behind her in several braids. She wore pelts of fur over her shoulders and a cape of feathers. Strapped across her waist was a large sword. Christine definitely wouldn't have messed with a woman of that caliber in her past life.

Before the cats cleared the final steps, Christine used her magic to roll an inconspicuous track of spikes at the top of the stairs. It was like a penalty system meant to puncture car tires for going the wrong way in a parking lot. There was the hope this would separate the rider from her trusty steeds. Christine knew all too well there was a lot that could go wrong.

She braced herself as the cats ran to the top of the stairs. In unison, the animals spotted the spikes and leaped over them. The chariot didn't clear the spikes and landed hard on them, making it go one way across the landing while the cats dashed the other way as their reins snapped.

The chariot fell to the side, its rider falling out and sliding across the marble floor and slamming into the wall. Her cats kept running down the hallway, galloping by priceless artwork as they snarled and growled, angered by their experience.

The impact knocked Freyja out for a moment. From Christine's spot perched around the corner, she didn't think that would last long. She slipped back into the corner and pressed her comm to her ear, ready to report both good and bad news.

CHAPTER SIXTY-FOUR

The crashing sound from the east wing made Paris cringe. She wished they had time to remove the artwork before that night. They hadn't been able to do anything that would clue the gods in on what they were planning. This event had to go on as if they weren't expecting two demigods to show up, meaning the Denon wing would be open where Freyja's necklace was on display and with it, many, many priceless pieces of art.

"Soooo…" Christine whispered over the comm. "Good news is that Freyja was knocked out when I took out her chariot."

"That's great," Paris said, moving in the direction where the goddess would have entered.

"Yeah, and if you get here right now, your job of trapping her in your wand will be easy," Christine continued in a whisper.

Paris halted. "I don't have her real name yet."

"Oh," Christine said. "Also, there's another little problem."

Paris tensed, putting her back up against a wall. "Which is?"

"Well, her cats weren't knocked out," Christine answered. "As I said, they aren't little alley cats. They are more like tigers who could take down a grown man or a giant. Or just about anything."

Paris groaned. "Where are they?"

"My best guess is they are headed your way," Christine said.

"Okay," Paris acknowledged. "So, I can't trap Freyja yet, but I definitely think we need to subdue the cats. Can you keep an eye on the goddess and let me know when sleeping beauty wakes up? I'm going to go and try to put her cats to sleep."

"You got it, boss."

Paris turned for the long corridor before looking over her shoulder at where Faraday was helping with last-minute trip-wires for the Cupid trap. The squirrel, who had heard everything over the comm, shrugged. "I'll stay here and put the finishing touches on this."

"Yeah, because I'm certain that you'd be an appetizer for Freyja's cats. Wish me luck with the giant creatures."

"Try calling them kitty, kitty," Faraday said, tugging on a wire to check its tautness. "I hear cats like that."

CHAPTER SIXTY-FIVE

Sully Wing, Louvre Museum, Paris, France

Paris had gotten the idea of Holly and Isha being disguised as statues when she had recently been at the Getty Villa Museum in Malibu. Holly had to admit, as she stood as still and cold as stone, it was a dynamite idea.

Three times Cupid had turned and looked her over, only to hear something over his shoulder and turn to gauge the room full of statues behind him. It would be very difficult for the god of love to spy Isha among all the Greek creations standing throughout the gallery. Then when Cupid was appropriately on edge, not knowing where the noises were coming from, Holly squeaked again.

The little man, who wasn't modest at all, swung around again to face Holly. Now it was time for Isha to close the deal.

Holly kept still as her friend came alive, out of statue form. She then lifted her wand from her robe. She made three quick successive movements before turning back to stone. The spells that followed did three things.

The first distracted Cupid's attention and the magic tore his crossbow from his shoulder.

Then the spell Paris had taught Isha made the crossbow fly across the room.

Finally, the most impressive part was the statue of Hermaphrodite was now holding a crossbow made of stone and pointing it at Cupid.

The god whipped around. He jerked his head back and forth. Then he caught sight of the goddess holding his prized weapon. Instead of flying over, Cupid screamed. It was such a high-pitched, aching sound. He flew to the closest statue and looked it over, then to the next one, and then to Isha, who was frozen. She was real, and if he got too close, Cupid was going to figure it out, which meant Holly had to create a diversion.

CHAPTER SIXTY-SIX

Denon Wing, Louvre Museum, Paris, France

Paris followed the sound of snarls. She thought it was probably the giant cats who belonged to an ancient Norse goddess and not one of the party guests. The guests had been sequestered to other areas by this time.

Paris had to admit she didn't really know how to deal with two creatures who belonged to a magical goddess of love who was heartbroken and looking for revenge. She was guessing they were as unpredictable as her. They were also loose in the Louvre and had somehow fallen under her jurisdiction.

"How I became animal control for large cats belonging to goddesses, I don't know," she said, approaching the long room known as the Salle Daru. It was two rooms from where Christine would have tripped the chariot, so it was a good bet for where the cats could be located. A quick glance inside told Paris she wasn't coming face to face with the kitties just yet. From the long stretch of the room, Paris could easily see them stalking back and forth and swishing their tails angrily in the next area.

Paris had no plan. She didn't have a spell to put the creatures to sleep and hurting them was out of the question. She couldn't very well leave them there. The idea all along was to separate Freyja from her guards. Paris hadn't figured out what to do with them with so many other details to arrange.

Pulling out her phone, Paris silently hoped that Mama Jamba had gotten back to her. She hadn't.

Paris' next wish was that Bermuda would pick up her phone and know what to do with two huge cats. Apparently, the gods were smiling down at her.

"Why are you calling me at this time?" the giantess asked when Paris pressed the phone to her ear.

"I'm in Paris."

"You are Paris," Bermuda corrected over the phone.

Paris pressed her back against the wall, not wanting to attract the cat's attention. "So, I have Freyja's cats hanging out in the Louvre and was hoping you had an idea of how to deal with them."

"Oh, dear me," Bermuda said, sounding tired. "You Beaufonts really know how to get yourselves in trouble. What are you doing in the Louvre? Cats aren't allowed in there."

"It's a long story, and I'm hoping you can help me," Paris said. "They are huge. Like enough to maul me. Any clues on how to put the kitties to sleep?"

Bermuda breathed into the phone. "You have to get rid of them."

"Yes, hence why I'm calling you for ideas."

"Well, isn't it obvious?" the giantess asked.

"Again, I don't usually call you when I've got two gods hanging out in the Louvre and two large loose animals prowling around in the next room when I can guess obvious answers. I need help now."

"Paris, open a portal. Then close it. Send the cats away. Then they won't be hurt, and they won't be your problem."

"Oh," Paris said, impressed by the simplicity of the solution. "I've got to get them to go through at the same time and then close it."

"I didn't say it would be easy. I said it would be obvious."

"Right," Paris said, biting on the word. "Well, thanks. I'm going to go round up some kitties."

CHAPTER SIXTY-SEVEN

Sully Wing, Louvre Museum, Paris, France

Breaking the statue spell, Holly tore from the room, knowing Cupid would follow her. He'd have to. It was terrifying, but he wouldn't have his bow. It was stone in Hermaphrodite's hands, a unique spell Paris had used for the situation.

Holly sprinted through the next room and heard the sound of beating wings chasing her. Cupid would have been alerted when she broke the spell and taken his focus off Isha. He would have noticed the missing caryatid, and now he was following Holly.

She didn't think she could outrun Cupid with his wings. She could hide, and he wasn't armed. All she had to do was get to a place where she could find a place to disappear and hope he didn't discover her. In the Louvre, how hard could that be? Holly thought as she tore through a room with several busted glass cases, figurines all over the place.

If they got out of this alive, Paris was going to have some explaining to do. The FGA would be indebted to the Louvre forever.

As Holly ran through the next room, she found it pretty ridiculous that a bunch of badly made vases were in high-security cases and considered so valuable. Holly was starting to feel frantic, hearing Cupid drawing closer to her. She didn't know what he'd do if he found her, but she was certain he didn't need a bow and arrow to harm her.

Realizing he would catch her if she continued through the next, large room, Holly threw herself to the stone floor and rolled underneath a bench tucked between two walls and nestled under a window. The light from the window over the bench kept her in the dark as she pushed back as far into the recess under the bench as possible.

The god of love flew halfway through the room, his wing beats seeming to speak of his indecision. He was lost and didn't know what he was looking for or where it had gone.

Holly bit down on her tongue, not daring to breathe as Cupid hovered in the air in the room next to her. She wasn't sure how much longer she could be silent. Her face was turning hot from holding her breath. The beat of Cupid's wings was making her heart pound harder.

When the god of love turned back the way he'd come, Holly knew she was safe. He was headed for the Venus de Milo. The trap was set for him. Paris was ready to cage the god.

CHAPTER SIXTY-EIGHT

Denon Wing, Louvre Museum, Paris, France

Easy-peasy, Paris thought, carefully stepping into the room, where the two large cats were growling and snarling and seeming to grow more restless by the second. Paris didn't *think* she could simply open a portal and have them hop through it like a fiery hoop in the circus.

To make matters worse, the room the creatures with claws and teeth had decided to stalk was none other than the one right outside the Mona Lisa. This one had a dozen paintings, all from notable seventeenth-century French painters. It felt very much like Paris was about to corner two bulls in a china shop and politely ask them to exit it.

When Paris sidled up to the doorway, Kitty One was inspecting a painting, sniffing it like he liked the way the oil smelled. She was pretty certain he was getting all sorts of cat boogers on the piece, and the curator would have a fit about it. Kitty two was even more naughty and had taken to gnawing on the frame of a particularly dark painting, trying to improve its appearance. Her job was to protect love, the planet, and apparently really old and bad artwork.

"Bad kitty," Paris found herself yelling and then tensed when the two creatures the size of panthers turned to face her, rather slowly as if they were trying to decide how best to kill that which had interrupted them.

The growl that fell from both their mouths came in unison, which would have been cute if Paris didn't know she was about to die by way of twin cats.

CHAPTER SIXTY-NINE

Backing up very carefully, Paris tried to smile at the cats who were slowly stepping in her direction. She didn't think it was because they were trying not to spook her, but rather they were planning their opportunity to pounce in unison. She should have been grateful for the voice in her ear, but it made her jump suddenly, which put the cats more on edge.

Kitty One let out a growl that sent chills down Paris' spine as Faraday chirped in her ear, "Cupid is headed this way. We're about to trap him."

"Okay, well, I'm playing fetch with cats," Paris said in a singsong voice, continuing to back up and watching the large creatures' every move. They were seconds away from springing at her.

"How's that going?" Faraday asked.

"Good," Paris said. "I forgot the ball."

"Oh, that's unfortunate," Faraday said.

"Yeah, but I have another plan," Paris said, taking a couple of steps and watching as the cats copied her quickness. They made up the space quickly and were just waiting for their moment to attack.

"What's that?" Faraday asked in her head.

"Run!" Paris yelled and whipped around. Running like hell, she motioned behind her as the cats leaped after her, creating a portal. The animals ran straight through it, and Paris paused briefly to close it. She hoped the large cats would enjoy life in the jungles of Peru where she'd sent them.

CHAPTER SEVENTY

Sully Wing, Louvre Museum, Paris, France

Paris couldn't believe that had worked and she'd gotten away from the cats. She raced in Cupid's direction, hoping he'd gotten trapped by the net. She still didn't know what to do with him.

As she sprinted back in the direction of the Venus de Milo, Paris pulled her phone from her pocket. To her shock, a message from Mama Jamba came through.

It read:

You didn't need this information before. Here are the names...

There wasn't any more to the message, and Paris nearly ran into a wall, staring at her phone, but then three more messages popped up one after the other. Paris read them. She couldn't believe Mother Nature and Father Time had picked such strange names for these demigods. It just proved they'd always had a sense of humor.

When Paris made it to the gallery where the Venus de Milo was on display, she hung back when she caught sight of the small, winged man circling around the marble statue. He had been disarmed due to Holly and Isha's bravery. Cupid thought he was alone. From across the gallery, Paris spied Faraday hanging out on a tall ledge, waiting for the perfect moment.

Cupid circled one more time around the statue of his mother before becoming enraged and balling up his fists. Then, like a bee darting for a target, he dove for her. Before he made contact with the ancient statue, which wasn't really his mother at all, Faraday released the nets, and they swept up and around the small, winged god, tying him up tightly into a ball. Cupid screamed and fought. He tried to break free, but the nets were reinforced. He was bound tightly.

Paris stepped out from her place hiding in the shadows and pointed Amantis at the god of love, feeling sorry for his torment, now and in the past. Even so, it was best if he went back to his world or at least to the world with his own kind. Cupid simply wasn't meant for this world. Not anymore.

Using the absorbing spell, Paris felt Amantis grow hot in her hand. The sapphire glowed brightly. The wand shook. It was hard to hold onto as she sought to trap the god inside the wand. Paris knew it was time to speak Cupid's real name as Mama Jamba had instructed.

"I trap you, Ted. You are mine because I have spoken your true name, given to you by Mother Nature and Father Time."

The small man screamed again as he continued to fight, then he disappeared from the net as if he'd never been there. When Paris lifted her wand, inside the clear sapphire, she spied a small face and knew it was Cupid looking out at her, wanting to escape his imprisonment.

CHAPTER SEVENTY-ONE

Denon Wing, Louvre Museum, Paris, France

No sooner had Paris trapped Cupid in her wand did Christine message over the comm.

"Sleeping Beauty has awoken and not gracefully," Christine said. "She jumped up like a terror and charged off in the direction of the necklace."

"I'm headed that way," Paris said, rushing back the way she'd just come to where the fake Brisingamen was on display. It was where Faraday and the Practical Love Department had set the trap for Freyja.

Paris had an inkling this was going to get increasingly difficult. She could feel something tugging at Amantis and knew it had to be Cupid fighting to free himself. Not until the gods were sealed into the book *Magical Creatures* would they be really gone. For now, they were bound, but they would fight. Paris had to carry this wand around with her with gods in it, hoping they didn't break free.

The room where they'd put the necklace was up ahead. Paris suspected the warrior would have made it there before her, which was fine. It was best not to fight that woman. Paris was fairly certain she'd lose.

Paris waited at the western exit until she heard a scream of protest. It was what she expected to hear when Freyja realized the necklace reported to be hers was a fake.

"Now," Paris whispered into the comms. As soon as she did, she heard a series of electronic sounds. Since she didn't hear any noises of pain, she guessed the goddess of love had been on the mark when she screamed.

Paris stepped into the doorway and saw everything had gone perfectly to plan. Freyja had been right in front of the case for the fake Brisingamen when she realized it wasn't her necklace. That's when Paris had given the order. Faraday hit a button which made a series of lasers spring up around the case, imprisoning the goddess for at least a moment.

The goddess was beautiful. Again, Paris felt sorry for the person who had lost so much and was simply acting out of pain. Like Cupid, Freyja wasn't meant for this world. She had to go back. She had to be taken down before Hathor got any more powerful.

Finding it more difficult than before, Paris pointed Amantis at the goddess of love and said the words she'd said before. This time, they seemed to rob her of her strength. Maybe she'd lost too much before when she'd trapped Cupid. Either way, her reserves were seriously low.

She opened her mouth to speak and found it hard to bring her voice up past a whisper.

That's when she felt a hand on one of her shoulders. Paris jerked around, afraid, but found Isha there, loaning her strength. Then another hand clapped onto her other shoulder and Paris spied Penny, sending her energy. From seemingly nowhere, Rudolf Sweetwater stepped up beside Paris and helped to lift the wand that felt like it weighed a hundred pounds in her hand. He looked at her and winked.

"You must do the spell and say the words, but our energy is yours to use," he said with conviction. "Trap her."

"No!" Freyja cried, her voice aching with pain as gold tears spilled over her cheeks. Paris ignored the demigoddess and spoke the words given to her by the gods.

"I trap you, Cat Wrangler. You are mine because I have spoken your true name, given to you by Mother Nature and Father Time."

The goddess shrunk in on herself. She screamed out again, pleading for mercy as she clawed at her face and cried tears that cut Paris' heart. Then she was gone. Amantis was so heavy that Paris dropped it to the floor where it clattered with two pairs of eyes staring out of the sapphire, begging to be released once more.

CHAPTER SEVENTY-TWO

Palace, Louvre Museum, Paris, France

"You did it!" Christine exclaimed, racing over from the Denon entrance, her face wild with excitement.

Paris smiled at her friend. It had been an incredibly hard task to accomplish, and she felt so depleted from the act of absorbing the gods into Amantis, even with the help of her friends.

"We did it," she corrected, looking around at her team, Christine, Penny, Holly, Isha, Faraday, and of course, Sherlock Holmes and King Rudolf Sweetwater.

Agent Barney Jasper stood to the side, a heavy expression on his face. "You did a fair amount of damage."

Rudolf held up his hand like he was in algebra class. "It was me, and I'll pay for all the figurines that were smashed."

"They are priceless artifacts and can't be replaced with money," Agent Jasper replied.

"Honestly, I got a quick look before I exploded the cases, and I could probably make something similar," King Rudolf argued. "Give me glue, paper, and clay. Oh, and a Sharpie. I will definitely need a Sharpie."

Barney sighed deeply, still in his tuxedo and looking very

different than the team, who were all dressed in black. The others who reported to Penny and Christine were also dressed similarly, and many were helping to clean up inside the Louvre. "There were also some incredibly expensive paintings that were damaged."

"Mostly just the frames," Paris muttered, remembering the harm the giant cats did in the Denon wing.

"It doesn't matter," Barney corrected. "We are indebted to the Louvre. It will take centuries to pay them to cover the cost of the destruction."

Again, Rudolf raised his hand. "I'll pay for it. I'm loaded."

Barney shook his head. "Then we will be indebted to the fae, and that never turns out well. This was FGA business, and we signed the contract with the Louvre. We'll cover it."

"I'm working on a way to create money for FGA," Paris said, looking sideways at Sherlock Holmes. He shook his head minutely, and she took that as a sign she shouldn't supply any details. "I need more time."

Agent Jasper sighed. "Well, regardless of the damage to the Louvre, you did what we set out to do. Two of the demigods have been contained. We have to capture one more who is located inside the Abu Simbel temple where her larger self is coming alive. We think the smaller version of her inside the building is what the statue is guarding."

"Actually," Paris began, drawing out the word. "I think it has to be me and Faraday."

There were sudden protests from everyone on her team, and the noise made Paris' ears hurt.

She held up her hand to halt their insistence. "I appreciate that you want to help, but the Small Temple of Abu Simbel isn't the same as the Louvre. It's just that, small and contained. Unlike here, we aren't luring the goddess to our territory. I have to go to her domain. I can't have you all in there. That would create more concerns for me. We really don't know what I'm walking into."

"That's exactly why we need to go with you," Christine argued.

Paris shook her head, but it was Agent Jasper who spoke for her.

"Agent Beaufont is right. Alone she can get a better handle on things. She knows what she has to do. If you all are in there, I can only think of the amount of damage that could be done to the temple. We'd be even further in debt."

"Good to see where your concerns lie," Holly said disapprovingly, crossing her arms.

"My concern is that we can persevere here but lose FGA," Barney explained. "The company is holding on by a thread after everything Agent Zelle did to us, and now this."

"It's okay," Paris said. "I know what I need to do, and with Faraday's help and a well-crafted plan, I can do it. If we all spill into that temple together, then that nasty goddess is just going to use us against each other."

"I've been studying the activity of the temple and more importantly, the large statue of Hathor that's coming alive. After tracking Cupid and Freyja's movements, I deduced the proximity of events fueled the goddess more."

"You mean the closer the acts of sabotage to love, the more power it gave Hathor?" Isha asked.

"That's exactly what I'm saying," Faraday answered. "If a bunch of us went into the temple, it has the opportunity to supply further power to the demigoddess."

"The statue will be fully mobile, and we will have bigger problems," Penny said.

"Quite literally," Rudolf agreed.

"If negative feelings fuel the goddess," Isha began, working it out as she talked, "then that means Paris and Faraday can't have any bad emotions when inside the temple."

"Yes, because we'll be in the belly of the beasts," Paris joked, wishing she could sit down.

"So again," Christine cut in, "you've got to distract and somehow disarm the goddess, but without our help or an elaborate plan or without knowing what traps she has set for you, and you have to do that with a smile on your face."

Paris faked a big grin. "I can do that."

"Although we don't know what traps Hathor will have or what attacks she could throw at us," Faraday said, "I think I have a way to disarm the demigoddess if we can distract her."

"You mean I need to distract her," Paris offered.

"After combing through Hathor's history, it seemed the only way to stop her was she had to be drugged. Then she could be contained."

"Great, so you have to slip a mickey to a demigoddess," Rudolf said. "You sure you don't want to bring me along?"

Paris laughed but shook her head. "Faraday, how do you plan for us to drug the goddess of war?"

"Well, I have a chloroform-type drug that should work on her," he explained. "It's demigoddess strength. All she has to do is inhale it. You'll have to distract her while I get it under her nose."

"Like with jokes?" Paris teased.

"Or combat," Barney offered.

"From the research," Faraday interrupted, "I found the Egyptians were often enticed by dance. Hathor distracted her father once by doing so."

"Paris needs to dance for the goddess of war?" Penny asked skeptically.

"It's an option," Faraday said. "It's about disarming her attention. Once we do that, Paris can absorb Hathor into her wand, and we're almost there."

Paris swayed her hips back and forth. "I can dance."

"What are you doing?" Christine questioned. "You're supposed to be enticing and entertaining. Not making her sick."

Paris groaned and stopped her bad dance moves. "I'll work on it later when I'm not so tired."

"You don't really have any later," Barney corrected. "You have time to rest, but the longer we wait, the more risk of Hathor growing to full power. Then she'll be loose and can really rise to incredible strength."

"Okay, well, I need a nap," Paris said through a yawn. "My dance moves will be great in the heat of the moment."

"That's the other thing," Penny argued. "Paris is exhausted, and she nearly didn't have enough strength to contain Freyja. How is she going to absorb a demigoddess as powerful as Hathor?"

"I think that I have a way to help with that too," Faraday said. "Usually, Amantis can serve as a battery to her magic, but currently, it's being used as a container."

Everyone glanced at the wand on Paris' hip. It felt heavy there, but Paris tried not to think about it or allow the demigods inside of it to tug her around, although they were trying.

The talking squirrel pointed to Penny. "Using that same idea of a battery, we searched the Louvre for an artifact that could be used in the same way as Amantis."

Penny pulled off a necklace that had been hanging around her neck.

"You took that from the Louvre?" Barney asked, his face flushing red as he pointed at the large blue stone hanging from the chain that Penny held out. "Are you insane?"

"We are borrowing it," Faraday amended. "The Louvre doesn't need to know, and they will get it back."

"They can keep that awesome replica of Freyja's necklace the Refinement Department made in the meantime," Christine offered.

Agent Jasper shook his head, obviously not comfortable with this idea even though it was a good one.

"Similar to how Paris fills up the magic bottle reserves for the Casual Romance department," Faraday began, "I was thinking each of you could charge up this stone. It's sapphire like the gem on Amantis, so I think it will take the charge and be in line with Paris' magic reserves."

"I'm down for that," Christine offered, stepping up and putting her hand out next to the stone.

"Me too," Isha said, also taking a step forward.

One by one, all the rest moved in tightly to the necklace, all of them putting their fingers close to the sapphire until only Agent Jasper stood back from the circle.

He sighed, resigned. "Fine, I'll help too." Taking the step forward, the director of the Basic Love Branch for FGA completed the circle.

The group worked fast together to send their energy into the stone, offering their power if and when Paris needed it. When they were done, Penny handed the necklace to Paris. She placed it around her neck and smiled at her friends and her team.

"Thanks for everything," she said, feeling ready to pass out.

Christine smiled back at her. "When you save the world, then we're the ones who will be thanking you."

"Everyone in the world should be grateful to you," Penny offered.

King Rudolf Sweetwater offered his niece a thoughtful expression. "Like so many great Beaufonts, yours will not be a job of glory and accolades, but one that will save this planet as your family has done countless times."

CHAPTER SEVENTY-THREE

The temples dedicated to Pharaoh Ramses II and his queen Nefertari took twenty years to build but have stood in Egypt for centuries. The Great Temple represented Ramses the Great and the gods Amun, Ra-Horakhty, and Ptah. The Small Temple was dedicated to Nefertari and the goddess Hathor.

The location of both sites standing close to each other was meant to be sacred to Hathor long before the temples were built. The placement of the temples was in alignment with the eastern sun twice a year, where it would shine directly into the sanctuary and cast light on the king and the gods in correspondence with Ramses' birthday and coronation.

Even though the Small Temple was considered lesser in size, it was a rare time in Egyptian art where the queen was depicted as equal in size to the king.

Paris studied the six large statues on the front of the Small Temple, knowing exactly which one was Hathor—the one full of color. The other five were the color of the stone around them, a tan with a hint of red.

The Egyptian sun was bright overhead. She'd only slept for a few hours before having to be there. She knew why she was under such a time crunch as she took in the sight of the goddess of war coming alive in statue form. Her feet, calves, hands, and forearms were full of color. Most of her body, chest, face, and head were still stone. Paris was chilled by the idea the goddess was trying to take real form as a huge statue. She didn't even come up to the stone figure's knee.

"Did you know that, ironically, that's not even Hathor?" Faraday offered, standing beside her in the hot sand.

Paris glanced down at the squirrel. "Do tell."

"I've been doing my research, and it's a common misconception that one of the figures here is Hathor," he explained. "Hathor is depicted inside the temple in several places, on pillars and murals. It appears Hathor is taking the form of Nefertari here, who is wearing the costume of the goddess."

"Who are these other blokes beside them?" Paris asked, indicating the other figures.

"Ramses II and their various children."

"Is it possible that since the statue isn't really her, that Hathor won't be successful at completing the ritual of taking her form?" Paris' voice was full of hope.

She lost her optimism when the squirrel shook his head. "The pharaohs and their queens idolized their gods, thinking they were the same. For all we know, Hathor possessed Nefertari at one point. Sadly, if fueled, Hathor will have no problem taking on the form of that statue, strolling out across the desert, destroying all in her path."

Paris gulped. "All that destruction will only make her stronger and grow bigger until she's large enough to split countries in two and then continents and then the planet."

Faraday shook from what appeared to be a chill, although they were standing in the hot sun. "Of course, it's an angry woman who tries to destroy the planet and not a man as everyone would have predicted."

Paris lowered her chin, regarding the squirrel with contempt. "Don't forget that Hathor was unleashed by a manly demon."

He held up his paws and shrugged. "Just pointing out it would be a woman who brought the planet down."

"A demigoddess," Paris corrected. "She's not going to be successful because we're going to stop her."

The two strode forward to enter the Abu Simbel temple, where it would be them and the goddess of war and most likely a few hundred scorpions.

CHAPTER SEVENTY-FOUR

The temperature dropped suddenly when Paris and Faraday entered Hathor's temple. Paris expected to be assaulted upon entering or stopped somehow, but the opposite was true. A cool breeze from inside the temple wrapped around her arms and legs and gently tugged her into the large space as if welcoming her and asking her to venture deeper.

Paris remembered what Faraday had learned. The demigoddess needed negative emotions to fuel her to full strength, and proximity made that happen sooner. It went to reason Hathor would want someone to visit the temple where she could induce fear and panic that would bring her to full strength faster. Paris drew in a steadying breath, reminding herself to stay calm. No matter what, she had to remain relaxed and full of good emotions.

Six pillars stretched from the floor to the towering ceilings at the front of the Small Temple. Paris was glad for the firelight that lit the inside of the cavernous temple until she realized someone must have lit it.

She glanced down at Faraday as she pointed to the first lit torch. "Hathor?"

He looked uneasy and then feigned a smile. "Isn't that so nice of her? She's a sweetheart."

"The sweetest," Paris said, plastering her own fake grin on her face.

A howl that didn't sound welcoming echoed through the chamber, followed by a chilly breeze that made the flames of the torches ripple in the wind. Paris rubbed her hands over her arms, tightening them around her, and forced her grin to widen.

"I love a nice cool wind," she said to Faraday in a singsong voice.

He was also clutching his limbs for warmth. "Not as much as I do."

She was inciting the goddess, so it shouldn't have been a surprise when the temperature of the temple suddenly dropped ten degrees. The cold made the sweat on her neck and back feel frozen. Paris tried to remain positive. If the demigoddess didn't have any negative emotions to fuel her, then she couldn't get any stronger.

She'd been relying on the other gods to help her. Now they were gone, she'd be relying on others in closer proximity to her to bring her back, and currently, that was Paris and Faraday. If they stayed even, and better yet, happy, the demigoddess would remain as she was until they trapped her.

Trying to ignore the frigid temperatures, Paris kept vigilant, knowing Hathor could be anywhere in the Small Temple, ready to jump out and fight. The demigoddess had a real form like Cupid and Freyja. It was just she wanted a bigger and better form so she could do more damage. In her smaller, more human size, Hathor shouldn't be underestimated. She was an Egyptian goddess, after all, and had once tried to be the demise of all mankind.

"The depictions on these pillars are fascinating," Faraday said, looking up at the first set of columns they came to. "They show Queen Nefertari playing music with the gods. The entire Small

Temple shows the pharaoh's offerings to the gods in hopes they would become like them."

"That is fascinating," Paris said through the shivers, pretending she was on an educational field trip and not a deathly mission to save the planet.

"Yes, and although my knowledge of hieroglyphs isn't good," Faraday continued, hopping close to one of the walls on the other side of the columns, "these will tell of how the king defeated his enemies and the queen worshipping Hathor. If you notice—"

Paris froze and not because she was freezing, but rather because of the noise of beating wings. Faraday glanced over his shoulder at her, obviously having heard it too. Unlike Cupid, this sounded like a lot of wings beating together at once.

"Whatever do you think that is?" Paris asked, trying to sound casual and not at all fearful of the noise growing louder and definitely headed in their direction.

"Something that might pass overhead," Faraday offered, also trying to sound casual. "I mean, it's not a bunch of scorpions scurrying across the ground, so that's good."

Paris held her breath as the sounds of squeaks filled the air. A cloud of black poured in from the far side of the chamber, signaling their first set of guests.

CHAPTER SEVENTY-FIVE

"Bats," Faraday muttered, biting on the word. "Why is it always bats?"

He was referring to the electro-bats they had faced when they were at Sad Lion Gaming Company. These didn't seem like a horde of angry bats that could electrocute them with their shared spark. They were regular old angry bats that appeared ready to suck their blood or maul them or both.

Not wasting a moment, Paris swooped down and picked up Faraday, looking in a rush for a way to escape. Over the rush of wings beating overhead and squawking from the beady-eyed bats, Paris felt the Small Temple shake. The stone floor under her feet shifted and the walls vibrated, sending dust and rocks raining down on them. She thought the whole structure could cave in on them.

"Happy emotions," Faraday reminded over the loud noises.

Paris realized her sudden panic was fueling Hathor. She paused and dared to close her eyes and draw in a deep breath. "Okay, I'm cool. I'm calm. I'm happy."

"Great," Faraday said, having climbed up closer to her shoulder. "While maintaining that maybe we could get out of here. The bats are angry and look ready to start dive-bombing."

Paris opened her eyes to glance up at the ceiling. It was mostly black, but she made out the forms of the bats. They looked bloodthirsty and ready to attack. Trying not to rush forward out of fear, Paris casually made her way to the opening the bats had flown through.

"Well, sorry to leave you chipper guys, but we're going this way, deeper into the temple, to find a friend," Paris sang, smiling up at the bats.

"Good job being positive," Faraday told her.

"Catch you later, bat brains." Paris waved up at the creatures, but this seemed the thing to set them off, either because of the gesture or because of the name-calling. In a rush, the bats swooped down, diving for them like large bullets.

The bats were fast, and many of them bit and scratched at Paris' face, head and neck as she ran for the doorway. They blurred around her and Faraday like a storm of black, making it hard to see where she was going. She knocked into them. The scream that erupted from her mouth was uncontrollable. Being attacked by a swarm of bats in an ancient Egyptian temple was one of the most terrifying things Paris had ever experienced, and that was saying a lot. The fear they produced had an immediate effect.

The floor quaked underfoot. Rubble rained down from the ceiling, and the sound of a large woman's laughter shook the entire temple.

Paris dove headfirst into the next set of rooms, trying to get ahead of the bats. She did a front roll, protecting Faraday in her arms before she popped up and threw her finger at the large slab standing beside the door she'd just run through. It slid at once over the opening, blocking out the charging bats, who made splat sounds as they hit the stone. Thankfully, none had followed them into this chamber, and she and Faraday appeared to be alone. Alone with their negative emotions of fear. They had to get over it fast before the entire structure collapsed on top of them, and Hathor came to life in giantess form.

236

CHAPTER SEVENTY-SIX

"Hey, what's the right way to hold a bat?" Paris asked, trying to catch her breath and keep her balance since the floor was vibrating intensely.

Faraday looked up at her. "What?"

"By the handle," Paris replied.

He shook his head at her. "Was that supposed to be a joke?"

"Not supposed to," Paris said as dust continued to rain down from the ceiling. "It was one. I'm trying to make us feel better. You know, erase the negative feelings of fear and impending death."

"We're still alive, so we're fine. Where are we?"

"Another room with pillars and hieroglyphs and torches of fire." Paris shook her head. "A little interior design wouldn't hurt, you know?"

"Remember how you mouthed off to the bats and that only angered them?" Faraday asked.

"Fine, I won't incite the goddess, but you'd think she'd have a couch or rug or something in her temple. I guess it is so much smaller than the guy's temple."

The walls shook again, although they'd stopped for a moment.

"Paris…" Faraday warned.

Paris snickered. "It's making me feel better."

"Well, then that's okay," Faraday said, relaxing as the trembling subsided.

"Hey, Batman told Wilfred it had been a long day and asked him to fill up the bathtub."

Faraday gave her a sideways expression. "Oh yeah? What did Wilfred say?"

Paris snickered, grateful the squirrel was playing along. "He said, Master Bruce, what's a tub?"

He hung his head with a great sigh. "These jokes may make you feel better, but they are making me feel worse."

Paris shook her head. "No, they aren't because the demigoddess has quieted down again."

Faraday glanced around at the chamber that did appear much like the one they'd been in before. The space was surprisingly not covered in dust and dirt and cobwebs as Paris would have expected. The firelight illuminated the carvings on the walls and columns, which depicted more stories of the pharaohs and the Egyptian gods.

"Yeah, I guess your joke-telling saved us," Faraday said, studying the space. "Remember, if you see another swarm of bats or monsters or the goddess herself, you must remain calm."

"When I see her," Paris corrected. "Yes, I've got my dance ready. I'm going to be so entertaining, she's going to be mesmerized. I can floss."

"That's good," Faraday chirped. "I hear it can lengthen your lifespan by up to a dozen years."

Paris chuckled. "No, not with my teeth. I meant the dance."

"I'm not aware of it," Faraday said. "Flossing is really good for you. Have you thought about adding it to your bathroom routine?"

Paris started forward, careful to check for bats up high and scorpions down low and whatever in between. "Now isn't really the time to lecture me on my hygiene habits, and no, I'm not a flosser. It's weird. Monkeys don't floss."

"That's awful reasoning," Faraday replied. "They are monkeys and also throw their—"

"Bananas," Paris interrupted, checking around the nearest column for a monster or an enraged demigoddess. She expected something to try to fluster her soon, and she was going to be ready this time. By ready, she wasn't going to scream and run and fear for her life, although she was aware the bats had scratched up her face and hands pretty badly. She hoped it wasn't anything she couldn't cover up for the wedding. She hoped there was a wedding and this wasn't the end of the world.

Faraday shook his head. "Did you know that up to forty percent of your teeth reside under the gum? You're missing all that."

"I can't believe we're having this conversation," Paris said, making for the next doorway.

"Because we're in the Small Temple of Hathor, the demigoddess of love and war?" he asked.

Paris shook her head. "Because you're a squirrel."

"Well, I care about such things and—"

There was a rush of air at Paris' back, making her freeze and interrupting the squirrel. Something fuzzy brushed up against her neck and then the back of her legs. She could have sworn that something dropped down behind her from the ceiling. Something large by the sound of the thud on the ground.

Glancing down at Faraday in her arms, Paris gave him a cautious expression, careful to keep her emotions in check.

He gave her a stern expression and mouthed the words, "Be happy. No matter what it is, be happy."

CHAPTER SEVENTY-SEVEN

Paris reasoned she could ignore whatever was behind them, clicking and making a loud racket, and never look at the creature. However, ignorance wasn't bliss. That would only fill her head with more imaginings that would lead to bigger worries.

Maybe the demigoddess had decided to join her and not make her run through this maze of the Small Temple. Then all Paris had to do was turn around, drop the squirrel, do a dance and then have him drug her. Easy-peasy.

Faraday, to get a sneak peek, crawled up and looked over Paris' shoulder. She felt him tense against her, his claws piercing into her skin.

Paris knew that no matter what was standing behind her, she was better off letting it kill her than allowing it to fill her with fear, which would bring Hathor to life fully. That's why she managed to grin down at Faraday.

"Hey, I just got a job as an Egyptian god," she said casually to the squirrel, feeling the creature behind her moving, sending a rush of air at her.

"Oh?" he asked.

"Yeah, and now I'm Set for life."

The smile that stretched across Faraday's face was scary as though a creepy clown was grinning. Paris decided to turn and face whatever was behind her.

Taking a step forward, she pivoted and at once realized she was facing something that was most people's worst fears.

CHAPTER SEVENTY-EIGHT

Paris had never been afraid of spiders. She didn't much care for them, but she didn't consider herself a Miss Muffet and wasn't going to pick up her dress and jump onto a chair and scream. Of course, if she was afraid of spiders, having one the size of a lawnmower inches away from her might have sent her into a panic attack.

Instead, Paris took a few steps back, mostly because she liked personal space.

Glancing down, she winked at Faraday, giving him an expression that said, "I got this."

Paris looked up at the hairy black spider with huge legs, too many eyes, and large pincers it was using to pick its teeth. She reasoned it had overheard their conversation about flossing and was getting to work.

"Hey, there, Buddy," Paris said, grinning at the spider.

"Buddy," Faraday mouthed.

"What?" she asked the squirrel. "Uncle John and I used to have spiders all over the apartment where I grew up. We called them our roommates. I named them."

Paris glanced around the cavernous chamber. "Do you live here? Is it lonely? I hope you like it? Do you have a name?"

"I don't think the man-eating spider is going to answer," Faraday said in a whisper.

As if in reply to Paris' questions, the spider clicked several times. She pretended to understand. "I could see liking living alone. I hope we're not bothering you."

The spider continued to click and twitch. His pincers were moving in various directions like he was pointing.

She said, "Yeah, totally."

"Do you understand the spider?" Faraday asked.

She chuckled, hoping her act was believable. "Of course. His name is Mr. Clicks. He's happy here living alone, but he likes that we've visited. He doesn't like that that mean demigoddess is creating so much trouble, shaking his house and making debris fall and messing up his webs."

As if she had read the spider's mind and not made all that up, Mr. Clicks' many eyes seemed to smile as if he'd finally been heard.

"Oh, wow," Faraday breathed. "Now I've seen it all."

"Well, I'm really sorry, Mr. Clicks. That meanie old Hathor is causing problems," Paris said, putting one of her free hands on her hip and really starting to groove with this whole relaxation business. "How about a joke? I'm known for them."

"She's known for many things but not her jokes," Faraday corrected, poking out from her arm where he'd been hiding from Mr. Clicks.

Paris cleared her throat. "We've started calling Granddad Spider-Man. It's not because he's got superpowers. He just can't get out of the bathtub."

Faraday groaned. "Two bathtub jokes… How is that possible?"

"It's a gift," Paris said, smiling at the spider and looking for his reaction to the joke.

Mr. Clicks tilted his head to the side as if all of a sudden he didn't understand the language she spoke, although Paris was pretty certain that had been the case since the beginning.

Paris shrugged. "Oh, well. I guess the pop culture reference was lost on you." She looked around. "Do you get Netflix here?"

"You're really asking him—"

Mr. Clicks began his reply with a series of noises.

"Oh, my, he's answering," Faraday said in disbelief.

"Of course he is." Paris glanced down at the squirrel in her arms. "He's civilized and has manners."

A moment later, the spider rose on a thick piece of silk as though he were taking an invisible elevator to the ceiling. Paris stepped back, waving to him. "See you later, Mr. Clicks."

The spider clicked in response and disappeared into the darkness.

Proud, Paris glanced down at Faraday, loving the expression of disbelief on his face.

"Seriously, only you, Paris Beaufont. Only you."

CHAPTER SEVENTY-NINE

The next chamber was unsurprisingly much like the last, with columns and hieroglyphs and torches of fire. Thankfully there weren't any bats. Sadly, there weren't any polite spiders. Paris could see having Mr. Clicks around. He seemed very pleasant even if he didn't get her jokes. Most didn't either, so she really couldn't fault him.

"So, how do you think we're going to find Hathor?" Paris asked Faraday in a low voice.

He twitched his nose. "Honestly, I think she'll find you, but she's hoping to get a rise out of you first, hence the bats and the giant spider."

"Oh, well, too bad because I simply came to see if she wanted to buy into my multilevel marketing business," Paris joked and then said loudly, "If you get in on the ground floor, you'll make a killing."

Something thundered overhead, making the walls shake.

Faraday tensed. "Maybe don't talk about killing to the goddess of war."

Paris rolled her eyes. "Hathor wants to destroy mankind, and

I want to make a profit off them." She raised her voice again. "I don't see how we're all that different."

A throaty growl echoed from the dark shadows, making Paris pause halfway through the large room. She looked around, noting several places where monsters could be.

"Maybe you don't have to be so loud," Faraday offered. "No reason to wake whatever is living in here."

"I thought it was just Mr. Clicks," Paris said with a shrug. "Maybe I'll wake Hathor. Come out and play!"

Faraday's claws pierced into Paris' arm, a movement that said, what are you thinking being so bold?

Paris huffed at him. "Come on. We don't have all day, or really even a day at this point. Remember that whole being exhausted thing."

His eyes darted to the sapphire necklace hanging around her neck as if to ensure it hadn't lost its energy.

Another throaty growl slipped from the shadows at their back. Paris cut her eyes in that direction, but no sooner had she done so when another one echoed in front of her. There was a scratching sound to the left of them. Then another one to the right. Whatever was approaching them had Paris and Faraday surrounded. She saw the outline of something emerge from the shadows, and all her lightness disappeared. The spiders might not have scared her, but bloody mummies with no eyes and open mouths and teeth did.

CHAPTER EIGHTY

Paris didn't think the light act of naming the mummies would work like it did with the giant spider. To her revulsion, there wasn't just one mummy but at least half a dozen. Paris would have backed up to get away but soon realized they were surrounded.

"Stay calm," Faraday urged as Paris turned around. Figures were limping in her direction, their arms covered in blackened bandages and reaching for her.

"Right," Paris mouthed, trying to decide if she could remain calm while she was sending combat spells at the creepy mummies who were drooling and growling and clawing the air in her direction. She didn't think so.

"Try talking to them casually like you did before," Faraday offered.

Paris opened her mouth as a mummy grabbed her arm and yanked at it as if thinking it might snap off. Another one reached for her other arm, the one holding Faraday, and pulled her in the opposite direction. Then a third mummy dove for her leg, and Paris was fairly certain they were going to pull her into pieces.

They were hoping to replace their own rotting flesh with hers. They smelled so foul it made demons seem not so bad.

To Paris' surprise, she was not panicking. She'd resigned her fate to this. If she died here by way of mummies, then so be it. Paris Beaufont would not be the demise of this world by allowing her emotions to get the best of her.

"Come on, guys," Paris said as the mummies reached for her, tearing at her hair and clothes. She was fully off the floor. Faraday had fallen from her grasp, but that was probably best for him. He could get away. "There's enough of me to go around."

At the rate they were pulling, there wasn't going to be any of Paris left. She was going to be yanked into pieces.

When Paris felt one of the mummies reach for her wand, she reacted instinctively, finally putting up a fight. She couldn't allow the gods to be released. Paris kicked free and rolled to the ground backing away, still trying not to allow her fear to brew to the surface.

The mummies were in front of her, some of them crouched, looking ready to spring at her as they snarled. Others were thundering forward. Paris didn't know how she was going to fight six blood-hungry mummies, and she didn't think it was possible to do so without feeling fear. She had too much to lose in this fight, starting with her life.

Paris was considering her options when all of the mummies looked up, howls and growls echoing from their mouths, and then like a net, something large and black dropped from the ceiling. There was an echo of screams and clicks and so many legs.

It took Paris a moment to figure out what was happening. Mr. Clicks was fighting the six mummies. For her! Sadly, it appeared as a mummy took a giant bite out of one of the legs he was going to lose.

When the chamber rattled, Paris worried she was allowing her emotions to get the best of her. Then she realized it was the Small Temple vibrating like before. Something was scuttling out of the shadows. A lot of somethings. A sea of black things on the ground.

Backing up, Paris joined Faraday by the door to the next room as they watched large spider babies descend on the mummies, seizing the advantage in the fight. Paris could hardly believe it. She was grateful for the laugh that popped out of her mouth, the strangeness of this situation keeping her emotions high, and the fear at bay.

She glanced sideways at Faraday. "Well, who would have thought. Mr. Clicks is a Mrs. Clicks?"

He waved as they turned for the next room. "Thanks, Mrs. Clicks and Family!"

CHAPTER EIGHTY-ONE

"Do you think we're going in a circle?" Paris asked when they came into the next chamber.

"Because that's the exit," Faraday replied back, pointing to a doorway that looked very much like the one they'd come through. Not only that, but the hot Egyptian sun could be seen through the opening.

"This can't be the end," Paris complained, turning around in a circle. "We didn't meet Hathor." She pointed to the opening where the bats had come through. "Should we do another loop and see if we can find—"

"Hey, look at this," Faraday interrupted, pulling her attention back toward the entrance. Lying in front of the archway on the stone floor was a small instrument. It had a metal frame and was U-shaped with several crossbars with hooks.

"What is that?" Paris walked over, about to pick up the instrument but hesitating.

"I think it's okay," Faraday said, sensing her hesitation. "It's a sistrum, a sacred musical instrument of the ancient Egyptians. You play it by dancing and shaking it."

Paris picked up the small instrument and found it surprisingly heavy in her hands. "What a curious way to make music."

"It happened to be one used in ceremonies to worship Hathor," Faraday told her.

"Oh," Paris said, studying the instrument. Her eyes widened, catching the squirrel's drift. "Ohhhhh…"

It was time to dance. Paris started circling the area, shaking her hips and jiggling the sistrum in her hand while she sang. It happened to be a newer one, but it worked. It was called, *Take You Dancing* by Jason Derulo.

Really covering the space, Paris started skipping and jiving, letting the soft clanging of the sistrum get her in the mood. Something was taking over her as she sang and danced, and soon she felt lost in the emotion.

"*Mmm-mmm-mmm. Let me take you dancing. Da-da-da-da-da-da. Mmm-mmm-mmm. Let me take you dancing. Da-da-da-da-da-da.*"

Paris was briefly aware that Faraday was looking at her like she'd lost her mind. In a way, she felt she had. She was definitely lost to the music in her head and that coming from the sistrum and the dance moves she was feeling.

Spinning around, Paris was about to go into the second verse when she suddenly halted. Not because of a swarm of bats. Or a giant spider. She definitely didn't face hungry mummies.

No, Paris was standing in front of the demigoddess of love and war, and she looked madder than hell.

CHAPTER EIGHTY-TWO

Paris took a few steps backward to take in the absolutely gorgeous woman. Hathor was so beautiful it hurt to look at her. She wore a golden silk gown and a headdress on her straight black hair. Kohl made her dark eyes pop more, and her red lips seemed amused as she smirked, taking in the halfling before her.

"Your dance was amusing," Hathor said, her voice deep and alluring.

Paris bowed, shaking the sistrum. "Why, thanks. I was hoping to entertain. You must be the goddess known as Hathor. It's a pleasure—"

"Save it!" the goddess screamed, making the temple around them shake. Paris looked to Faraday, who was standing by the entrance and making a weird motion she couldn't quite make out. Not wanting to alert the demigoddess' attention to Faraday, Paris glanced back at her.

"I know why you're here," Hathor continued, starting to stroll to the right.

"Because I want you in my multilevel marketing business," Paris said, taking this opportunity to glance in Faraday's direction. He was indicating the exit. It appeared he was telling her to leave. Why should she do that when she'd finally lured the goddess out of hiding? No, she needed to subdue Hathor and then trap her.

"I have to admit," Paris continued, "it's definitely a pyramid scheme."

The goddess turned, her golden dress flying out around her. "You speak too much."

"Right, should I get back to dancing?" Paris asked, starting to twirl around and shake the sistrum.

The goddess had never seen moves like that based on the confused expression on her face, but Paris' dancing didn't appear to be distracting Hathor enough.

It did allow Paris to pass by Faraday, who whispered to her, "Jump out of the exit when I tell you." He pointed to the bottle of potion in his paws meant to drug the demigoddess.

At first, Paris didn't understand what he meant. Then, as she danced, it was as if the moves helped her to put it all together, and she understood. The squirrel, as if she didn't already know, was a genius.

"Stop it!" Hathor exclaimed, her voice shaking the very earth.

Halting Paris glanced to the side, catching sight of Faraday and the exit.

"You have taken the gods meant to restore me to full power. You are trying to make a fool of me. Instead of relying on them, I've decided I'll do something even better than becoming my statue form." A wicked grin flickered across Hathor's face as she held out a hand. "I'll possess you, and then I'll maim the world as the powerful halfling with demon blood."

Paris tried to laugh, knowing that negative emotions would fuel the goddess. Then she tried to move, feeling panic at the idea of becoming possessed by Hathor. She was screwed. The demigoddess had paralyzed her and was taking her over. This was how it was going to go after everything. Paris wasn't going to save the world. She was going to be the instrument for its very undoing. She was going to fail, epically delivering to Hathor exactly what she needed to be successful.

Unable to move, feeling her energy recede and something invade her body, Paris felt the biggest violation of her life as the Egyptian goddess took her over. There was no fighting it. There was nothing she could do. For once, she was powerless and alone.

On the heels of those thoughts, something flew through the air.

Faraday screamed as he launched himself at the beautiful face of the demigoddess. It took only a second for Paris to realize she had control over her body again.

Hathor scrambled back, clawing at the rodent who had wrapped himself over her face, beating her in the side of her head with his tail and scratching at her face and hair.

He looked over his shoulder, a crazed expression on his face. "Leave. Leave now for a whole minute."

Paris wanted to argue as she watched him lift the potion bottle from the place tied around his neck and realized what he intended to do. There was no time, so she did the cowardly thing and dove out the exit of the Small temple as he threw the bottle of drugs strong enough to work on a demigoddess to the stone floor, where it burst into a cloud of green smoke.

As Paris rolled out into the heat of the Egyptian desert and looked back at the entrance to the Small Temple, she could only wonder what the drug would do to the little squirrel.

CHAPTER EIGHTY-THREE

The minute Paris waited outside of the chamber dedicated to the Egyptian goddess Hathor felt like the longest of Paris' life. She knew enough to know why Faraday asked for that. This would be the amount of time it took for the drug to dissipate and therefore not affect Paris. It would have also knocked out Faraday. If it was strong enough to drug Hathor, a demigoddess, then what could it do to him?

Worry constricted her heart at the thought he'd sacrificed himself for her. She had been about to be possessed, and the brave squirrel sprang into action. He did what he thought was best, breaking the drug meant to be inhaled in the chamber after Paris vacated.

She glanced up at the statue of Hathor and saw that not much color had grown on it, which meant her fear and worry weren't fueling the goddess. Which hopefully meant she was knocked out. It was time to reenter the chamber, trap Hathor, and seal her and the others away. Before that, Paris was going to help Faraday.

He couldn't be dead. She couldn't accept that. She wouldn't.

The chamber felt different than before. When she entered, she found the beautiful demigoddess stretched out on the stone floor, red scratches lining her face. Beside her was Paris' best friend, and to her relief, his chest was rising and falling. He was still alive, but like Hathor, he wasn't moving. She had to hope he awoke.

He had to.

Paris couldn't allow his bravery to be wasted. It was time to cage the demigoddess. She pulled out Amantis and held it in one hand, pointing it at the sleeping woman on the stone floor of the Small Temple.

In her other hand, she clasped the sapphire on the chain around her neck and drew on its energy as she spoke the words given to her by Mama Jamba.

"I trap you, Lava Face. You are mine because I have spoken your true name, given to you by Mother Nature and Father Time."

Hathor's eyes sprang open, and Paris worried the spell hadn't worked and she hadn't absorbed the demigoddess. Suddenly Hathor screamed, in pain and pleading for mercy. She clawed her face and cried out into the cold air one last time. Then she was gone.

Amantis was heavy. More than she ever thought she could carry. Paris dropped it to the floor where it clattered, now with three pairs of eyes staring out of the sapphire, begging to be released once more.

CHAPTER EIGHTY-FOUR

Unsure if she could bring the heavy wand all the way to the Great Library, Paris called Paul to meet her at Abu Simbel Temple. The Great Librarian seemed fascinated by his surroundings as he studied the Small Temple. Paris' eyes were only on Faraday, sleeping on her jacket where she'd nestled him after checking on his vitals. She'd also called everyone she could think of for help: Mama Jamba, Papa Creola, Mae Ling, Willow, Aunt Sophia, her mother and father, and even King Rudolf Sweetwater.

They had all responded but only with messages, and they were all the same. He will awaken when the drug wears off.

When would that be? Paris wondered, her insides constricted with worry. What if he was out for days or months, or even years? She couldn't fathom doing everything she had to do without her best friend beside her.

"You have the spell?" Paul asked, holding Bermuda Lauren's book, *Magical Creatures*.

Paris pulled out the paper Elvira had given her. She'd looked over the spell when she received it, but it didn't make any sense. Not only because she didn't understand the magic it used. There was that.

More importantly, Paris didn't understand the language it was written in. She'd asked her father about it, and he said that when the time came to do the spell, she would know what to do. He also instructed her not to practice it beforehand and never again to speak the forbidden language of the demons unless she must.

Paris didn't really understand what was so forbidden about the demon's language or why she couldn't have practiced the spell, but she always did what her parents told her. If her father told her not to do the spell, then she wasn't going to until that very moment.

"Okay, first, you're going to need to put the demigods back into the book," Paul said, holding out the thick leather volume.

Paris glanced down at Amantis, wondering if she could lift the heavy wand. Putting her hand around the sapphire around her neck, she drew on the strength lent to her by her friends. It pooled in her core and allowed her the power to lift the wand she hadn't had seconds prior. It was such a wonderful and wild thing to know her friends could help her even when they weren't there.

The wand was heavy but manageable in her hands. Paris touched it to the book, wondering how she released the demigods into the book without letting them loose. That part had been Paul's job without her knowing it or them having discussed it.

The Great Librarian closed his eyes as the tip of the wand touched the book and began chanting. "From the pages of a book, you fled. Bound to the words, you are once more. One, two, three, all find your place back in the volume only ever to be read."

One by one, the demigods appeared like sparks, their light only flickers. Paris spied Cupid's wings, Freyja's hair, and Hathor's piercing eyes. They flew like wisps of smoke from the wand's tip and then sunk into the book.

When the last had receded, Paul closed the cover and looked at Paris. "You must seal it, or the demigods can escape once more."

Paris unraveled the piece of paper. She opened her mouth to speak and blinked at the words, not understanding how to say them. She shook her head, totally confused. Paris didn't know how to recite or work the demon spell.

Paul pointed to his head. "You're trying to do the spell from here. Don't."

She shrugged, at a loss. "That's how I do magic."

"No, as a magician and a fairy, you do it with head and heart," he said. "That's how you keep the balance. The problem with a demon is they have no balance. They only care about satisfying their craving. That craving is to lust after the heart until they steal all good emotions." He pointed to his chest. "Recite the spell from here. You'll have no clarity. You'll have no objectivity. You will have the power to seal the spell."

Paris refocused on the paper in her hand, considering his advice. She opened her mouth again, and a voice that didn't sound like hers and words she didn't understand echoed from her lips.

A force unlike anything Paris had felt before ripped from her chest. It was a visible light, and it reached out and wrapped around the book, briefly covering it in fire. Paul dropped it where it banged to the stone floor and quickly extinguished as though it hadn't been on fire seconds prior.

The Great Librarian picked up the book and held it to his chest. "It is done. Thank you."

Paris was grateful this chapter was over but knew that what Tomár had started was far from it.

CHAPTER EIGHTY-FIVE

Fiftieth Floor, Saint Valentine's Office, Matters of the Heart, FGA Tower, New York City, New York

"What does your father say?" Saint Valentine asked from the other side of his desk.

Paris let out a weighty breath. She was still sleep-deprived, but that was all Faraday was doing, she couldn't find it in herself to shut her eyes for long. Paris kept waking up to see if her best friend had awoken from his drug-induced sleep, only to discover he hadn't.

Paris glanced at Agent Barney Jasper beside her before looking at Saint Valentine. "He and my mother have been tracking the demon expert, Renswick, since that's who Tomár was after, knowing he had the counterspell to seal the demigods back in the book, *Magical Creatures*. They kept losing both of their trails, but they are still trying to track them both down."

"Now the demigods have been shut back away and the wards reinforced on the Great Library, do you really think Tomár would go after Renswick?" Barney asked.

"It's hard to say," Paris replied, having asked her father the same question. "Renswick is a demon expert and knows the weapon that we'll need to stop Tomár once and for all."

"Does he know this?" Saint Valentine asked, his wise eyes calculating.

"We don't know," Paris said, "but most likely he does."

The leader of FGA sat back in his elegant desk chair. "What Tomár does will affect love again. He wants to die, and that's the way to do it."

"Or he's going to be out for revenge," Barney said.

"Either way, we have to be vigilant. We can't let down our guard knowing how powerful this demon is and what lengths he's gone to destroy love."

Paris sighed. "I'll keep in contact with you both on what my parents learn. If they discover what Tomár is doing next, I'll let you know."

"Thank you," Saint Valentine said, looking old and tired, as tired as she felt. "We need to stay ahead of him. Although I worry that we don't have the resources to do that."

"Sir, I'm sorry about the damage at the Louvre—"

Saint Valentine paused her, holding up a hand. "Agent Beaufont, you were willing to sacrifice your life and those of your friends to put three demigods back where they belonged. You haven't rested properly in days and have worked harder than anyone I've yet to meet. The fact that we incurred a large bill from the Louvre really isn't my concern. We will pay it off eventually. Honestly, they should overlook the whole matter, but they tend to like to have us indebted to them."

"I'm trying to secure a funding source for us, sir," Paris continued.

"I appreciate that," Saint Valentine said with a charming smile. "For now, what I think you deserve is a day off. A whole weekend, I dare say. I hear that you have a wedding to attend."

She grinned back at him. "Yes, my uncle's."

"Well, then you have enough time to get ready for it and

maybe even get a nap," Saint Valentine said, motioning her to the door.

Paris stood, awkwardly looking between him and Agent Jasper. It felt like there was more to say, to figure out. There were so many plans for them to discuss.

Saint Valentine read her mind. He nodded to the door again. "Everything can wait until Monday. Go enjoy your family."

"Okay," Paris said, turning and making for the door.

"Oh, and Agent Beaufont," Saint Valentine said.

"Yes?"

"I shouldn't be surprised, but I find myself constantly in that state of being when it comes to you," Saint Valentine said matter-of-factly, his hands casually clasped on his desk. "You don't just exceed expectations as an agent for FGA. You blow them away. I will gratefully pay any debt you incur to the Louvre or any other place because what you do is priceless to me, FGA, and this world. I know you don't do any of this for the praise, but you're going to get it regardless, and it's definitely not enough. Still, thank you, Agent Beaufont, for your service. I dare say, get ready for more responsibility because I wouldn't be a wise man not to give someone like you more of it."

Paris felt something tender in her chest and knew it to be pride. She released a small smile, so tired she thought she might cry if she wasn't careful. "You're welcome, sir. It's my pleasure to serve."

CHAPTER EIGHTY-SIX

Little Pleasures Farmhouse, Outskirts of Boulder, Colorado

Paris had to admit the plum dress wasn't so bad as she stood at the front of the wedding ceremony next to her mother and Aunt Sophia, who were dressed the same. Paris glanced at Uncle John, handsome in his tuxedo. Beside him, her father stood with her Uncle Clark.

The Little Pleasures Farm was magical, with lights in the trees and chairs and an aisle and altar at the front of the forest. Hemingway had thought of everything, arranging the setup for the wedding. The guests were all looking their best as they sat with wide smiles, waiting for the bride to come down the aisle.

Paris knew that Pickles, Uncle John's terrier, was the ring bearer for the ceremony. She was surprised when the dog came trotting down the aisle with a basket of flower petals in his mouth and shook his head, making them spill out onto the runner. The guests all laughed at the cute display. Paris realized that if the dog really wanted to steal the show, he could change into his form as a chimera. When she spotted someone taking their place at the far end of the audience, Paris knew no one could steal the show and why Pickles had been the flower dog.

Standing in a tiny tuxedo and holding a pillow with the rings was Faraday. The squirrel had awoken! Just in time to not only attend the wedding but take a place in it. Paris wanted to scream out with joy, but she kept her emotions buttoned down. Her mother caught sight of the tenderness in her expression.

"Our familiars don't quit," Liv mouthed to her daughter.

Paris smiled. She felt so grateful as Faraday scurried down the aisle, back to his old self. It was good news for a lot of reasons, but mostly because he and Paris had more bad guys to stop and more love to help bring to the world.

The music cued that Alicia was about to appear, and everyone stood, turning their attention to the bride as she took her place at the far side of the procession. The Italian was gorgeously dressed in white and wearing a smile full of true happiness.

Paris couldn't think of two people who deserved to be in love as much as her Uncle John and Aunt Alicia. They had sacrificed so much for her. They'd been apart to keep the world safe. Now they were being rewarded with true love.

As Alicia made her way to Uncle John, Paris' eyes connected with Hemingway's. She knew that love was about sacrifice, but it was also about finding your way to someone over and over and falling in love again each time.

That's what Paris had wanted for the world. She hoped she could bring that to all who wanted it. Because Paris Beaufont truly believed if people were in love, the problems of the world would simply disappear.

CHAPTER EIGHTY-SEVEN

"I can't believe you're wearing a tuxedo," Paris said, kneeling and checking Faraday. He appeared to be fine, with no residual effects from the drug.

"I can't believe you're wearing a dress," he teased.

"How do you feel?"

"I'm fine," he said. "I always knew it was a possibility that I'd have to drug myself to take down the evil demigoddess. You were successful with sealing the three away, it seems?"

She smiled. "Thanks to the help of my friends." Paris turned to welcome King Rudolf and Sherlock Holmes over, who had just gotten drinks from the bar and handed Paris a glass of champagne. Faraday hopped away to receive praise from Paris' mother and father, who would also want to gush over his suit. There was no way Liv could have ever gotten Plato into a tuxedo.

"You were brilliant at the Louvre," Uncle Rudolf said, clinking his champagne flute against Paris'.

"Thanks to you," she said, looking between the unlikely pair. "I was grateful for both your help in the end."

"We were in the area," Rudolf said, winking at Sherlock Holmes.

"Yeah, about that," Paris replied. "Why weren't you searching for Subfar?"

Sherlock Holmes stepped in closer to her and leaned down low. "We were being followed every time. I'll go after the Protector of Wealth, but only once you contain the person who I think will compromise his safety if I do locate him."

Paris glanced around the wedding party, where people were eating and drinking and dancing. She located Subner, who was grumpily standing next to Papa Creola. Next to him was Mama Jamba, wearing a giant hat full of feathers and flowers.

"Subner," she guessed.

"Yes. I fear Subner will swoop in once we find his brother and murder him. Then the Protector of Wealth will be no good to you."

"Yeah, I need to figure out how to get them to reconcile things," Paris muttered, sipping on her champagne. "I haven't figured that out yet."

"That might require finding the Protector of Wealth first and getting him to straighten out his shifty ways," King Rudolf offered.

"That means I have to do something with Subner in the meantime," Paris said.

"It means that you need to abduct and hold Subner," Rudolf said with a laugh.

"Not only do I not know how to do that, but how am I supposed to abduct a man who knows what I'm going to do before I do it?" Paris asked.

"I think we can help," Rudolf offered, winking at Sherlock again.

To her surprise, the great detective nodded in reply to this. "Tonight, we relax. We celebrate."

Sherlock held up his champagne flute and Paris joined him, clinking her glass against his. "Thanks for all your help. It means a lot."

Sherlock gave her a serious expression. "Agent Beaufont, from my observations, what you do for so many is vital. I'm happy to help. You've given me purpose again, and I didn't even know I'd lost it."

Rudolf clapped the detective on the back and laughed. "I'm always finding things I didn't know I lost. I went a whole month without one of my children, and then someone turns up at the door and asks if I want Captain Morgan back."

Sherlock turned, shaking his head. "Don't repeat that story. It makes you look like an idiot."

King Rudolf laughed again. "Oh, if you want to hear something that makes me sound like an idiot, listen to this."

"You look beautiful," a familiar voice said at Paris' side. She looked up to see the person she owed her life to.

"Uncle John," she gushed, throwing her arms around his shoulders and hugging him tightly. "I'm so happy for you."

He hugged her back. "Thank you, Pare. I know you didn't want to wear the dress, but you are gorgeous in violet or whatever color Alicia is calling it."

She giggled. "Well, I'd wear just about anything if you wanted me to. I can't imagine not being part of this."

"It's because of you that this is possible," Uncle John said, looking around at the wedding. The space was full of magic, although no spells had been cast.

She blushed. "Oh, no. I'm the reason you and Alicia couldn't be together for so long."

He gave her a stern expression. "Pare, you're the reason that so many can wake up tomorrow next to the person they love, me included. Don't ever guilt yourself for what we did to protect you. Yes, we sacrificed everything to protect you, but it was because we knew the truth. If we didn't, we might as well give up on the planet right then. Mama Jamba made it very clear to us." He opened his mouth like he was going to continue but was edged to the side as Mother Nature appeared next to Uncle John. She looked small, although her hat was huge.

"I told him and all the rest, give up today to protect that child," Mama Jamba chimed. "Give up everything. Anything you love, don't consider for a moment not letting go if it protects Guinevere Paris Beaufont. Because if anything happens to her, then kiss this world goodbye."

Uncle John gave Paris a look of pride. "After what you've done, saving the world from demigods, how can we all not know that we were right to make those sacrifices? Because you were protected and are here, you are saving our world and looking beautiful doing it."

Paris was speechless. She was grateful when Mama Jamba leaned forward and pinched her cheek. "We've had our moment, and you've had yours with Faraday. You've spoken with Rudolf and Sherlock, and I agree on your mission."

Paris gave Mama Jamba a curious expression but didn't ask her to elaborate.

The old woman's periwinkle eyes sparkled with mischief as she pointed across the reception. "There's a man over there I think you need to dance with. He's too handsome not to."

Paris followed her finger and saw Hemingway, looking very fine in a tuxedo and smiling at her from across the room.

"Yeah, I think you're right," Paris said over her shoulder, waving to Mama Jamba and Uncle John as she found her way to Hemingway and into his arms.

The pair didn't have to say a word. They danced to the music and held each other and enjoyed that for the moment, everything was right in the world. Sometimes when two people who are so very right for one another find each other, they heal the world by being together.

Paris Beaufont and Hemingway Noble had that kind of love. What they didn't know was that they would help the world to have a love like theirs. For right then, they'd enjoy their affections while only their friends and family watched, in awe of young and true love.

269

THE STORY CONTINUES

The story continues with book five, *The Savvy Renegade*, available at Amazon.

Claim your copy today!

SARAH'S AUTHOR NOTES

APRIL 20, 2022

Thank you so much for taking a chance on this new series. Thanks for buying and reviewing the books. Thanks for supporting LMBPN and for being awesome! If you're reading this, you are definitely awesome!

I loooooove libraries! Like heart them to the moon and back. I realize that as an author and you as a reader, we are the ones who would love libraries. Well and also the homeless. I've found that the homeless like libraries too. That's because they are quiet and warm and dry and have comfortable chairs, perfect for napping. More on how I know that later.

But seriously, I don't love libraries because I'm an author. I'm an author because of my love of libraries. Before I wrote books, I had a boring job at a university in Southern Oregon. The people were awesome. What we did, providing education for the community was fantastic. But the job, well it was soul sucking.

I worked on an urban campus in the middle of downtown. That part was cool with the Siskiyou Mountain range all around us, nestled in the Rogue Valley. It was snowcapped much of the year and from the main classrooms we had lovely views. And we had homeless... Again more on that later.

I don't do lunch. I just never have. I'm not the colleague who will pop out with you to grab a bite to eat to get away from the grind of the day. I work from home now and my lunch routine involves eating pistachios and berries over my laptop because I'm all about efficiency. You all want books, right?

Side note…because my name is Sarah Noffke and I derail everything. So I love release days for books. And I love it when a book comes out on midnight and I wake up and bunch of you have already read it in a few hours. And I love it when you're like, "Awesome book." But then I don't so much like it when you're like, "Where's the next one?"

Hey, reader! It's in my brain. Give me a minute. I have to sleep. Not much though. And I don't take lunch breaks.

But yes, I try and not keep you waiting for long. So please don't think I'm ungrateful that some of you read my books so fast and then want more. I like that. It's just funny when I've spent two to three weeks doing nothing but spinning ideas into plots and trying to create 70k words of awesomeness and some of you read it in hours and are like, "Give Momma more!" Okay, maybe you don't say that, but you get the idea. Keep reading. Keeping asking for books. And I'll keep writing them as fast as I can, no lunch breaks allowed.

Okay, back to the university and me not lunching. See, I didn't forget. Anyway, my colleagues quit asking me out to lunch after a year. Usually I took my lunch breaks to get all my work done so I could cut out early. A lot of times I took it to meditate and relax. But most of the time, I went to the county and university library next to the building where I worked. It was a short walk and a beautiful library as it served as the collection for the county and the students at both the college and the university where I worked.

On these antisocial lunch breaks, I would browse the aisle and drift along looking for my next read. Stop me if I've told you this story…I used to run my hands over the spines of the books with my eyes closed and walk down the aisle and randomly stop. I'd open my eyes and whatever book I paused on was the answer to my problems or the one to fix things or the one I was looking for. It took me many, many more years to realize that I was looking for a book that hadn't been written yet…because I hadn't written it. That's how I knew I had a story in me that needed to be told. And later, I realized that was why I was so unhappy at that job, although I loved education and what the college did. I was meant to be writing books. So it was libraries that made me into an author.

I always have had libraries in my books. This was my 91st book to write and really most all of them have libraries in them. Not that one about bugs in space though. That just didn't fit. But all the rest really do. They are always really grand and full of mystery and like the one in the House of Fourteen, if you don't know what you're looking for, then you'll get lost. So it only made sense that in the Sophia series and then this one, that I have the Great Library. I mean, talk about a cool place. As soon as a book is written in the world, it appears there. Every book in the world! The coolest place, in my opinion.

So yes, this book was all about my favorite place. A library. And what would happen if something in books came alive.

Okay, you're wondering where all this rambling is going. Well, back in the day, after I browsed the aisle of the library, found my next read, then I'd snuggle up with the book in one of the cozy chairs and sit in the warmth of the library looking out at the snowy Siskiyou mountains. Often I'd be surrounded by homeless people who were pretending to read books, but just nodding off, enjoying having shelter and also a great view.

Later when I became pregnant with Lydia, I was sleepy all the time. Usually it was frowned upon to sleep in my office. Silly bosses. One time I snuck off to the study room to sleep, but then some silly students were like, we need this for studying. And that's when I remembered my favorite place and realized that it was the ideal location to sleep. And so, for about six months, over every lunch break, I could be found sleeping in the library surrounded by snoozing homeless people. Nothing better than sleeping around books.

On that note, I have to ask a question to the Bird Killer. Hey, Mike, what's the weirdest place you've ever slept? I'm off to nap now…

Much love and Peace,

Tiny Ninja

MICHAEL'S AUTHOR NOTES

WRITTEN MAY 13, 2022

Thank you for not only reading this book but these author notes as well!

The weirdest place to sleep?

One of the weirdest places I remember sleeping is in the back of a car under the windshield above the backseat. I was fairly small (obviously) and enjoyed lying there while we drove somewhere as a family.

Looking back, I'd like to scream at my parents, "WHAT THE HELL ARE YOU THINKING? IF YOU CRASH, I'M DEAD! I HAVE A GREAT LIFE AHEAD OF ME!"

(Note to Michael: My mother (whom you've met) rode from Chicago to Los Angeles in just that spot in 1945. She was fourteen. The dog (~25 pounds) was up there with her. She had to ride there because the car was packed, moving back to LA after the war. Strangely, she says she enjoyed it too...for about ten miles.)

Someone got the message about safety in cars (this was 1970 or so), and/or I got too big to sleep in the back.

Then some asshole developed seat belts, and I cursed the day they were born.

The second weirdest place to sleep?

I admit to having slept outside in made-up tents, no tents, etc., but since camping is a huge industry, I'm not sure that can be considered weird.

Now, the following location is weird to me as I so rarely drink alcohol that seeing me passed out on a pool table in a bar is a weird situation. First, I'm almost never in a bar. I don't like the vibe (my mother was an alcoholic) or the noise (can't hear for shit), and the drinks don't tempt me.

However, a group of friends and I had just seen a Metallica concert in the late 80s and decided one seriously cold night in Houston, TX to walk to a local pub. Now, I was used to getting my eight or nine hours in. Why? I don't know. Perhaps because I needed to grow a bit more. Either way, we finished the concert late, and I was not about to tell my girlfriend and friends no.

I was always the designated driver since I never drank alcohol at the shows. This time, it wasn't just because I didn't like it. I was broke as hell.

You can guess the rest of the story. We get there and hang out. I'm sitting on the pool table (no one playing), and next thing you know...

I zonk out.

There, Sarah. Did that answer your question? Unfortunately for you, I haven't slept in any really strange places.

That I remember at this moment.

;-)

Ad Aeternitatem,

Michael

P.S. If you want, you can read a couple of short stories I have shared in the Michael Anderle newsletter here: (No requirement to sign up.)

https://michael.beehiiv.com/

ABOUT SARAH

Sarah Noffke is a prolific USA Today Best-Selling Author, who writes YA and NA science fiction, fantasy, paranormal and urban fantasy. Most of her stories draw on her experiences living on the West Coast, growing up in Texas or traveling the world.

Her passion for art, culture and literature drives her to create stories that are full of whimsey, humor and philosophy. Her books appeal to readers who enjoy an escape, a bit of magic mixed with science and the unexpected--like a dragon who tells bad jokes and has a video game addiction, but fights for justice.

Noffke's books are top rated and best-sellers on Amazon. Her books are available in paperback, audio and in Spanish, Portuguese, German, Dutch and Italian.

To stay up to date with Sarah, please visit her website and subscribe to her newsletter: www.sarahnoffke.com

For a complete list of books by Sarah and a suggested reading order, please see: www.sarahnoffke.com/reading-guide/

BOOKS BY SARAH NOFFKE

For a complete list of books by Sarah and a suggested reading order, please visit:

www.sarahnoffke.com/reading-guide/

BOOKS BY MICHAEL ANDERLE

Sign up for the LMBPN email list to be notified of new releases and special deals!

https://lmbpn.com/email/

For a complete list of books by Michael Anderle, please visit:

www.lmbpn.com/ma-books/

CONNECT WITH THE AUTHORS

Connect with Sarah and sign up for her email list here:

http://www.sarahnoffke.com/connect/

Michael Anderle Social

Website: http://lmbpn.com

Email List: https://michael.beehiiv.com/

https://www.facebook.com/LMBPNPublishing

https://twitter.com/MichaelAnderle

https://www.instagram.com/lmbpn_publishing/

https://www.bookbub.com/authors/michael-anderle

www.ingramcontent.com/pod-product-compliance
Lightning Source LLC
Chambersburg PA
CBHW032355310726
48973CB00007B/2020